Imperfect Past

Jessica Casavant

Yellow Rose Books

Nederland, Texas

ISBN 1-932300-34-1

First Printing 2004

9 8 7 6 5 4 3 2 1

Cover design by Donna Pawlowski

Published by:

Yellow Rose Books
PMB 210, 8691 9th Avenue
Port Arthur, Texas 77642-8025

Find us on the World Wide Web at
http://www.regalcrest.biz

Printed in the United States of America

Acknowledgments

When I first started working on *Twist of Fate*, little did I know that this group of friends that appeared to me in my sleep, would not let go, and would insist on having their own stories told. With each story their voices are getting stronger. They really do feel like family.

Every book surprises me. This is especially true of *Imperfect Past*. The friendship between this group of women, most specifically Jamie and Darcy, came out of the blue as their story evolved. All I could do was follow where they wanted me to go.

Thanks to all my readers who keep asking for the next one in the series.

To my editor Day, for once again holding my hand, and for pushing me just a bit further with every story. I am lucky to have found you.

Donna, for another great cover.

To everyone at Regal Crest, most especially my publisher C. LeNoir, for continuing to do great work.

To Cathy for never questioning why you fell for someone who disappears for hours at a time.

For Cathy.
For shining a light into my darkest corners.

Chapter
One

DETECTIVE JAMIE SAUNDERS stared out her office window and sighed. It was a day following innumerable other days of sweat and hazy skies. There were no puffy white clouds or balmy breezes, only a wall of humidity and smog nearly thick enough to swim in. Even the thunderstorm the night before had barely caused a ripple of relief. Reports on the news cheerfully promised more of the same. In those long, lazy, first days of summer, the unusually early heat wave was moving into its second pitiless week and was competing for headlines with those heralding a missing eight-year-old girl, as the biggest story in Boston.

Jamie glared at the air conditioning unit rattling in her window. The noise, she was now convinced, was just for show as she felt the dampness at the base of her neck. She stretched, trying to work the stiffness from her back, then continued typing her report.

Murder victim number eighteen had been a medical student at Harvard, with dreams. Now her life was neatly summarized on two pages in triplicate. Jamie stared at the pictures and shook her head, trying to fend off the headache nibbling around its edges. They had been lucky with this one when the boyfriend had confessed.

She finished the report and placed it in the solved cases tray. One of these days she just might get around to filing the stack away. When the telephone rang by her right elbow, she absently reached for it.

"Saunders."

"Meet me near Hatch Shell, below Longfellow Bridge." Alex's voice was tight, and she hung up without adding anything further.

Jamie stood up and grabbed her suit jacket, grimacing as she thought of the heat outside. *Just once I would like to ease into my week*, she thought grumpily.

Jamie drove along the Esplanade, one of many parks that

squatted along the seventeen mile stretch of land that ran beside the Charles River and parked her car by the Community Boating Boathouse. The activity underway spoke volumes about what had been discovered. Police divers were already scouring the bottom of the murky, polluted waters, looking for evidence. The entire detective contingent from the major case squad was there, too. That usually was not a good sign.

When Jamie stepped out into the heat, she located her best friend standing to the left of the official group. The tall, attractive brunette turned, and their eyes met. The look in Alex Ryan's eyes was fierce, and in an instant Jamie knew who the newly discovered victim was, and her face tightened. She strode across the parking lot and was met halfway by her partner.

"Is it the kid?"

Alex looked at her, her startling blue eyes a little wild. "We don't know yet."

Jamie swore quietly. The dead were her business. She lived with them, worked with them, and studied them. She dreamed of them. A decade as a cop had toughened her, given her a cold, clinical, and often cynical eye toward death and its many visages. Murder no longer shocked her, but it continued to repel.

She followed Alex to the river's edge, ducked under the yellow police tape, and saw the two black duffel bags. Intent on the first bag, she only partly registered that one of the newer uniforms was throwing up against a tree. Jamie looked down, and for a moment forgot that she shouldn't be shocked. Inside the bag was the naked torso of a young child. Instinct told her that it was the dismembered body of eight-year-old Sarah Timley who had gone missing two days before. Then Jamie looked down into the second bag and saw the child's head.

She concentrated on keeping her ferocity and fury from her face. "Who's got this?"

"Kodalski."

Jamie shifted her eyes to her left, looking for the detective in charge of the Sex Crimes Unit. She found him standing at the water's edge, staring into the iron gray water. He was built like the linebacker he had once been, except for the extra pounds in the middle that refused to go. Jamie watched him as he surreptitiously wiped at tears. Unwilling to invade his privacy, she looked away, feeling her own eyes burn.

As a police officer, she always held on to hope: hope that she could find missing children; hope that she would be able to be the protector she had been sworn to be; hope that she could find the predators that lived in her city. But moments like these made it difficult to believe in hope; they only made her believe in hate.

Chapter
Two

"WE OBVIOUSLY HAVE a monster, or monsters out in our community, who have perpetrated an unthinkably heinous crime on a totally defenseless, innocent child. I want to absolutely reassure the Timleys and the entire city that we are not missing a beat on this case. The officers you see around you today are here to knock on every door in this neighborhood, to uncover the smallest bit of evidence that will ultimately lead to the apprehension of the guilty party. Let there be no mistake about it: we will be successful in bringing the perpetrator or perpetrators to justice."

The words echoed through Jamie's mind as she stood listening to the chief of police speak at the edge of the neighborhood park. It was a call to duty that no officer could ignore, and there was a strong police presence — Jamie and Alex included — standing by to begin the door-to-door canvass of Sarah's neighborhood.

Though the Timley case wasn't theirs, Jamie welcomed the opportunity to assist in it. The order had come down as a result of a meeting the night before, when the chief had met with the homicide unit head, as well as with the staff inspector of the sex crimes unit, to review the evidence that had been collected to date. Dissatisfied with the progress on the investigation, the chief had given the order for the door-to-door canvass. The objective of the canvass, Jamie knew, was to find anyone who may have seen the little girl being abducted, and to sweep up information about any suspicious individuals living in the neighborhood.

As the chief of police wrapped up his press conference, Jamie reflected that he was looking his age. His face was stamped with the permanently weary look of a man who has seen too much of the underbelly of society.

Jamie moved away from the press gathering where reporters clamored their questions at the chief. Her thoughts flickered to the day they had discovered the remains of the eight-year-old. Now, on the sidewalk in Sarah Timley's neighborhood, close to the scene of the disappearance, Jamie was unable to shake the memory of the child's head — her blonde hair still in a ponytail — discarded in a bag like so much unwanted garbage. She felt the biting edge of the wind nip at her neck and shivered with it. She wasn't sure if it was the cold or her dark thoughts. The earlier heat wave had disappeared as unexpectedly as it had arrived

Jamie's jaw tightened and she fought to clear her mind and go about her day with detached professionalism. A glance at Alex's set face told her that her partner was struggling with the same difficulty.

As the wind continued to pick up, Jamie glanced up at the sky and the shifting, ever-darkening clouds. The sky was threatening rain, and while it would be a welcome relief to the days of endless heat they had been having, she hoped the rain would hold off for a little while. There was nothing worse than racing to find evidence before the rain washed it away.

The chief had said that over two hundred officers had been assigned to the task force. And as Jamie looked around at the ever-increasing activity in the neighborhood, it was easy to believe. She joined Alex, who waited by the curb of the sidewalk, and they started the painstaking work of looking for minutiae.

The two detectives went about their search with meticulous concentration, looking for any marks or other evidence of a struggle that would indicate the spot where the abduction had taken place. More than once they squatted or got down on their knees for a closer inspection. Years of being partners had them working silently, their movements synchronized.

Other teams checked back alleys and questioned young people living in the vicinity to determine if there were other shortcuts Sarah might have taken home from her best friend's house.

It took Jamie and Alex the entire day to complete their examination of the sidewalks. At the last pavement square in their search area, Jamie stood up from her crouch and winced as she tried to stretch the ache in her lower back. Despite the intensified search, they had not found anything to pinpoint the spot where Sarah had been taken.

Jamie narrowed her eyes and stared across the street, reading the same fruitless findings from the body language of another detective team. *Nothing. How can a child disappear in broad daylight two houses away from her home and leave no trace?*

"Are people so wrapped up into their own little worlds that they wouldn't notice a child being taken against her will?" Alex asked as she also looked around.

"Maybe there was nothing to notice. Maybe it was someone she knew." Jamie rubbed at a spot of dirt on her right knee. She met Alex's frustrated eyes and sighed at the futility of their search. With nothing to show for her day's work, Jamie didn't want to go home—even though she had been on duty for sixteen hours, and couldn't remember her last meal.

Alex shoved a hand through her short, dark hair and glared at nothing tangible. Without saying another word, she and Jamie joined the door-to-door search.

It was nearing midnight as they went up to the last house on the block and rang the doorbell. Frustrated, tired, and hungry, Jamie glanced up at the plain white stucco façade and impatiently rang the bell again.

Alex looked at her but said nothing.

Finally, after what seemed like an interminable wait, Jamie saw the lights come on and she forced herself to patience.

The door was opened by a heavy-set man wearing a ratty bathrobe that might have once been called green. He glared at their badges.

"What?"

"Good evening, sir. I'm sorry to disturb you. I'm Detective Saunders and this is Detective Ryan. We are working on the Sarah Timley investigation and are conducting a door-to-door search. Could we take a look inside of your home?"

His watery eyes blinked. "What?"

"Your home, sir. We would like to look around," Alex repeated.

"My house?"

"Yes, sir."

He looked at them, suspicion evident on his coarse, florid face. "Why?"

Alex gave him a smile that was meant to be reassuring. "We're going door to door in this neighborhood to make sure we didn't miss anything. It's just a formality."

"Formality? I don't want no cops in my house. Unless you have a warrant, you can just get the hell off my front steps."

He moved to slam the door but Jamie's foot blocked it. Then she moved so quickly that even Alex was taken by surprise.

Despite his weight and height advantage, the man found himself pinned against the wall like a rag doll with Jamie's nightstick against his throat. His face reddened as he started to feel the constriction of his air passage.

"Now you have a choice. Either you can let us search your house and do our job, or you can become intimately acquainted with this stick. What will it be?" Jamie pressed harder and the man's eyes bulged.

Alex looked on, trying to figure out if she should intervene. "James..." she said softly.

Jamie ignored her, attention focused solely on the man. "Ready to show us how hospitable you can be?" Unable to interpret his responding gurgle, she said, "Nod if that is a yes."

As much as the nightstick would allow, he nodded, as the sweat rolled down his face.

Jamie released the pressure and stepped back. When she glanced over at her partner, the look on Alex's face almost made her smile.

"Would you...would you like a glass of water?" the man stammered once he got his breath back, trying desperately to remember how to be hospitable.

As if a switch had been flipped, Jamie smiled at him. "That would be nice. Thank you." She moved further into the tiny vestibule.

Alex gave the man a quick look, then followed her partner inside.

The strong smell of fried foods and unwashed body odor assailed them as they moved through the dark house toward the back. Turning on lights as they went, they reached the tiny kitchen, which gave a view of the neighbor's brick wall.

Jamie made a face at the pile of dirty dishes stacked high in the sink. She watched as he searched his empty cupboards for a clean glass.

"I haven't had time to do the dishes," he stammered as he banged another cupboard door shut.

Jamie smiled at him. "That's okay, sir. I don't need the water." *Or the potential fatal disease,* she thought as she looked at the dirty pots sitting on the mustard yellow stove. She met Alex's disgusted look and made a face in response.

They conducted their search of the tiny one storey bungalow with absorbed attention, but found nothing of interest—nothing but dirty clothes, two inches of dust and empty beer cans under the sofa, and old copies of *Reader's Digest* meant to hide the stash of nudie magazines.

The rancid smell of dirty socks had Jamie's eyes watering as she moved about his bedroom. The bed was unmade and the mattress stained with substances Jamie did not want to guess at. She rejoined Alex in the narrow hallway that divided the bedroom and bathroom from the living room. The look on Alex's face was priceless and Jamie swallowed a laugh.

After another cursory look around the living room, they left the house, and Jamie took a long gulp of air as she stood on the steps. Criminally messy housekeeping was hardly grounds for suspicion in a kidnap, but because she hadn't liked his attitude, Jamie stayed on the front steps, took out her notebook, and wrote down the address and the details of the exchange. He joined the "people of interest" list that they were generating after each interview and search. Each person of interest would be revisited later by a different team. *I just hate it when someone slams a door in my face.*

"You okay?" Alex asked Jamie as they walked back to their car.

"I'm sick of this," Jamie admitted.

"Of what?"

"Death," Jamie responded, her tone flat.

Alex studied her with concern. "James..."

Jamie waved it away. When she noticed the bald headed man hanging back near one of the police vans, she frowned in annoyance.

He saw that he had been noticed and called out, "Hey, Saunders, you want to tell me why you're asking people what kind of cleaning agents they use or why you're searching for power tools?"

"Cranford, you want to tell me why you're still so ugly?" Jamie got into the car.

Alex shut the passenger door and grinned at her partner. "You might get quoted on that one."

Jamie smiled. "I don't have a problem with the media doing their job, I just don't want to stumble over them when I'm trying to do mine."

She started the car and, after a quick glance in her rear view mirror, pulled away from the curb. Then she looked over at Alex and grinned. "Plus, he *is* ugly."

Chapter
Three

HOPING FOR A different perspective away from the officious hubbub of the police department, Jamie ignored the lunch crowd in Darcy's café and pored through the tips that had been flooding in to the police hot line. The calls, as they came in, had been logged, summarized, and prioritized.

The vicious murder of eight-year-old Sarah had galvanized the city of Boston. One week after finding the body parts stuffed into two black duffel bags, and after the door-to-door search of the young girl's neighborhood turned up no new information, the team of detectives was still scouring the river for further clues and awaiting the results of the DNA testing performed on samples taken from the body. The waters of the Charles, meant to wash away all evidentiary elements of the crime, hadn't done a very good job. They had found the containers that held the child's remains so quickly, a lot of forensic evidence was still intact, or so they believed. An article in the Boston Daily Globe revealed that the police had begun collecting saliva samples from all males who lived or worked in the vicinity where the girl had disappeared.

But despite the best efforts of the Boston P.D., eight days after Sarah became the city's nineteenth homicide victim of the year, her killer remained on the loose and the press was starting to ask the obvious question: were any of their children safe; and how long was too long to wait for a murderer to be dragged away in handcuffs?

As a seasoned investigator, Jamie knew that a week without an arrest was hardly reason to panic. But still, the fact that they had nothing concrete was maddening. They had already followed up and cleared the more promising tips, and now they sifted through the ones that were unlikely to bear any fruit. She sighed; she needed a break from the creepy thoughts crowding her mind, from the endless grief of the family that was too much to witness.

Jamie shuffled her notes as she thought of the Timleys. No one could know the heart of a grieving parent. It was anguishing enough to feel keen loss from a distance, at a safe remove, where the hurt was diluted and tolerable. She could only try and do justice to Sarah by helping find the killer.

Drawn by the sudden noise of outside traffic, she looked at the front door of the restaurant...and noticed a woman entering. Even in a crowd, this woman was definitely a standout. Tall and lean, with long brown hair that fell in a wave to her shoulders, she hesitated in the entrance as she scanned the room as if looking for someone.

Deductive reasoning was Jamie's forte, and she watched from a back table as she toyed with fanciful thoughts of who the stranger might be. Part of her instinctively registered that the woman was unsettled, upset. It was there in her body language, in the tight way she held on to her purse.

Jamie sipped her wine as she continued to stare at the newcomer with interest, then froze when her stare was returned. Her heart lurched at meeting the woman's eyes. She was embarrassed at being caught, but she didn't look away. Jamie felt herself warm under the frank assessment of cool eyes and she almost screamed when a server blocked her view for several seconds. When the server was out of the way, the woman was still staring at her and Jamie sensed the woman's surprise. *But at what?* Then the woman broke eye contact as she settled in at a small table and turned her attention to the menu.

Jamie looked at the police reports and tried to concentrate on the words. She felt rather than saw the woman's eyes return to her. She fought the urge to lift her head, but her heart raced at the possibility that the woman was showing some interest.

Several minutes later, Jamie gave up pretending an interest in her paperwork and looked up. Her heart skipped a beat as she stared into deep green eyes. A faint smile might have appeared on the woman's face, but a heavy-set man with a sun burnt face, apparently fortified by too many glasses of Scotch, approached the woman's table. Jamie frowned in annoyance at the interruption, half amused at herself for caring. She returned her attention to her notes but looked back up at the noise coming from the woman's table.

"I couldn't help but notice a pretty little thing like you sitting here all by your lonesome," the man said in a slurred voice.

"I'm waiting for someone," the brunette said, keeping her tone pleasant.

"Yeah—waiting for me." He pulled out a chair and settled

his substantial bulk in front of her. "Why don't I buy you a drink?"

She indicated the glass of wine on the table. "No thanks. Already got one."

"Oh, yeah." He chuckled. "Well then, I'll join you." He turned to look for the waitress and waved his hand to get her attention, missing the look on his companion's face.

But Jamie saw the mixture of panic and frustration on the woman's face. She watched as the brunette struggled for some inoffensive way to rid herself of the unwelcome intrusion. Without really thinking about it, Jamie gathered her papers into her briefcase and crossed the café to the woman's table.

"Hey, sorry I'm late. Couldn't get out of the meeting any earlier," Jamie said breathlessly as she pulled up a chair.

Impulsive though it had been, now, seeing up close what she had glimpsed from a distance made her more than happy that she had acted on her notion. The startled eyes, looking up at Jamie in surprise, were a rich green flecked with gold. The hair was not brown, but a rich toffee color, streaked with gold as if sun kissed. Her lashes were a shade darker than her hair.

Jamie was pleased when the initial startled look turned into a smile and dimples appeared on both sides of the woman's mouth.

"Oh, that's okay. I was just telling this nice man that I was waiting for you."

Jamie turned cool gray eyes to the intruder. "Hello. If you don't mind, we really would like to be alone."

He looked as if he was about to argue, but Jamie's quiet and deadly expression stopped him. He swallowed nervously. "Sure, sure. Didn't want her to get lonely, that's all. Excuse me."

Jamie almost laughed at his hurried exit.

The woman watched him go, then turned her attention to Jamie. "Thank you. It was becoming a sticky situation."

Jamie smiled. "You're welcome. I'm Jamie."

The brunette accepted her hand and smiled. "Shane."

Their eyes held for several seconds. Jamie looked away as she withdrew her hand.

"Can I buy you a drink?" Shane offered. "After all, it's the least I can do for you saving me."

"When you put it that way, how can I refuse?"

Shane motioned the waitress over, and then they silently waited for her to return with their order.

"So, do you often go around rescuing people like that?" Shane asked after they had been served.

"Hardly ever, and only if they're beautiful. I don't bother

with the ugly ones." Jamie grinned and Shane laughed. "Did I come across as very brave?"

Shane smiled. "Very."

Jamie returned Shane's smile. "Good. I have no idea what I would have done if he had stayed. Probably poured a glass of whatever was on hand over his head."

"Do you come here often?" Shane asked with a wry smile.

"I practically live here. One of my closest friends owns the place." Jamie glanced around, then back at her companion. "I've never seen you here before." She toyed with her glass.

"No?"

"No. I would have remembered." Jamie flicked her eyes to her tablemate, then back to her glass.

Shane smiled, flattered, yet cautious. "I stumbled onto it. I had a meeting here in Cambridge and parked just up the street. Afterwards, it was such a nice night that I thought I would do some window shopping. When I saw the blue sign outside, I decided to stop in for a drink. It was an impulse."

Or was it fate? Of all the bars to stop at, she had picked Murphy's and tumbled into something she was unsure of.

Jamie sensed the tension under the light tone. She studied Shane for a moment and met her eyes. Something very close to fear flickered in the clear green eyes and then retreated. Intrigued, Jamie wanted to find out more about her. Instinct told her she wouldn't get anywhere with her questions. *What does she have to hide?* She glanced at the hands lying on the table. She was relieved that they were ringless.

Seeing Jamie's glance, Shane didn't know whether to be pleased or worried. She met Jamie's eyes. *She has the deepest, darkest eyes. Eyes that look through you. No, not through you — into you. To the secret places no one is allowed access to.* She could have sworn that Jamie knew everything about her from just that one look. And it worried her.

Jamie was intrigued by Shane's curious, yet vaguely worried expression. "So, do you believe in love at first sight?" she asked with a smile.

Shane gave her a startled look and cleared her throat. "You don't know anything about me, about my life."

"I know that you have a great smile. I know that you obviously have great taste, since you picked me up."

"I didn't pick you up, you picked me up."

"Really?" Jamie grinned wickedly. "That's not how I remember it."

Shane answered with a slow and easy smile. "I see. Short term memory problems?"

Jamie shook her head. "Selective memory. I like the sound of that better."

Jamie's smile sent heat rushing to Shane's extremities and she shifted in her chair.

"So, now that we're in love, what do we do about it?" Jamie asked playfully.

Shane relaxed a bit. For right now, she wanted to play along. "I don't know. In novels, isn't this the part where we ride off into the sunset?"

Jamie shook her head. "I have to kiss you first, I think. The hero," she pointed at herself, "that would be me—sweeps the damsel off her feet." She pointed at Shane. "That would be you. Then we kiss, and *then* we ride off into the sunset."

Their eyes met and Shane felt her cheeks blush. "Well...there is *that*. Are you always this impulsive?"

Jamie grinned. "Hardly ever. And only with beautiful women."

Shane had to smile. Despite her disquiet, she was curious to see how far their banter went. "What do you do, when you're not rescuing women?"

"When I'm bored, I don a cape and fight crime and mayhem. You?"

"I'm working on a cure for cancer."

Jamie puzzled over the attraction that had come swiftly, and which they now danced around, not quite touching it. "When you're not looking for miracle cures, what else do you like to do?"

Shane looked at her, then away. "Read, run, swim. Sometimes I'll even sit by the water and do nothing, just breathe. How about you?"

Jamie toyed with her glass. "Interestingly enough, the same." She pushed a suddenly unsteady hand through her hair as she felt the electricity of attraction dance over her skin. "Though lately I've also taken to murdering plants as a hobby. I'm just trying to see if I have a green thumb."

"Do you?"

"It's hard to say. The plants don't live long enough to prove it conclusively." Shane laughed out loud and Jamie enjoyed the sound of her laughter.

THE SONG ENDED and Jamie pulled away reluctantly. Curious to know how the woman would feel in her arms, she had asked Shane to dance. Now she knew. She felt Shane studying her with a serious almost intense look.

"I have to go." Shane's words came out husky.

Lost in the first flush of arousal, it took a moment for the words to register on Jamie. "What? What? Why?"

Shane shook her head. "I'm sorry. I have to go."

For a fraction of a second, Jamie tightened her grasp on Shane's arms as if readying to stop her. Amazed at her own reaction, Jamie released Shane then stepped back, a puzzled look on her face. "Why?" she asked softly.

Shane didn't meet her eyes. "I'm sorry." She hurried out of Murphy's without a backward glance.

As Jamie watched her leave, possible explanations bounced around in her mind: *She's married, in a relationship, straight.* Unbelievably, none of it mattered. There was something there. She had never felt such a raw reaction to anyone in her life. She wasn't so unschooled as to believe that it hadn't been mutual.

She ran outside the restaurant, scanned the street, and caught a glimpse of gold a block away. She reached Shane just as she was getting into her car. Jamie grabbed the door, keeping her from closing it. Shane stared at her, lips parted.

"Please don't go," Jamie panted.

Shane sighed, looking unhappy. "Just let it go."

"Tell me you didn't feel it and I'll go," Jamie said.

Shane opened her mouth. One little lie and this would be over. She met Jamie's eyes and her body reacted. She closed her mouth.

Jamie grinned in triumph. "Let's go somewhere to talk."

Shane almost looked amused. "Talk?"

Jamie smiled. "Will you follow me? My car is just over there." Seeing Shane's hesitation, she bent down and closed her mouth over her quarry's.

As her mouth opened under Jamie's, Shane thought, *I wonder if this is what danger tastes like — something dark that pulls at me until it feels like I'm going under.*

Jamie pulled away and with a quick determined look, she crossed the street to her car. She turned to see if Shane was waiting for her. Relieved that Shane was still there, she got into her car and started it, her eyes on the rearview mirror.

Jamie kept glancing in the rearview mirror, convinced that Shane would stop following her and disappear, never to be seen again. Several minutes later, she pulled into a quiet residential street and turned onto a shady driveway, and was relieved when Shane pulled up behind her. Jamie got out and waited for the golden haired woman to catch up to her.

"Is this your home?" Shane asked, heart hammering as she neared Jamie.

"Yes." Jamie unlocked the front door and stepped aside to let Shane in.

"Do you bring a lot of women here?"

The tone was light, but Jamie heard the interest behind the question. She concentrated on closing the door and threw the keys onto a small table nestled in an alcove near the door. "I've never brought anyone here."

"Never?"

Jamie looked into the living room off to her right for a moment as she considered her answer, then turned her head to Shane. For some reason, she wanted to be completely honest with this woman. "Never. I didn't want the memory of their presence to interfere with my private space." She paused. "Until now."

Shane's heart tripped and her body warmed under Jamie's thoughtful gray eyes.

"Would you like a drink?" Jamie asked, breaking the intense eye contact.

"No."

Jamie turned and stroked Shane's arm and was gripped with a flash of pleasure that raised goose bumps along her skin. She hesitated and Shane brushed her lips, retreated, teased and then touched again. Jamie hungrily closed her mouth over Shane's. She devoured Shane's lips with a desperate impatience and then broke off, leaving them both gasping.

Jamie gasped. "This is rash and reckless and—"

"—totally irresponsible."

"But I can't help it."

"Neither can I. Oh, God, kiss me again." Shane groaned.

The breeze that fluttered the curtains of the open windows was cool. Within the two women were a furnace that stoked higher and higher.

"I want to—"

"I want you to—"

Jamie, frantic for more of Shane, fumbled with her shirt buttons.

Shane, eyes reflecting the same desperation, pulled her shirt open.

There was a rush to touch, a hurry to feel, and little time to savor. In their haste, clothes ripped, tangled; buttons scattered on the hardwood floor. Their partially clad bodies were slick, heated as they came together. Legs, arms—there was no way of knowing where one started and the other ended. They never made it upstairs, never even past the living room, where they tumbled to the smooth, polished oak floor.

Jamie knew she wouldn't last as need poured through her. When Shane's cool fingers found her wet and ready, Jamie was already coming in a wild, wet burst.

"Jesus!" Jamie's eyes, dark with arousal flew open. "Jesus. What was that?"

Shane collapsed over her, small shudders dancing along her body. "I don't know. I don't know."

They looked at each other and Jamie saw the same stunned caution in Shane's eyes that she felt. The first trickle of fear, of panic at how out of control she had felt, was still feeling, enveloped her. *This was too quick. Too rash.* She closed her eyes, but could not help the faint smile curving her mouth.

Shane wanted to feel that mouth on hers again. Desperately, like one starving for water. She danced her fingers on the smooth skin of Jamie's arm, her rib cage.

Jamie opened one eye. "I think my brain has leaked out of my ears." Shane's laugh — low and sexy — sent fresh arousal spinning through her.

"We might need to try this again," Shane said.

Jamie opened the other eye. "Yeah. I think so. Let's try to make it upstairs this time."

Shane's grin was wicked. "We can try."

Slowly, Jamie pulled Shane's shirt over her head. She knew what Shane felt like, but she wanted to see what her hands and mouth had touched. She wasn't disappointed. Shane was lovely. Jamie liked seeing her hands on the smooth tanned skin, liked watching the breasts respond to her stroking, the dark nipples hardening under her fingertips, liked hearing Shane's hum of pleasure when her mouth lowered to them.

"You like this?" Jamie asked

"Yes."

She took a dusky nipple into her mouth and sucked it, causing Shane to clasp her head and moan softly. "Too hard?"

"No."

Jamie held Shane's face between her hands and kissed her so passionately that her body arched off the floor and straddled Jamie's firm thigh with her long legs. Shane's hips moved and pushed against her as the throbbing between her legs increased. Jamie skimmed her hand over Shane's breasts, down her ribcage, onto her smooth stomach. "Look at you. You're stunning." She fitted her hands into the "V" of Shane's thighs, covering her mound with her palm, her fingers tapering downward, inward into her softness. "You're already..."

"Yes."

"So soft, so..."

"Oh!" Shane gasped.

"Wet." Jamie rose above her for a silky, sexy kiss that ended when Shane gave a soft cry and climaxed around Jamie's fingers, against her thumb.

Moments later Shane opened her eyes and saw Jamie smiling down at her, her eyes a soft, warm gray. "I'm sorry."

"Sorry?" Jamie asked, laughing softly. "Why?"

"I couldn't hold it."

"I'm glad," Jamie whispered.

Shane groaned. "Let me touch you."

"You don't have to."

"I need to know how you taste." Shane urgently savored Jamie's neck...shoulders... mouth with her own mouth. Her lips sucked and nipped Jamie's breasts; her hands felt the weight of them. She lowered her mouth — tasting, searching. The fire was still there, but smoldering rather than blazing. Jamie's body stilled, even her breathing had stopped.

Shane slipped her tongue inside, slow and gentle as it stroked and licked the inner walls, pushing deep then retreating. Sure and quick, her tongue darted out to press firmly against Jamie's aching center. Jamie's low moan spurred her on.

Shane felt her own body tighten and react, her own wetness increase. She had never come without direct stimulation, but knew she could now. Her tongue — hot and questing — felt the thickening ridges, her eager mouth gathered the increasing wetness, and her teeth gently toyed with the hardening tip; then her lips sucked greedily.

"Oh God, Shane, I'm so close."

"Hold on to it," Shane whispered urgently.

But unable to hold off any longer, Jamie let herself go as she bucked against the hot mouth. As the waves rolled through Jamie, she stayed suspended in the moment until, with one last cry, she fell back against the floor, Shane's head against her stomach. With her heart still racing, Jamie tried to form a coherent thought, but her mind was completely empty. When Shane's soft tongue flicked against her sensitive clit, she almost arched off the floor.

"Stop. Mercy." She groaned. Her arms felt like lead as she tried to reach for her sweet tormentor.

"Mercy?"

Jamie lifted her head at the amused tone. "Let's at least make it to the bed."

Shane's tongue flicked against her and her body shuddered almost painfully.

It was a mystery to them both how they managed to make it

upstairs.

"Please don't go. Stay," Jamie whispered as she fought to stay awake.

Struggling against her own exhaustion, Shane watched Jamie succumb to sleep. The whole evening had been so unbelievable, that for a moment she was sure she was dreaming. Then the reality of what had just happened settled over her and with it, the misgivings. *What am I doing here? With this woman?* Instinct told her that the night would come back to haunt her. And for a brief moment, she knew to be afraid.

Chapter
Four

SHE WAS GONE. Jamie looked around and knew without searching the house that Shane was gone. Her anger surged, followed quickly by disappointment. Swearing, she stood in the room naked, head tilted as she listened to the quiet of her house. *She's gone. And I don't even know her last name.*

She grabbed the phone on her bedside table and hit "one" on her speed dial.

"Somebody better be dead," the cranky, sleepy voice answered.

"Hey, Darcy."

"Jamie? What time is it? Is everything okay?"

"Yeah. Listen, did you see the woman I was talking to at your place last night?"

There was a pause. "Are you fucking crazy? It's six o'clock in the fucking morning and you're calling me for that? I only answer to emergencies before nine a.m. This is not an emergency. I'm hanging up now."

"No, wait. Wait. I'm sorry, I know it's dumb, but did you see her?" Jamie asked in a sheepish tone.

"It's more than dumb." Darcy sighed as she tried to shake the sleep from her brain. "Look, James, last night was a bad night in the kitchen and I hardly even noticed that *you* were there. What's going on? You don't have another crush on a straight woman do you?"

"No. Nothing like that. Don't worry about it. Go back to sleep." Feeling foolish, she hung up in the middle of Darcy's curse.

Clearly she had lost it. So it had been a one-night stand, so what? It wasn't like they had promised each other anything, including the decency to say goodbye.

Her front door buzzer sounded and her heart started to race in hopes that Shane had come back. *Maybe she went out for coffee.* Jamie hurried to the door. Her smile turned to a frown when she found her best friend waiting on the other side.

"Get dressed. There's been a murder. I'll need your help," Alex said bluntly as she scanned the room. She gazed at the discarded clothing on the floor and her eyebrow shot up in amusement.

Seeing where Alex's attention was, Jamie bent down and grabbed her clothes then turned to go upstairs, ignoring the silent question.

"Where?" she asked as she started up the stairs.

"The Colonnade."

"Who's the victim?

"Chief Justice Reynolds. This one's going to be hell. I've already got the mayor's office breathing down my neck. Walters took the initial call, but he's been moved to the Timley case so we can concentrate on this one." Alex turned and frowned when she saw Jamie wasn't moving. "Are you getting dressed or what?"

"Yeah, yeah."

In the car, Jamie sat lost in thought.

Alex glanced at her. "Want to stop for coffee? You look like shit," she added, with a smile to soften the insult.

Jamie nodded. "Gee, thanks."

After stopping to grab a coffee, they parked close to the hotel. Already word was out and the television news trucks were parked along the street, while curious locals pressed onto the sidewalk and gawked into the entrance.

Alex swore. She turned to Jamie. "Just what we need—a media circus. Someone must have tipped them off because we haven't released anything, pending notification of the next of kin." She shook her head, frustrated. "We're still trying to find them. I hear there was a wife at some point, but we're still searching."

Jamie slowly got out of the car, her expression carefully neutral. "There was a wife, but a brother in Florida is the one who should be notified."

"Yeah? And you know this how?" Alex asked, curious.

Jamie took a sip of coffee as she avoided her friend's eyes. "He was my father." She turned and headed toward the entrance, leaving behind a stunned Alex.

INSIDE THE SUITE, Jamie looked around, trying to imagine her father in this room. There were no personal touches, no hint of what kind of life he had been leading. She found the dark red stain where the body had rested and felt nothing, except relief that she could walk around the suite and study everything with cool detachment. He was just another victim after all. She didn't acknowledge feeling relieved that he was dead. *How often have I wished it so?*

She heard Alex behind her and avoided meeting her eyes. "What do we know?" she asked calmly.

Taking her cue from the brusque tone, Alex pulled the notepad from her back pocket and flipped through a few pages. "There's no sign of forced entry. There's a wound on his forehead that indicates he might have fallen or had been pushed, causing him to hit his head. While he was lying on the floor, he was shot in the back of the head. There was no sign of a struggle or robbery gone bad. His wallet was still in his pants pocket. That's about it so far." She studied Jamie. "Jamie, are you—"

"Where is the body now?" Jamie asked.

"Morgue."

Jamie nodded, stepped closer to the stain, and envisioned the trajectory that the body might have taken on its way down. She looked around the room for anything that seemed out of place, her eyes unable to be still. She studied the half full glass of whisky on the table, and felt her stomach roil at the memory of her father drinking the same when she was a child. The fingerprint tech had already dusted the table and the glass, and the residue showed the prints against the side of the table.

Jamie felt Alex watching her. She lifted her head and finally met Alex's eyes. "We'll talk later, okay? Let's just get this done."

Alex closed her notepad and nodded. "Fine. Let's go find out what Jim's got."

They left the suite and made their way to the elevator. While waiting for its arrival, Jamie glanced up at the recessed lights in the ceiling and noticed the red light blinking by one of the tiny spots. She nodded toward it. "Have we asked about a camera?"

Alex followed Jamie's line of sight and saw the light. She had missed it on their way in. "Let's stop at the front desk and ask about it."

THE ASSISTANT HOTEL manager swallowed nervously as Jamie fixed her eyes on his bouncing Adam's apple. "I'm sorry, Detectives, but I'll need a search warrant before I can give you the security tapes."

Jamie glanced at the polished name tag on his dark suit. "Look, David, is it? You know and I know that I'll get one. You also know that if I have to run out to a justice of the peace to get a warrant, it'll waste my precious time in finding the killer, who is, running loose in *your* hotel. What if he's still here? It wouldn't be good for business if that got out, especially if he was to kill again when we could have done something about it."

Jamie tapped her fingers on the marble front desk as David's Adam's apple bobbled up and down and he looked nervously around.

"Now I'll ask you again, can we get a copy of your security tapes from the tenth floor? And I would suggest you just nod and tell me yes."

Jamie gave him a heated stare and he blushed, but nodded. When he picked up the telephone, his hand shook, and Jamie felt almost sorry for him.

David hung up the phone and his face looked almost gray. "There seems...there appears to be an issue with the tape."

Of course there is. Jamie, who had been studying the lobby, looking for anyone who looked out of place, or who was paying attention to them, focused her attention back on the manager.

He swallowed hard and wiped the perspiration from his forehead. "You see...we tend to... How can I explain it?" He blinked as he caught Alex's sharp blue eyes narrow. "We usually record over the tape. We are concerned for our guests' privacy you see and—"

"Why install the damn cameras if you are so concerned with privacy?" Jamie shot back.

David had no response for that and his mouth opened then closed, looking like a guppy. "We have the tape, but unfortunately it covers part of today as well as a part of yesterday."

"Which part?" Jamie waved his answer aside. "Never mind. Just get me whatever the hell you've got." As he scurried to the back office, Jamie turned to Alex who was leaning against the front desk, watching a pretty blonde cross the marble lobby on impossibly high heels.

"Why is it that in detective shows, there's never a problem with the videotape?"

Alex grinned. "Same reason why British whodunits always have a butler."

"I hate real life," Jamie muttered causing Alex to laugh.

Chapter
Five

WHILE WAITING FOR the video technician to cue up the videotape, Jamie carried her lukewarm coffee to the window of the media room and stared out at a day that was too sunny to match her mood. She had to shake it off. *I'm mooning over a stranger when I should be concentrating on the cases. That's pathetic.*

After watching Jamie for a moment, Alex joined her at the window. "Why didn't you ever tell me about the judge being your father?"

She was both puzzled and hurt. They had been friends since high school and she felt betrayed by the omission, unsure for the first time about how close they really were.

Having expected the question, Jamie sighed. She had run away from her paternity for years, and now knew she couldn't avoid it any longer. "It's something that we as a family tried to forget." She sipped but did not taste her coffee. "He was a bastard, and took off when I was eight. The marriage ended; his existence was erased from our family's memories the day he walked out." *Or was kicked out*, she amended.

Alex studied Jamie, hesitating. She sensed pain and...something else. But Jamie's face remained blank.

Jamie looked at her. "I'm sorry I never shared that with you, but my mother asked us not to discuss it, and after a while, it was almost as if he had never existed for us."

It was as logical a reason as any, but Alex was not totally satisfied. *I'd bet my pension that there's more to the story than a bitter divorce, but this is neither the place nor time to discuss it.*

"Okay." Alex turned and went back to the technician, who sat hunched over his video console, adjusting levels.

Troubled, Jamie sighed. She knew Alex was hurt, and that they would be talking about this again. Years of closeness would make a confrontation inevitable.

"Ready for you," the technician called out.

Jamie walked to the console, and without another word they

turned their attention to the monitor.

The quality of the playback was not very good and the beginning of the recording was for the current day, indicated by the date and time in the lower left corner. Seeing the familiar police activity and even herself on the tape made Jamie swear.

The recording stopped abruptly at about the time that Jamie had enquired about the existence of a tape, and the video cut to the previous evening. For over half an hour, they watched the coming and goings on the floor, looking attentively for anyone near Judge Reynolds' door.

As the playback crawled through the evening hours, Jamie started to fidget.

"What's wrong with you?" Alex finally asked.

"Caffeine withdrawal."

Alex chuckled. "So, go get us some coffee."

Jamie shook her head. "Us? No way. It's your turn. I've gotten the coffee the last three times. We had a deal, remember? I ran out into that huge storm the last time, and ruined my favorite shoes, and you said..."

"I don't want to hear that storm story again," Alex interrupted. "It was just a little rain." When Jamie's eyes narrowed and she opened her mouth to argue, Alex lifted a hand. "Fine, I'll go, just so I never hear that story again."

While Alex stepped out to grab a coffee, Jamie continued to watch the tape. She rubbed at an ache in her lower back and tried not to think about the reason behind it. Almost absently, she noted the woman who stepped off the left elevator and turned right. Something about the way she moved looked familiar.

Jamie's interest perked up. "There. The woman just hesitated by the door. Can you rewind this and make it larger?" she asked as her teeth worried her bottom lip.

The technician rewound the tape and fiddled with a dial for a second, then started the playback again with the image enlarged.

The quality was even worse with the picture blown up. Jamie stared at the screen as the scene was replayed at half the speed. She watched in total concentration as the image of the woman reappeared on the screen. Tall, shoulder length golden hair, she hesitated in front of the door, and for a fraction of a second, her head turned toward the camera.

Jamie stared at the frozen image and felt the shock vibrate through her body as her stomach plummeted. *Shane. It's Shane.*

"Anything?" Alex's sudden reappearance at the door caused Jamie to jump.

"No. Nothing," Jamie replied, too quickly.

Her answer surprised the technician who threw her a startled look.

Jamie hit the eject button. "Another dead end."

Jamie's stomach muscles clenched at what she was doing. The shock of seeing the woman she had just spent the night with appear near a murder scene hours before their meeting had her reacting without thinking. *She could be innocent.*

Alex studied her friend. She had not missed the tech's reaction or Jamie's. Something felt off. Her pager went off. She glanced down at it.

"We have to go. They're releasing the photographs of the black bags to the media in the hopes that someone will link them to the murder. Are you coming?"

Jamie, who had also felt her pager vibrating, nodded. "Yeah, I'll be right there."

Alex left, and Jamie squarely met the technician's speculative look. "Thanks for your help, Harry. I'll take the tape and drop it off to Evidence."

Harry almost refused, but then thought better of it. He handed her the tape and turned his attention back to the controls.

Jamie felt the weight of the tape in her hand and knew that she was about to cross a line.

Chapter
Six

II SIMPLE CAN'T be. Coincidence? Highly unlikely. She must have some connection with the Chief Justice. To my father.

Jamie wasn't sure she wanted to know what that connection was. In fact, she was dead certain she *didn't* want to know. She dragged a hand down her face then propped her elbows on her desk, stared into space, and tried to arrange her chaotic thoughts into some semblance of order.

First — without a doubt, unbelievable as it was, the woman on the tape, that frozen image had been the face of the woman with whom she had spent Thursday night mere hours after the murder. A face she would not likely forget. The face that had immediately attracted her as its owner stood in the entrance of Darcy's bar. She had spent hours admiring, studying, caressing it. She had come to know that heartbreaking face intimately.

"Strange but true" — a hackneyed adage that was nonetheless apt. Gullibility was forgivable; obstruction of justice wasn't. Why hadn't she admitted to Alex that she recognized the woman in the video? She could have laughed and said something like, "You'll never believe who I spent the night with last night." She hadn't. Truth be told, Jamie had never even considered identifying Shane. From the heart-stopping moment she'd recognized her on the tape and known with absolute certainty who the potential suspect was, she knew with equal certainty that she wasn't going to reveal her name...or their acquaintanceship.

The memory — sweet and sharp — of where she had last seen that face, the expression on that face as they made love, had left her with few options. Even now just thinking about Shane sent arousal spinning through her. She felt the ache deep within. She was concealing Shane's identity, at least for the moment. And with her silence, she willfully breached every rule of ethics the department had, violated the law by hiding evidence and impeded a homicide investigation, her own investigation no less.

She couldn't even imagine what the consequences might be. A part of her, an irrational part, wanted to find Shane and force her to admit to something, anything. Another part, equally irrational, wanted to beg Shane to run away with her. Jamie clenched her teeth and a muscle jumped in her jaw as she thought about seeing the toffee-haired woman again.

ONE OF THE detectives burst into Alex's office. "We've got something."

Alex called out to Jamie but got no response from the cubicle next door. She shrugged and nodded toward him. "What do we have?"

"We've been interviewing the people in and around the judge's offices. Co-workers, paralegals etc. We missed her on the first run through." He paused for effect.

Alex fought off her impatience. "Missed who?"

He smiled, pleased with his announcement. "His secretary. She was more than happy to tell us what she knew. It seems Reynolds had a bit of a confrontation a few hours before his death with another judge. She couldn't hear the conversation, but it was pretty heated and this judge slammed out of Reynolds' office."

"Do we have a name?"

"Shane Scott."

Alex stood up and shrugged on her jacket. For a moment she considered waiting for Jamie to return from wherever she was. But Jamie had been acting strangely ever since she'd heard about her father's death, and Alex didn't want to lose time. She would call Jamie from her cell on the way. "Let's go."

OVERWHELMED WITH GUILT, Shane nervously paced her living room floor. *I should have said goodbye. I should have wakened Jamie and told her I was leaving; but she looked so peaceful, I didn't have the heart to wake her.*

Ruefully shaking her head, Shane acknowledged that cowardice was another compelling reason she had let Jamie sleep. She had been nervous about waking her, about what would be said or asked. Though they had carefully stayed away from discussing anything beyond the moment they were caught up in, she instinctively knew that Jamie had hoped to wake up to her, with her.

The possessive arm thrown over her waist as she slept spoke volumes about unconscious want. And Shane had wanted to stay, had wanted to wake her, to share a coffee with her. To make love to her again. Instead, she had sneaked out in the darkness without even leaving a note. She could almost picture Jamie waking up alone, her hand automatically reaching out for her.

Shane somehow knew that Jamie was not one for one-night stands, and her disappearance would hurt her. She would be angry. She would feel used. *But what else could I have done?*

She pushed a trembling hand through her tousled hair. The previous day had started badly and gone askew from there. She didn't regret spending the night with Jamie. Couldn't. It had been too much like a dream. Even now her body tingled at the remembered feel of her. It had been the most unbelievably erotic experience she had ever had, and yet even that didn't quite explain the yearning she felt—like an ache under her skin. Their connection had been immediate. She was certain that they had both recognized it from the start. Regardless, Shane had run away from it, and she knew that was mostly because of what had happened earlier in the afternoon.

That earlier confrontation had been ugly. The feelings of rage and impotence flooded her once again as she remembered. Apprehension consumed her. *Where are they? Where are the pictures?*

If only she hadn't panicked the second time around and fled without more than a cursory search, she might have been lucky enough to find them before they could fall into the wrong hands. Finding them would have meant that she could escape from the nightmare, a waking nightmare that had consumed her life for years. She lived her life in fear, waiting for the axe to fall.

The ringing of her doorbell interrupted her pacing. With a quick frown, she went to open the door.

A uniformed policeman stood to the right side of a tall, dark-haired woman with unusual blue eyes. Knowing what had brought them to her home, Shane's heart plummeted. Her life was about to be pitched into chaos. To conceal her anxiety, she smiled pleasantly. "Can I help you?"

"Shane Scott?"

"Yes?"

"I'm Detective Alex Ryan, a homicide detective with Boston P.D. I'd like to talk to you about the murder of the Chief Justice, the honorable Tomas Reynolds."

"Judge Reynolds? I don't—"

"You were seen arguing with him on the afternoon he was murdered, so please don't waste my time by pretending that you don't know what I'm talking about."

She and Alex locked eyes as if taking each other's measure. Shane relented and stood aside. "Come in."

"Actually, I was going to ask you to come with us."

Shane swallowed, although her mouth was already dry. "I'd like to call my lawyer."

"That isn't necessary. This isn't an arrest." Shane looked pointedly at the stoic policeman, and Alex smiled. "Volunteering to be questioned without an attorney present would go a long way toward convincing me that you're innocent of any wrongdoing."

"I don't believe that for an instant, Detective Ryan." Shane smiled as she scored a point.

Alex acknowledged it with a faint nod.

Chapter
Seven

AS SHE ARRIVED back at the office, Alex finally located Jamie. "Where were you? I tried you on your cell and your pager."

"Grabbing a sandwich. What's up?"

"We've got our first suspect in the Reynolds case."

Jamie felt her heart race as she fought to keep the shock from her face. "What? How?" *Is there another tape?*

"We got to Reynolds' secretary who told us of an argument he had with another judge a few hours before his death. Her name is Shane Scott. We've brought her in for questioning."

Jamie rubbed her palms on her pants. "Did you arrest her?"

"Came in voluntarily."

Jamie considered the ramifications of the news. Alex's interrogation techniques could wring a confession from a saint. When she saw Jamie, would she reveal that they knew each other?

To be on the safe side, Jamie wanted to postpone the inevitable face-to-face meeting for as long as possible. She was unsure of what her reaction might be at seeing the woman who had been haunting her thoughts.

She waited for several minutes until she thought she had her nerves under control, then slowly walked to the meeting room where she knew the questioning was to take place. With a deep breath, she pushed the door open.

Alex sat at a table with a tape recorder in front of her. Also present was Stacey Nash from the DA's office. Jamie knew that her inclusion was primarily political. Except for rare occasions, her office didn't become directly involved until the detectives felt they had enough evidence to press formal charges. The importance of the victim, and now the suspect, had her in attendance — most likely more to calm jittery nerves in the mayor's office than to lend a hand. Jamie swallowed her resentment at the woman's presence as she nodded in Nash's direction. Shane was sitting at the table, her back to the door.

Alex looked at Jamie as she entered. "There you are. Miss Scott, this is Detective Jamie Saunders."

Jamie braced herself as Shane turned and looked at her with shocked eyes. Jamie met her eyes for only a second, and the non-verbal exchange was as meaningful as if they had spoken.

Jamie wanted to ask, "What have you done to me?" And mean it in more ways than one.

She had been thunderstruck that Thursday night. She had thought, no hoped, that seeing Shane again, under bright fluorescent lighting and in a far less romantic setting, would have less of an impact. Just the opposite. She felt like she had been punched. And the vivid memory of how Shane had felt in her arms had Jamie gritting her teeth.

Shane's face remained composed and betrayed no recognition. "How do you do, Detective?"

"Ma'am."

Hearing Shane's voice was as stirring as if the judge had touched her. Jamie could almost feel her warm breath against her ear again, whispering her need. She deliberately crossed the room to stand on the other side, trying to put distance between Shane and her feelings.

Shane fought against the sudden panic tightening her chest. The shock at seeing Jamie again was as unexpected as it was unsettling. Especially now, especially under those circumstances.

I spent the night with a detective. She fought to keep her hands from trembling. *It can't get worse, can it?*

The door swung open and attorney Ken Landry arrived looking flushed, rushed, and apologetic. "I'm sorry, Shane. I got here as soon as I could. What's this about?"

Landry had a solid reputation and an excellent track record as an attorney. Jamie was not surprised that he was the one Shane called. She had often thought that he would be the one she would want to use if she ever needed a lawyer.

Alex nodded at him in acknowledgement. "We have some questions we'd like to put to Miss Scott in connection with the murder of Chief Justice Reynolds."

Landry's jaw dropped. "You've got to be kidding me."

"Unfortunately, no, she's not," Shane said dryly. "Thank you for coming under such short notice, Ken."

He waved away her thanks and turned to Alex. "Can you explain how the hell things got to this point?"

"Certainly," Alex said calmly. "Judge Scott was one of the last people to see Judge Reynolds in his office. We would like to ask her a few questions about that day."

Landry stared at Alex, then at Shane. "I would like a few minutes with my client before we proceed."

Alex nodded and preceded Jamie and Stacey out of the room. Alex turned to them as they waited in the hallway. "What do you think?"

"Cool customer," Stacey responded.

Jamie said nothing, but she could feel the nausea creeping up her throat.

BACK IN THE conference room, Alex smiled pleasantly at Shane. "Thank you for agreeing to meet with us, Your Honor."

Shane nodded a faint acknowledgment.

"Can you tell us where you were last Thursday night at approximately ten p.m.?"

Jamie tensed. *She was fucking my brains out,* she thought as she waited to be outed.

"I was out having a drink."

"Alone?"

"Yes."

"Did anyone see you?"

Shane shrugged. "I have no idea. I would imagine. Obviously, whoever served me."

"Which bar?"

Shane briefly hesitated. Jamie knew that only she saw it because she had anticipated it.

"I don't remember," Shane said.

"You don't remember?"

Shane pushed back a lock of hair that had fallen over one eye. "Look, Detective, I had a bitch of day. I had a meeting in Cambridge, then I decided to do some window shopping and stopped at a little bar to have a drink and relax for a few hours. If I walked around, I could probably find it again. But to be honest, I really didn't pay much attention to the name of the place."

"Where in Cambridge?"

"Around. I started on Elm Street and went from there."

"Who were you meeting?"

"A potential client. Under client-attorney privilege I have to keep the name confidential."

"Then I'm sure that you won't mind if we have a look at your date book just to confirm the meeting."

Shane nodded once.

"How long did you walk?"

"I don't know—maybe half an hour, an hour. I really wasn't keeping track."

"Convenient," Stacey whispered.

Shane heard her and her face tightened. She tried to ignore the comment. She was very aware of Jamie, her senses tuned to the presence against the wall.

She forced herself not to turn around. She didn't want to look at Jamie, didn't want to read the anger and suspicion in her eyes. Worse, she didn't want to remember how she'd felt in the cop's arms and forced her mind away from thinking about Jamie, about their night together. Instinctively, she knew Jamie was trying just as hard not to think of that night. The awareness was battering at her in waves.

As Alex studied her, Shane had a disquieting thought. *She senses it. She doesn't know what yet, but she senses it.*

Alex raised an eyebrow, then shifted her eyes ever so slightly to Jamie—who was a study in bored nonchalance: leaning against the wall, arms crossed, staring into the distance. Only the tightness of her jaw gave her away. Alex knew her too well not to notice.

Jamie's eyes met Alex's and for the briefest of moments, something turbulent and wild flashed in the gray eyes. Puzzled, Alex returned her attention back to Shane.

"Can anyone substantiate your alibi?"

Shane reflexively glanced at Jamie.

Alex noticed the glance and narrowed her eyes, then she turned her attention back to Shane.

"No. Like I said, I was having a drink. Hundreds of people could have seen me that night or none at all. It's such an everyday occurrence, why would they remember me?"

Jamie frowned at that. *Why indeed?*

"So, Miss Scott, why don't you tell us again about your relationship with the Chief Justice?"

"We were colleagues."

"Colleagues?"

"Yes. Colleagues."

Alex waited, the silence stretching, but Shane did not add anything into the quiet. *Two can play at this game*, Alex thought, pushing her frustration down. "Do colleagues see each other after work?"

"Occasionally."

"When, for instance?"

"On special occasions, like a birthday or anniversary."

"Any other time?"

Shane met Alex's cool blue eyes, knowing she was fishing.

"When working on a particularly difficult case, we often bounce ideas off of each other."

"Did you do so at any time?"

Shane smiled. "At different times we all do, depending on our case law experience and the particular points of law being debated."

"Have you ever been to Judge Reynolds' residence?"

As Shane hesitated, Landry said, "Don't answer that."

"You heard my lawyer."

Alex tapped her fingers on her front teeth as she considered her next question.

Watching from the corner, Jamie fought off the urge to pace. Instead she pushed her hands into the front pockets of her pants and fixed her eyes on Shane, trying to decipher something, anything from her body language.

"Would you allow us to take a look at your phone records?" Alex asked.

Shane looked almost amused. "Not without a subpoena."

Alex nodded. She had expected as much. "You told us that on the night in question, you were walking around and ended up at a bar."

"Yes, that's what I said."

"You also said that you stayed there for a while, had a drink, then left," Alex said. Shane nodded. "Did you leave alone?"

Shane hesitated and she fought off the urge to look at Jamie. "Yes."

"What did you argue about?"

"What?" Her shock was almost imperceptible.

Alex was not fooled by it. "I said what did you and Judge Reynolds argue about the day of his murder?"

Shane's chest tightened. She felt everyone's keen interest in her answer and struggled for nonchalance. "I don't believe we argued. If we did, I don't remember the topic."

"You don't remember?"

"No. We've often had heated discussions when debating cases." She shrugged as she forced a smile. Even to her ears the answer sounded lame.

Alex smiled. "Our witness does not recall a heated discussion but rather a full blown argument."

Shane did not answer and the silence stretched.

"What—"

"Are you prepared to do anything here today?" Landry asked.

"I'm just asking questions, trying to be thorough," Alex answered calmly.

Her tone and mild words did not fool Shane. "I've been as cooperative as I can be, but I'm due in court in half an hour. I need to leave, unless you are prepared to file charges."

Alex shrugged. "Not at *this* time. You're free to go." Thoughtfully, she watched the judge and her lawyer depart, then turned to Jamie. "You were quiet."

Jamie shrugged. "You seemed to have everything under control."

"That never stopped you before."

Jamie's jaw tightened. "You're reaching, Alex."

"What?"

"With her. You're reaching. We've got nothing, except a witness who says she might have seen her argue with our victim. Pretty flimsy." She tried not to think of the videotape in her office. *What more does it show?*

"We've started with a lot less before." Unperturbed Alex turned her attention to Stacey. "What did you think?"

"Pretty cool lady."

Except in bed, Jamie thought, jaw tightening. *Except when she's about to come and she begs you not to stop.* She swore silently at her thoughts and turned her attention Stacey. "Well, that's helpful."

Stacey smiled. "You know I think you have a problem."

"Excuse me?"

"You seem a bit too quick to want to believe that our pretty judge is innocent."

Jamie worked to keep her anger under control. "What the hell does that mean?"

"I saw you watching her through the whole interview. You could barely keep your eyes off of her. Be careful you're not thinking with some part of your body other than your brain."

Jamie felt her face redden and a vein throbbed in her forehead. She took a step toward Stacey before Alex grabbed her arm.

"Easy," Alex said.

Jamie angrily shook off Alex's hand. "You have absolutely no clue. What I'm trying to do is make sure that we build a solid case here. You remember what the hell that is? I'm just making sure that we're not going off half cocked in our rush to find someone to pin this on. What the hell do we have? A witness who might have overheard them arguing? Where's the motive, the physical evidence? Hell, I argue with people every day. Does that make me a potential murder suspect? All I'm saying is let's be thorough in our investigation and not simply decide ahead of time what the outcome should be."

Stacey paled at the barb that referred to a previous case of her own where painfully personal involvement had motivated her to stop an investigation before the evidence was followed to its conclusion.

Alex, who had been directly involved in that investigation, stepped in to stop the argument before it progressed beyond words.

"Enough. Both of you knock it off," she said. "I've got better things to do than to play referee for a couple of immature know-it-alls."

She glared at both of them until she saw they were listening. "I'm sort of agreeing with Jamie here. The main problem I have with her being a suspect is that she didn't have an alibi."

Stacey threw a look at Jamie and then more calmly turned to Alex. "I'm confused. Are you thinking that by not having an alibi, she appears more innocent than if she did?"

"Not necessarily. It just makes me wonder if she's waiting to see how far this goes before springing an alibi on us."

"Like she's holding one in reserve, just in case?"

"Something like that. Unless we find evidence that she was in that hotel room, or we discover details of that argument that provide us with motive, I'm not sure we have enough to charge her."

Jamie frowned. She wanted to punch something. She pushed off the wall and walked to the door.

"Jamie, wait a moment?" Alex went to her. "Are you okay? I know this must be hard." She hesitated, trying to figure out how best to handle Jamie's relationship with the deceased.

"I'm fine. I just need to stretch my legs." Jamie left without another word.

Alex looked after her, puzzled. *Something's wrong with her, and I'm going to find out what it is.*

Chapter
Eight

A SHORT TIME later, Jamie checked Alex's office and was told that she had stepped out for lunch. Back in her own office, Jamie closed and locked the door, then with heart hammering, she inserted the tape into the VCR. She looked quickly around the tiny office before pressing play. She felt guilt mixed with trepidation as she fast forwarded to the image of Shane stepping out of the elevator. Her eyes followed Shane as she walked to the door, but the tape ended before she could see anything else. She didn't know whether or not to feel relief that she couldn't know for sure what Shane had been up to that Thursday evening.

She rubbed her eyes, feeling strangely close to tears. *What the hell am I going to do?* She ejected the tape and, after briefly debating about it, placed it in the bottom drawer of her desk and locked it.

Jamie left the building and walked down the street. Her thoughts were chaotic, her feelings too close to the surface. She tried to grasp any one of her thoughts: Shane, her father...*Father.* She hadn't thought of him that way in years, the memory of his presence in her life ruthlessly erased. Therapy had soothed away some of the ragged edges left by the past. Hatred, fear, and guilt had all softened to a dull throb.

She barely registered the thought that the dead man was her father; he had stopped being that a lifetime ago. Part of her knew he deserved what he had gotten. *The bastard.* She suddenly realized that she should tell her mother.

LEAVING THE POLICE precinct, Shane drove with one eye on the rearview mirror. She recognized her symptoms as paranoia but she figured she was entitled, having spent the previous hour being questioned in connection with a homicide. With Jamie Saunders in the room, knowing she was lying. Of course, Jamie had also been lying, if only by omission. *I wonder why? Curiosity? To see how far I would go?*

She had fully expected the detective to denounce her as a liar. *Maybe she was protecting her own reputation. Maybe her colleagues don't know that she's gay. Maybe that was part of it.* For today at least, Jamie had been more interested in keeping their night together a secret than in impeaching her statement and nailing her as a suspect. *But that could change. I don't have much time.*

HESITATING, JAMIE STOOD on the sidewalk, just looking at the tiny bungalow. The shutters had been painted a muted green; her mother's prized roses were in full bloom on either side of the walkway. Now that she was here, she was at a loss. She hadn't considered how she would broach the subject of her father. That topic had not been brought up in this house since that horrifying night when he had walked out for good, a shotgun aimed at his chest providing the motivation.

The front door opened and her mother stepped out onto the porch and squinted into the sun. She was an older, shorter version of Jamie — fuller in the face, her hair a quieter shade of blonde, her face faintly lined. Only her eyes, a soft blue, were notably different. Jamie had more chiseled features, and she had inherited her father's eyes. Jamie knew that thirty years later, her eyes still brought a jolt of pain to her mother.

"Hi, honey. This is a surprise." Her mother smiled in delight.

Jamie shrugged as she climbed the steps to the small front porch. "I was in the neighborhood." She nodded at a couple of white wicker chairs in the corner that looked cozy. "Those are new."

"My reading corner," her mother replied, astute eyes reading the tension in her daughter's body. As if that weren't enough of an indicator, her eyes were a dead giveaway — the dark, turbulent gray when Jamie was upset. "Want some iced tea?"

"Sure."

They stepped into the cheerful little house, the scent of lemon wax mixing with that of freshly cut flowers. Jamie followed her mother to the back, where the kitchen looked out over a neat yard. She perched on one of the stools next to a large breakfast nook and silently watched her mother efficiently pour them each a glass of iced tea from a pitcher.

Her mother turned and caught the quiet interest. "Honey, what is it?"

Jamie smiled ruefully. *I never could keep anything from her.* Except for that one terrible secret that had, when exposed to the light of day, destroyed her family. "Have you seen the news lately?"

Her mother chuckled. "Never. I refuse to watch anything that will depress me." She took her glass and started walking to the front of the house. "Let's go sit on the porch."

Jamie followed slowly, feeling the tightness in her chest. Her mother patted the flowered cushion beside her and Jamie settled there, a familiar scent drifting toward her. *She always smells of lemon and something soft.* That smell evoked everything that was good about her childhood. Her mother put an arm around her shoulders, and they sat quietly for a moment.

"I'm working on a new case."

Her mother stayed silent, knowing Jamie would reveal what was bothering her in her own good time.

"A murder." Jamie took her mother's hand, feeling the strength and the fragility in equal measure. "The Chief Justice was killed last Thursday." Even now she could not bring herself to call him "dad."

She felt the stillness in her mother's body, the brief tightening of her hand. Felt the slight shudder that then followed. She looked at her mother who stared at the brick house across the street, her face pensive.

"Funny, for years I did wish him harm. But in time, that sentiment dulled as I tried to focus on the good."

Jamie stroked her hand. "I'm sorry, Mom." *Sorry for destroying your life, sorry for destroying the illusion,* she thought but did not voice.

"Sorry?" Her mother turned to her. "Oh, honey, don't." She cupped Jamie's trembling chin with her hand and lifted her face to look deep into her eyes. "You are my angel. Having you was the good that I kept remembering. I stopped hating him a long time ago. The man is dead, and I'm sorry that he died by someone's hand." She settled her hands in her lap with a sigh. "Truth be told, though, I'm not sorry he's dead."

"Neither am I."

"Will you tell Emma, or do you want me to?" her mother asked, knowing that Jamie's sister probably had not heard the news, either.

"I will." Jamie leaned her head against her mother's shoulder as she had when she was a child, and felt the soft stroking of her mother's hand on her head. They sat quietly. "I love you, Mom."

"And I love you."

Chapter
Nine

"Daddy?"

"Hush, sweet pea. You don't want to wake your sister." She felt his hands on the front of her pajama bottom. *"Remember the game I taught you?"*

"But, Daddy –"

"Shhh. Be a good girl."

"Daddy, it hurts..."

Jamie bolted up, a scream dying on her lips. Disoriented, she frantically searched the dark room and slowly clued in to the dream. She shoved a trembling hand through her tousled hair as she gulped in air. It had been years since she had been visited by those images. She rubbed a hand over her face and felt the wetness. She glanced at the clock beside the bed — three o'clock. The silence pressed down on her and panic spread through her body. *I'm safe. I'm safe,* she kept repeating to herself. After a brief hesitation, she reached for the telephone.

"What?" the grumpy voice answered on the seventh ring.

"Darcy? It's Jamie."

There was a pause. "James, this is starting to be a bad habit."

Darcy's voice had always fascinated Jamie. It always sounded like it needed sleep cleared from it. Tonight the voice was deeper than usual as if she had just gone to bed.

"I'm sorry." Then a thought dawned on Jamie. "Oh. Darcy, are you alone?"

"As a matter of fact, yes. Not that it's any of your damn business."

The grumpy tone almost made Jamie smile. "Can I come over?"

Something in Jamie's tone alerted Darcy, who sat up, pushing the tangled waves from her face, immediately concerned. "What's wrong?"

"I don't want to be alone."

Darcy absorbed the quiet words. "Honey, are the demons back?"

Jamie swallowed hard, trying not to cry. "Kind of."

"I'll leave the back door open."

"Thanks, Darcy."

"Forget it. I was just sleeping. *Alone*."

Jamie hung up, then stood up on trembling legs. Darcy was the only one of her friends who knew any part of the sordid story. Years before, after too many glasses of wine, Darcy had stayed overnight and had been awakened by Jamie's screams. As Darcy held her, the story behind the nightmares tumbled out in a rush of words as if it had been too long held back. The secrets; the waiting for the sound of footsteps outside the bedroom door; the horrific visits in the middle of the night as her sister lay sleeping in the bed next to hers, until the night when Jamie had woken up and heard her sister crying. She had known then that her father had been visiting both of them.

To protect her sister, she had gone to her mother the next day and told her everything. She had been eight years old and even now, thirty years later, she could see the look on her mother's face: the shock, the disbelief, the pain. And she had been the one to cause it; it had been her fault.

Over the years, whenever the screaming in Jamie's head got too loud, Darcy had always been there—non-judgmental, dropping everything to be with her when needed—until the nightmares came with less and less frequency. Jamie couldn't remember the last time she'd had one. *Until tonight.*

She drove to Darcy's apartment above Murphy's and let herself in. Darcy had turned on all the lights and was in the kitchen getting the vodka ready. Her thick auburn hair, which she usually wore up or tied back, fell in a wild mass of curls down to the middle of her back.

Seeing Darcy standing in the kitchen looking sleep tousled and grumpy, Jamie was struck with the realization that her friend was stunning—an unusual thought to be having at that particular moment.

Darcy had always worn her sexuality comfortably, at ease with it. It was just genetics after all, she often said when complimented. She rarely considered her effect on people. And over the years, neither had Jamie. But when she let her hair down—both figuratively and literally—the impact was powerful. And for a moment, Jamie felt it, shivered with it.

Darcy gazed at Jamie with quiet blue eyes. Without a word, she handed Jamie a tumbler. "I've got a fire going in the other room." She walked into the living room.

Jamie was grateful for Darcy's matter-of-fact tone as she followed.

Darcy settled her long form onto the brown leather couch, then raised a brow at Jamie.

With a quiet smile, Jamie went to the couch and settled beside Darcy.

Darcy wrapped her arms around Jamie, who relaxed into her embrace as they sat watching the fire as it hissed in the grate.

"Do you want to talk about it?" Darcy asked, softly.

Jamie sighed. "Same nightmare. It's been a long time."

"What brought it on, do you think?"

Jamie hesitated. "He died. It brought back a lot of stuff I thought had been dealt with, I guess."

"You have dealt with it, James, to the best of your ability."

For a while they watched the flames flicker and take shapes, comfortable in the silence. Jamie smiled as Darcy caressed her hair, the touch soothing. She relaxed further into her arms, inhaling a scent that had, over the years, become as familiar as her own.

"Why do you suppose we never got together?" Jamie suddenly asked.

The question startled Darcy and she took time to think about it. "I dunno. Maybe because relationships often come and go, but true friendships can last a lifetime." She looked at Jamie. "I guess I'd rather have you in my life for a lifetime."

Expecting a typically Darcy flippant remark, Jamie stared at her, touched. "You sometime surprise me, Darcy." She smiled tenderly.

Hiding her embarrassment, Darcy grinned. "Don't get used to it."

Jamie settled back into Darcy's strong arms. A feeling, soft and sweet, stole over her as she felt the arms tighten around her. *Safe. I'm safe here.*

Chapter
Ten

JAMIE WAS AMBIVALENT about Alex wanting to attend the Chief Justice's memorial service. But she was fascinated, in a detached sort of way as they stood outside and watched the people who had decided that the service was worth attending.

Tomas Reynolds' will stipulated that he be cremated. A memorial service had been scheduled, and the morning dawned bright and sunny. By ten o'clock, the Cathedral Church of St. Paul was packed to capacity. The famous and infamous were there, as were those who had come to gawk at the famous and infamous, including the current junior senator, the mayor, and the entire court of appeals.

Some had never met Judge Reynolds, but deemed themselves important enough to attend an important man's funeral. Almost without exception, most of those in attendance had disparaged the deceased while he was alive. Nevertheless, they filed into the church shaking their heads and mourning his tragic, untimely death. The altar overflowed with floral arrangements.

Outside, inconspicuous beside one of the faux Greek pillars, a police photographer was snapping shots of everyone who was in attendance. Killers often returned to the scene of the crime or appeared to watch the mourners.

As soon as she and Alex entered, Jamie caught sight of Shane sitting in the front, her head bowed as if she were praying.

Jamie and Alex scooted into a pew in the back of the church just as the service started. Jamie tuned out the scripture readings and eulogies as she mulled over the details of the case. The case. That was all it was to her. Her father's death, his murder, was reduced to the level of an investigation.

The pressure in her chest intensified. She looked across the packed church and was surprised that her vision was blurred. She blinked as more tears came. *How can I be crying for the bastard?* She clenched her hands in her lap, and a shudder carried the grief through her body. She rubbed impatiently at the wetness on her cheeks and she focused on the back of Shane's golden head.

"*Daddy, I'm afraid.*"

"*Of what, sweet pea?*"

"*The monster. He's in the closet.*"

"*Don't worry, honey. I'll take care of him.*" He walked to the closet and opened the door and made all kinds of noise. "*There. He's gone.*"

She smiled at him. Her daddy would always protect her.

"Are you okay?" Alex asked, as Jamie shifted restlessly.

"I'm fine. See anything of interest?"

"No."

As the hymn rose around her, Jamie started to panic, sweat breaking out along her spine. She took a breath and all of a sudden felt lightheaded. "I'm going to go check on things outside."

Without looking at her, Alex nodded.

Jamie squeezed past her partner and slipped outside. She blinked at the bright sunshine and nodded once at the uniforms slouching against the unmarked car alongside the curb. She stood still, trying to calm her jittery nerves and barely felt the breeze that carried the scent of something sweet.

I'm losing it. Maybe I should make an appointment with my therapist.

Jamie had stopped seeing her a few years before, when she thought she had done enough work on understanding herself to take a break. But now the hard won peace seemed to have evaporated. Being reduced to panic attacks in church was not a good sign.

A familiar car pulled up to the front of the church. The red Mustang convertible had been a weakness and an extravagance that suited Darcy to a T. Darcy got out of the car, her impressively long legs catching the attention of the officers. She flashed Jamie a smile that Jamie returned.

"What are you doing here?" Jamie asked.

"Sure as hell not paying my respects." Darcy squinted into the sun. "Alex told me about the funeral, and I thought I would come by just to make sure the bastard was dead."

The remark was so outrageous that Jamie stared open-mouthed at her for a moment. Darcy looked back, her mouth curving. Jamie started to laugh; it felt good. She leaned her head briefly on Darcy's shoulder, inhaling the familiar spicy scent. "I'm so glad you came. I think I was in the middle of a full fledged panic attack in there."

"How are you now?"

"Better." Jamie was surprised that she meant it.

Years before, she had stopped questioning why being with Darcy made her feel protected; it just did. But on this afternoon, the thought crossed her mind again. She studied Darcy's smooth profile, her full unsmiling mouth, and flutters bounced in her stomach that, for her, usually signaled attraction. *Surely not this time.* She shifted, trying to quell the rising feeling. "Listen, I —"

The church bells pealed. The service was over. She glanced back at the oak doors and swore silently. Darcy looked at her. "What were you going to say?"

"Nothing important." The doors swung open with a dull thud, and the crowd spilled out of the church. Jamie sighed. "I have to go." She glanced at Darcy, who was smiling at the gawking officers. "Don't toy with them."

Darcy grinned and shrugged. "Habit."

Jamie shook her head and turned to leave, but stopped. "Can I come over later?"

Darcy lifted an eyebrow in surprise. "Why would you even ask that? You always come over."

Jamie smiled tentatively. "I mean after you finish work."

Darcy froze as she met Jamie's gray eyes. Something tangled in her stomach but let go before she could name it. "Sure. I'm not closing tonight, so come by anytime."

"No hot date then?"

Darcy paused as she tried to remember the last time she had had a date. "Fuck, I guess I'm going through a dry spell." They laughed.

Jamie impulsively kissed her on the cheek, tempted for one brief instant to lean closer. She pulled back reluctantly. "I'll be over later."

WHEN JAMIE ARRIVED at the café, Darcy was leaning against the oak bar flirting with a pretty brunette in a very short skirt. Darcy had changed into faded jeans and a loose, charcoal gray sweater; her hair was tied back carelessly and she looked casually sexy. For some unfathomable reason, this irritated Jamie.

Darcy turned and flashed a quick grin in Jamie's direction but her grin faded at the look on Jamie's face. "Are you okay?"

"Just edgy."

"Want a drink?"

"Not really." Jamie shifted, unable to put words to what she was feeling.

Darcy leaned over and whispered something to the brunette, who laughed and nodded. Still smiling, Darcy turned and caught Jamie's intent look. "What?"

"A new prospect for that long overdue date?"

Darcy gave her a curious look. "As a matter of fact, no. Natalie is engaged to Billy and is just killing time until his shift is over."

Jamie felt foolish. Billy was one of her pretty boy bartenders. She frowned, rubbing an impatient hand along the back of her neck. *What the hell is wrong with me?*

"She lets me practice my lines on her though," Darcy added with a grin.

Jamie shook her head. "You don't need any practice, Stretch. Believe me, you're dangerous enough."

Darcy studied Jamie for a moment. Something didn't feel right. Almost like a note that was off-key. "James, let's go for a walk."

Bundled into jackets against the cool evening air, they started walking without any particular direction, gazing into windows, reading the menus plastered on entryways. As they passed a roadhouse, the tantalizing smell of mesquite floated past them. Music drifted from a bar across the street. The sidewalks were alive with people walking home from a movie, from late business, from a visit to friends. A subway train rumbled underground. Taxis were coming back from the theaters, traveling to little clubs on the side streets.

Jamie took a deep breath and slowly eased it through her body. She needed this, this aimless drifting that allowed her to empty her mind and just concentrate on the noises and smells around her. There were almost no stars in the inky sky. As they continued walking, their footsteps echoed softly on the pavement. They didn't say anything, felt no need for words. The silence between them was easy.

They crossed at a traffic light and as they got to the other side, Darcy grabbed Jamie's hand and held it as they continued walking. Jamie shot her a quick glance, but Darcy's attention was on one of the displays in an antique shop. Jamie curled her fingers against Darcy's hand and let Darcy lead her as they resumed walking.

Darcy grinned when a woman in a tight, blue running suit ran past and shot the auburn beauty a quick look. The look was subtle but effective. Darcy was more amused than interested. She felt the sudden tension in Jamie's hand and turned to her. Jamie was glaring after the jogger with what looked like annoyance.

"Jamie?" Curious once again at the mixed signals she was

sensing, Darcy stopped walking and released Jamie's hand. "Is everything okay? Do you want to talk?"

Jamie didn't understand why she suddenly felt so resentful of the attention Darcy was getting. No, resentful was the wrong word. *I feel...*Puzzled, she stared at Darcy, then it hit her with a sudden, stabbing clarity. *Jealous? I'm jealous?* She forced a smile. "It was just a bad day, Darcy. I'm feeling off, that's all."

Jamie started to walk and Darcy followed. But the air between them had shifted, and Darcy puzzled over the undercurrents that pulled at her. Then she saw a green and orange neon sign that was as colorful as Christmas lights and she stopped, delighted. "Mario's. I forgot he was still here. We have to stop. Tonight calls for a hot chocolate." She grabbed Jamie's hand again and pulled her to the pastry shop with the gaudy window displays. "Wait here."

She went in, leaving Jamie standing outside the door lost in thought as she watched the traffic go by. A few minutes later Darcy returned and handed a cup to Jamie while she kept the second. Jamie's cup overflowed with whip cream.

"I ordered extra whip. This is guaranteed to improve any mood," she said with a grin.

Darcy's pink tongue slowly licked the foam from the top of her cup. Fascinated by the movement, Jamie stared at her, unable to look away.

Becoming aware of the stare, Darcy met Jamie's eyes and her heart lurched against her ribcage. She held the gaze until Jamie broke it to take a sip.

"This is too sinful to be having on a weeknight," Jamie injected into the charged air.

I probably misread her look, Darcy thought. She forced a smile. "I know. Decadent isn't it?"

"I'll have to run an extra ten miles tomorrow, but it might just be worth it." Jamie took another sip, closing her eyes with pleasure.

Darcy grinned. "A taste of heaven." She slowly stroked Jamie's upper lip with her thumb. "You've got foam all over the place."

Jamie went very still at the feel of Darcy's finger against her mouth and for one crazy moment, she was tempted to seek more. She blinked once as she focused first on Darcy's mouth, then lifted to the waiting blue. Darcy looked at her, unsmiling, and Jamie read the awareness in her blue eyes, an acknowledgement that the temptation was somehow mutual. Jamie smiled. Then they broke contact almost simultaneously.

Whatever it was had passed, and Jamie filed the fleeting

moment away to think about later. But as Darcy took her hand for the walk back, Jamie smiled to herself. Despite the difficult day, the last hour had evaporated her tension, replaced it with a different kind. The kind that left her breathless and in knots. And she had no doubt that the reason for it was the woman walking beside her. Once again Darcy had made the bad things better. Without thinking, Jamie pushed a strand of Darcy's hair that the wind toyed with behind Darcy's ear.

Darcy turned her head to Jamie as they stopped at her front door. "Want to come up?" she asked softly.

The question was simple, the meaning unclear. And Jamie's need was huge. Shaking her head, she sighed. "No, it's best that I don't." She kissed Darcy on the cheek. "Good night, Stretch."

Chapter
Eleven

JAMIE THOUGHTFULLY STUDIED the autopsy report. "So, he had a stroke."

Alex nodded. "That could explain the wound on his head. He was sitting there having a drink, stood up, and then keeled over—hitting his head on the floor. Remember, it was only after he was already down that he got popped. Whoever it was, was trying to make sure he was dead."

Jamie paced the office. "This changes the complexion of things. This may no longer be murder, but rather attempted murder. The timing between his stroke and his being shot might be too close to ever know for sure."

"Yeah." Alex rubbed her chin. "It can't change our investigation. At the very least, we have attempted murder. We have to proceed under the assumption that he was murdered. As long as we have evidence of foul play, I have to continue the investigation. I'm waiting on the rest of the CSA's findings. They found two other sets of fingerprints and a strand of hair that was patently not Reynolds'." The door opened and an assistant walked in with a folder. "Speaking of the devil—"

"The tests results are in." He handed Alex the folder.

She glanced at the piece of paper inside and then smiled. "Well, well, well, it appears that our star suspect has not been telling the truth after all."

Jamie felt sick inside, and turned away. Whatever relief she had initially felt at Alex's statement about the stroke had evaporated as she watched Alex's eyes narrow at the folder's contents.

"I'll ask Judge Scott to come in for further questioning," Alex said.

The trap was being set. Jamie could sense it. *I need to get out of here.*

SHANE WAS IMMEDIATELY on her guard as Alex ushered her and her lawyer into the interrogation room and seated them at the table where Jamie was already waiting. Alex appeared too confident with her quiet manner, her faint amusement. Shane glanced at Jamie, who was studiously avoiding Shane's eyes. Alex stood across from Shane and her voice commanded everyone's attention. "I'll ask you one more time — and I would suggest you think carefully before answering: were you in Judge Reynolds' suite on the night in question?"

Shane tried not to look at Jamie, but couldn't help herself. Their eyes met and she felt Jamie's gray eyes like a physical touch. Her mouth parted, almost as if she were out of breath.

"Don't answer that," Landry cautioned.

"I don't mind. I have nothing to hide. No, I was not in his hotel room on the night in question."

Alex nodded. She had expected the denial. She flipped through her notes. "Then how would you explain your fingerprints inside the room? Well?"

"Well, what, Detective?"

"You lied to us, didn't you, Miss Scott?"

"Don't answer, Shane," Landry said.

"I want to, Ken."

"I strongly urge you not to say anything."

"But I want to answer." She turned her attention to Alex.

Alex met Shane's eyes and felt the impact of her presence. Shane really was an attractive woman. But there was something more in her eyes, something haunted and almost calculating as they stared back at her. Alex narrowed her eyes.

"I did not lie, Detective. You asked me if I was in Judge Reynolds' suite the night of his murder, and I was not. But I *have* been in the suite on previous occasions working on a case."

She's clever, Alex thought with grudging respect. "Well, that's convenient, isn't it? When were you in his suite?"

"A few days prior to his death. We were working on a death penalty case and I dropped some opinions over."

"I see." Alex rubbed her lower lip thoughtfully, then she glanced at Jamie and was jolted by the look on her face. Jamie stood and moved out of Alex's field of vision. Alex turned back to Shane. "It's interesting that you seem to have a prepared answer for everything."

"Is that a question?" Landry asked testily.

"Just an observation. I guess that's all for now." Alex thoughtfully watched them leave, then glanced at Jamie. "Something doesn't feel right."

Jamie tensed. "What doesn't?"

Alex stood up. "Her whole demeanor, her whole story. It just doesn't add up."

Jamie frowned. "It doesn't not add up, either."

"That's just it."

Chapter
Twelve

RAIN DRIPPED FROM the leaves in steady musical plops, and the air shimmered with the weight the storm had left behind. The day was leaking into dusk as Jamie leaned against the tree and stared at the windows of the brownstone. When a light came on in an upstairs room, she pushed upright, her mind made up.

Jamie went to the front door and rang the bell. A few minutes later, she saw the peephole darken and the door opened, revealing Shane wrapped in a towel, her hair dripping wet.

"What are you doing here?"

"I wanted to talk to you."

"That's not a good idea. We shouldn't be speaking."

"I'm aware of that. Nevertheless..." Jamie shrugged.

Shane stepped aside. Jamie walked in and closed the door behind her.

As they stood in the foyer, Jamie studied Shane and couldn't control her body's reaction. Her anger rose at that realization as she fought to keep her mind on what had to be done. "Did you know who I was when you walked into Murphy's that night?"

"No, I —"

Jamie slammed her hand against the wall, startling Shane, who jumped nervously. "Don't lie to me, goddammit. Don't you lie to me. Did you know who I was?"

"No, I swear." Jamie's nearness made Shane's body ache.

"But you recognized me somehow. Where? Where did you recognize me from?"

"I didn't. I don't..."

Desperation settling over her, Jamie grabbed Shane. "What are you hiding? I know you're hiding something. Why didn't you say anything about me when you were first questioned?"

"Why didn't you?" Shane asked.

"I know you're lying," Jamie said softly, almost to herself. "Except I can't figure out what you're lying about. Did you kill the Justice, Shane?" She shook Shane slightly.

"No." Shane struggled against Jamie's firm hold, her robe slipping dangerously low.

Jamie shook her head. "You knew who I was when you walked into that bar. You made sure I would see you, making enough commotion to get my attention. Why? Was it a set up?" She leaned closer. "Tell me, *Your Honor*? What are you hiding? Were you his lover?"

"What?"

"Were you fucking the Chief Justice?"

"Go to hell." Shane pulled away.

"Thanks anyway. I've been there since I first laid eyes on you."

Jamie's bitter words slashed at Shane. "Don't," she whispered.

Jamie tried not to let the pleading expression in Shane's eyes sway her. "That's not what you said when you came the first time. Or was it the second time?"

Shane shook her head. "Jamie, please leave. Don't ask me anything else. Don't put me in the position of having to lie to you."

"That's a joke. You've been lying since I met you. Look at me and tell me you didn't come after me that day."

Shane stared at her. "I didn't. Not really."

"Not really." Jamie clenched her fists at her side; she wanted to release the unbearable pressure by punching something. She swore as she pivoted away. Fighting against the wave of helplessness that was rising in her, she turned back. "What else have you lied about?"

"I haven't."

Jamie stepped closer and rubbed Shane's lower lip with her thumb. "So beautiful. You lie so beautifully."

"I'm not lying, Jamie."

"You played me so well. Why?" She parted the full lips with her thumb. "Why did you come home with me?"

Buried in the question was a plea that called to Shane. She closed her eyes, fighting the arousal spreading through her body. She opened heavy lids. "For this. Just for this." She groaned as she pressed her mouth to Jamie's.

At the feel of Shane's mouth, Jamie lost all control. With an oath, she thrust her tongue deep in response and pushed Shane against the wall, her firm thigh pressing between bare legs. She parted the loose robe and was steeped in the remembered scent and feel of her body.

Shane pumped her hips against Jamie's jeans clad leg, need

pouring through her. "Oh God, Jamie, touch me. Please." She grabbed and pulled Jamie's shirt from her pants, and greedily found and stroked her velvet skin, the full breasts, and squeezed the hard nipples.

"Damn you. Damn you," Jamie snarled as she moved against Shane, feeling the pressure build. She entered Shane with her fingers without any gentleness and found her wet and ready.

Shane bucked against Jamie's fingers, knowing she was about to come, too wrapped up in the incredible feeling pulsing through her to stop it. "Yes, yes. Faster." Shane shoved against Jamie's hand, and the climax came fast and sharp, and she cried out as she grasped Jamie's back.

Jamie closed her eyes and emptied her mind as she rode the firm thigh. She bit Shane's neck as the climax slammed into her.

They half supported one another as they tried to catch their breath. Jamie took a shuddering, gulping breath. It had been primal and angry but she had been too far gone to stop it. She was disgusted with herself, with her lack of control. She felt undone by the madness of being so close to Shane again.

Jamie opened her eyes to look at Shane, and shook her head as if to clear it. "I'm sorry. I'm sorry, Shane; I shouldn't have... Did I hurt you?"

Shane opened her eyes and gently brushed Jamie's blonde hair from her forehead with a trembling hand. "You have to believe that it's never been like this with anyone," she whispered.

Jamie sighed. "God help me. You're so lovely, Shane. Every time I see you, it's like the first time. The light's different, the angle, but it strikes me just as it did the first time. Tell me what you're hiding. I know there's something. Maybe I can help you."

Shane straightened and pushed her away, giving her a long, level look. "You have to go. You can't be seen here."

Desperation spread through Jamie. "Was there something between you and the judge? Was he threatening you in some way?" She felt rather than saw Shane's sudden tension.

"I'm sorry. Just go, Jamie."

Resigned and frustrated, Jamie walked the few steps to the front door, then stopped and turned. "You're going to have to come clean about what you know one of these days." She wanted to mention the video but didn't. She took a last look, then closed the door.

JAMIE CAUGHT THE shadowy figure out of the corner of her eye and got her arms up and deflected the blow.

"What the fuck are you doing here? Have you lost your mind?" Alex shouted as she shoved Jamie against her car.

Jamie struggled against her hold. "Let me go."

"Shut up." Alex pushed her inside, then went around the car, got into the driver's side, and slammed the door with barely restrained anger. "What the hell are you doing at our suspect's house in the middle of the night?"

"What are you doing following me?" Jamie asked.

Alex slammed a fist against the steering wheel. "I wasn't, you fool. I was watching our suspect to see where she goes at night. Imagine my surprise when I saw you going in, hoping like hell that I was mistaken. Are you fucking crazy?"

"Possibly."

"What were you doing in there?"

Jamie looked at her and shook her head. She was sure Alex would never understand, especially since she didn't herself. "Nothing."

Alex swore as she shoved an impatient hand through her short dark hair. "You better start leveling with me, 'cause I'm not in the mood to play guessing games right now. I'm this close to kicking your ass from here to New York City and back. Now start talking. Do you know this woman?"

"No. Not really."

"Not really?" Alex whipped her head around and stared at Jamie. "Spill it."

Jamie looked out of the window. She could still feel Shane's imprint on her body. "I just...I just wanted to talk to her."

"Why?"

"Because. I was trying to get at the truth."

"Truth? Truth about what? You *do* know her don't you?"

Jamie shrugged. "We had a one-night stand." She hunched defensively and couldn't meet Alex's stunned eyes.

Alex swore loudly. "I knew something felt odd. When? Why didn't you say anything?"

"At the time, it didn't seem important."

Alex stared at Jamie as if seeing her for the first time. So many thoughts flitted through her mind that for a moment she was speechless. She took a deep breath, fighting off the urge to snap something in two. "Well, now it is. You're jeopardizing our investigation, your career, possibly mine. For what? Are you willing to put yourself on the line for someone you don't even know?"

Alex was right. Everything she said made sense. Still, Jamie couldn't help herself. She was wrapped in a sexual haze and it flowed through her veins as addictive as any drug. "Yeah, I'm willing to put it all on the line."

"For a quick fuck?"

Jamie turned to her. "Alex, I can't explain it. It just feels so..." She shook her head.

Alex looked at Jamie, torn between her love for her and her duty as a police officer. Jamie was her best friend and they had been through so much over the years. Jamie had been there for her when she needed her. But now she was being asked to obstruct justice. *The damn fool.* Frustrated love flooded through her. She took hold of Jamie's arm. "I want you off this case. *Now.* And I want you to promise to stay away from our suspect."

Jamie pushed away from her. "I can't do that. I need to see this through."

"Then you're crazier than I am. I'm going to ask that you be taken off this case. For your own sake."

"Do what you have to do, Alex. But I'll do what I have to do." Jamie slammed out of the car.

Alex punched the dashboard in frustration and stared into the darkness. "Goddammit!"

FOLLOWING THE CONFRONTATION with Alex, Jamie drove around for hours, unsettled. The fact that she couldn't think rationally about this case, about this woman, scared her. Somehow, it had all gone off the rails. She really didn't know what she was going to do. *How am I supposed to handle this? I need to talk to someone. Someone who can be objective.* Ordinarily she would have talked to Alex, but under the circumstances that was out of the question.

She thought of Darcy, but felt she had already imposed on her enough. And thinking of Darcy had her stomach jumping for reasons she was determined not to explore too closely. *Lauren. I can go to Lauren.* Their friendship had the ease of old friends, where weeks could go by without speaking to one another, and then all of a sudden they would reconnect, as if no time had passed at all.

Lauren was surprised when she opened the door. It was unusual for Jamie to show up unannounced, but a quick glance discerned the misery on her face. "Are you going to just stand there in my doorway, or do you want to come in?"

"Yes...no..." Jamie shifted from one foot to the other.

"Okay, why don't I help you decide?" Lauren smiled gently and pulled Jamie inside. "Want a beer?"

"I...I don't know." Jamie pushed an impatient hand through her already tousled hair.

The trembling in Jamie's fingers was not lost on Lauren, who hid her concern with a practical shrug. "Well, I'm having one. I'll get you one just in case."

Followed by Jamie, she went to the kitchen, retrieved two beers, and placed a bottle on the table for Jamie.

Jamie stood in the doorway undecided, lost.

"Jamie, what is it? What's got you so twisted?"

Jamie met Lauren's golden eyes. They had been friends since college, and for years Jamie had been half in love with her. Too scared to declare herself to Lauren, she had buried all emotions except friendship. The feelings had eased over the years, especially after Lauren had fallen head over heels in love with Madison, another of Jamie's close friends. Now they were closer than ever, settling into an easy friendship with few demands. But Jamie would always have a tender spot for Lauren. She sighed. "A woman."

Lauren hid a smile. That answer had been almost predictable. "You met someone?"

"Yes...no."

Lauren lifted a brow. "You didn't meet someone?"

"I kind of did, but not in the normal sense." Jamie paused. "That didn't come out right."

"Really?" Lauren replied dryly.

Jamie shot her a look, sat down, and placed her elbows on the table. "I met someone a couple of weeks ago. It was the most unbelievable night of my life. Then the next morning, she was gone. And that was that. Except it's not, and she's back, and I'm in the middle of something that's just...She's..."Jamie rubbed her eyes. "It's complicated. I can't discuss it." *And my friendship with Alex is in jeopardy,* she thought.

Hiding her worry, Lauren knelt next to Jamie and wrapped her arms around her.

"This is not what I had planned for. She's not what I was looking for. It's so —"

"Life's full of surprises, isn't it? Some of them are a real kick in the ass," Lauren replied, not unsympathetically. "I'll tell you something Madison once told me. In life you can't keep sitting on the sidelines placing little side bets on what the outcome is going to be. You have to play the game; 'cause if you don't play, you can't win."

Jamie looked at her. "Madison said that?"

Lauren smiled. "Yeah."

"Well, Madison's an idiot."

Lauren laughed, and her amusement escalated when she met the puzzled eyes of her lover in the doorway.

"Should I be jealous?" Madison slipped out of her jacket and threw it on the back of one of the chairs as she walked into the kitchen.

"Absolutely. Jamie's the only woman besides you that has my heart." She kissed the top of Jamie's head, and with a last gentle rub of her back, straightened and went to greet Madison. Her stomach did the usual flip as she kissed her, lingering for a moment. "Hey."

"Hey back." Madison pulled away reluctantly and gave Jamie a friendly slap on the back. "Hello, stranger. Haven't seen you in weeks. How are you?"

"Busy. Just dropped by to see if I could talk Lauren into running away with me." Jamie stood up. "She's not ready quite yet."

Madison grinned as she went to the refrigerator to grab a beer. "Give it time. I'm still not picking the towels up off the floor after a shower." She met Lauren's eyes and smiled. Lauren gave an amused shake of her head.

Jamie kissed Lauren. "I should go. Thanks for the beer." She nodded at the untouched bottle on the table. She gave Madison a quick hug, and left.

"What's wrong with her?" Madison asked.

"A woman." Lauren was troubled. "I've never seen her scared before, but I'd swear that she is now."

Madison frowned. "She's scared? Of what? This woman?"

"I don't know." Lauren exchanged puzzled looks with Madison. Jamie was and had always been the steadiest of them all, the one who could be counted on when things got out of control. Lauren found it as unsettling as it was unusual to believe that for once Jamie was in need of their help.

Chapter
Thirteen

JAMIE PUSHED OPEN the torn screen door and stopped in the entrance, immediately assaulted by the smell of cigarette smoke, spilt beer, and countless other odors best not to try and identify. Her feet stuck to the worn wooden floor, and she tried not to think about what kind of substances had been spilt on it. Her eyes stung as she narrowed them against the thick smoke that hung in the room.

Near the door, the regulars were glued to wobbly stools lining a large oak bar that might at some time have looked impressive. Some kept one eye on the baseball game playing on the old television set on a platform above them in the corner of the bar. The colors were washed out and the picture was blurry, but it didn't seem to matter. To the left, a pool table took up most of the space, and four men nursing their beers interrupted their game to watch her with interest.

Jamie squinted and tried to see through the thick blue haze. She wasn't surprised to find Barney sitting in his usual spot by the jukebox. She sauntered across the bar to him.

"No. No way."

"Hello, Barney."

The short, balding man scowled. "Whatever it is, Saunders, I didn't do it."

Jamie smiled, unperturbed. "Barney, sit. I'll buy you a beer." She motioned to a small table.

He looked at her suspiciously. "Shit, you got that look on your face."

"What look?"

"The one that says I'm not going to like what you have to say." He sat down and rubbed nicotine stained fingers over his bald head. "Make it a pint."

Jamie grinned, sat opposite him, and motioned to the waitress for two. She watched her unwilling companion until the waitress placed the glasses on the table with a thud, and he took a sip. "Watcha been doing lately, Barney?"

He nervously licked his fleshy lips. "Come on, let me enjoy my beer before springing whatever you've got."

Jamie laughed at his woebegone look. She had always liked him, even when she knew he had been skimming from the snitch fund to pay his gambling tabs. He had been a good investigator once, but alcohol and gambling weaknesses had caught up to him. She had used his investigative talents more than once. Sober, he was one of the best. Even half tanked he put a lot of the rookies to shame.

"I need a favor," she started.

He sighed. "Here it comes. And since you're alone, I'm not going to like it."

"I need you to do a deep background on a possible suspect we've got."

"Do we want him guilty or not?"

Jamie rubbed her chin. "I'm not sure. And it's not a he." He raised a brow as she handed him a small slip of paper. "Her name is Shane Scott. She's a judge. We think she might know something about the death of the Chief Justice."

"Jesus fucking Christ. A judge?" He dropped the slip of paper as if burned. "No way."

She calmly picked up her beer and took a sip as he continued his eruption.

He fixed his pale blue eyes on her. "Must be serious if you've come looking for me to do the research."

Jamie shrugged, trying for nonchalance. "There's some noise."

He nodded. "Where's Ryan?"

"She's working it from another angle. Keep her out of this one."

He nodded. "You're not acting with lust in your heart, are you, Detective?"

She threw him a cool look and stood up. "Just find out what you can. And fast."

Chapter
Fourteen

"NEED A RIDE?"

Lost in thought, it took a moment for the words to register, then Jamie noticed Madison leaning out of the driver's side of a parked car.

"Hey, Doc."

"I was in the neighborhood. Thought I could buy you a cup of coffee."

Jamie narrowed her eyes. "You wouldn't happen to be checking up on me, now would you, Doctor Williams?"

Madison put on an innocent expression. "Never. Anyway, it's either me or Darcy."

Jamie shook her head and smiled. "Put that way, how can I say no?" She got into the car.

Madison drove to a small coffee bar a few blocks away. She glanced at Jamie and took in the shadows like soft bruises under her eyes, the deep lines around her mouth.

They grabbed a coffee and decided to stroll along the little shops and art galleries.

"You know, whenever your name comes up in front of Alex, she just grunts and walks away. Are you two fighting?"

Jamie glanced at her. "Not exactly. We just had a difference of opinion."

"About this woman you're all twisted about?"

Jamie tripped but quickly recovered. "Where did you hear that?"

"Lauren."

Jamie swore to herself.

"She's worried about you, so am I. What's going on? Who is this girl? Anyone we know?"

Jamie shoved a hand through her hair, not wanting to have this conversation. "No. I met her...by chance."

"What's she like?" For the first time, Jamie looked at her fully and smiled, but the look in her eyes made Madison's heart lurch.

"She's beautiful. Witty. And I hardly know anything about her."

Madison gave her a worried look. "Jamie..."

Jamie waved her hand. "I know. It's just hard to know what is sheer lust and what could be more, because we haven't had any chance to really spend time together."

"Why?"

"It's complicated."

"You keep saying that."

"I know. I just...I never thought I could catch someone's eye that way, someone so beautiful. I don't know how to handle it."

Madison looked at her in surprise. "You're kidding me, right?"

Jamie frowned. "Why?"

Madison took her hand and they stopped for a moment. "You're beautiful, Jamie. You also happen to be the sexiest woman I know."

Startled, Jamie willed the warmth in her cheeks to go away.

Madison grinned. "Are you blushing?"

"No."

"You are too. Oh, my God! I made Saunders blush," she yelled out.

Jamie felt her blush intensify. "Shut up."

Madison emitted a sharp laugh. "I gotta remember this the next time you give me grief about something."

"Yeah, yeah, whatever." Jamie took a step and then looked back.

Madison, realized that whatever was going on, was serious to Jamie. She strolled next to Jamie past several blocks trying to figure out what to say to her friend.

"Is she married?"

"What?" Jamie looked at her. "No, it's nothing like that." She sighed. "I just don't know if I can trust her. I think she's lying to me."

Madison frowned. "Jamie –"

"Don't worry, I've got a plan."

"A plan?"

They stopped next to Madison's car.

"Sure. I've got to go." Jamie gave Madison a quick hug, then strode down the sidewalk before Madison could say anything else.

Madison stared after her, more worried than before. *We're gonna need the big guns,* she thought. They would need to involve Darcy.

Chapter
Fifteen

ALEX SAT LOST in thought and tapped her pen against an open folder. Did they have enough to persuade a judge to give them a search warrant? She continued to tap.

Stacey, who had dropped by to get an update, watched Alex with growing exasperation. Alex had mumbled no more than two words to her since her arrival and now, along with the tapping, looked distracted and uninterested in her questions.

"Should we wait for Jamie before going for the search warrant?" Stacey asked again.

Alex stared out of the window, thinking about the events from two nights before. *Jamie and our suspect. How could she be so dumb?* she thought angrily. *How can she jeopardize everything for someone she doesn't even know?*

Stacey grabbed the bouncing pen from Alex's hand. "For crying out loud, Alex, what's wrong with you today?"

Alex frowned. "What?"

"I've asked you the same question three times now. Do we have to wait for Jamie, or should we proceed with the warrant request?"

Alex sighed, her face set. "No, we don't have to wait for her."

Stacey opened her mouth to ask where Jamie was and snapped it shut at the look on Alex's face. Something had happened between them. Instinct told her it was related to their case, but she let it go for the moment.

"Okay, then let's go talk to a judge."

DARCY SHUT THE cash register and walked to the end of the bar. Jamie, looking glum, had been sitting there for the better part of an hour. "You know, Saunders, that frown of yours is going to scare away all of my best customers."

Jamie continued to stare at her drink. "Sorry."

Darcy took a couple of shot glasses from the glass shelf behind her and placed them on the polished oak bar. She grabbed a bottle, poured out shots, and handed one to Jamie, who automatically accepted it.

Following Darcy's lead, Jamie tossed it back, grimacing as the heat spread down her throat.

"Spill it," Darcy demanded.

"Spill what?"

"Whatever's got you glowering at my bar, not appreciating my best stuff, worrying your friends...you name it." Darcy shrugged. "What's up with you? Why are you and Alex fighting?"

"We're not fighting," Jamie said through clenched teeth. "Can't a person have any secrets around here? What's between Alex and me is between Alex and me."

Darcy nodded. "Sure. But for right now, you're sitting in my bar looking like you've just lost your best friend, so I'm entitled to demand answers. It's one of those perks."

Jamie met Darcy's eyes. *How come I've never noticed how dark her pupils are?* she thought. Wasn't it strange how small the world became when looking into someone's eyes? Why hadn't she ever noticed that before? She felt like she was drowning in their depths, and shook herself as she pulled her mind back. "I met someone."

Darcy stared at her, wondering why she felt less than thrilled. "You did?"

"Yeah." Jamie put her elbow on the bar and rubbed her upper lip with her finger.

Darcy frowned. Jamie didn't look happy about it. "Who is she?"

"A judge."

Darcy whistled, impressed. "Where'd you meet her?"

Jamie paused. "Here."

"Here?" Darcy frowned. "Wait a minute, was that the girl you were calling me about the other morning?"

Jamie shrugged. "I didn't know her last name then. I sort of took her home without getting that particular detail."

"You what?"

"I picked her up here and, well, one thing led to another." She shrugged, not meeting Darcy's eyes.

"That was a stupid thing to do." Darcy almost shouted it.

Jamie stared at her in surprise. "What?"

"You don't just pick somebody up for the night."

"Are you kidding me? I mean, that's rich coming from you. You're the queen of one-night stands. In fact, it's like a religion with you." Jamie was livid. "Really, Darcy, when was the last time you stuck around long enough to develop feelings for anybody?"

She has me there. Darcy couldn't figure out why, but the thought of Jamie having anonymous sex irritated her. The vague twinge in the pit of her stomach unsettled her, and she rubbed at the ache. "Never mind." She frowned, fighting the urge to break something.

Jamie stared at her, feeling angry and defensive and something else she couldn't quite put her finger on. Of all the people she knew, she thought Darcy would understand. She felt an ache deep in her chest. She met Darcy's uncertain eyes.

Jamie stood and grabbed her jacket from the stool beside her. "Forget it. I've got to go. I'll see you around." She rushed out the door.

Darcy stared at the closed door and frowned. She poured herself another shot and tossed it back, then slammed the glass down. Aware of curious looks, she stalked back to the kitchen.

WITH A SINKING sense of dread, Shane knew instantly that the police car parked in front of her house had nothing to do with a burglary. Two uniformed policemen flanked her front door. As she got out of her car, she noted that the scene was being played out in front of her interested neighbors.

She glared at Alex who was chatting with another man. "What the hell are you doing here?"

"I have a search warrant." Alex produced the document from the inside pocket of her suit jacket.

"I'm calling Ken Landry."

Alex shrugged. "Be my guest. But we don't need his permission to come inside. We don't even need yours." She motioned her men forward.

Shane's stomach twisted as they slipped on plastic gloves, as if she was contaminated. She couldn't just watch her home being invaded, so she got in her car and drove away. Then realized that she had nowhere to go, nowhere she could go and hide.

JAMIE WATCHED A car pull up in front of her house. The occupant made no move to get out. The car looked familiar. Shane's car. She sighed, went outside, and stopped a few paces from it.

"They're searching my house," Shane said.

Jamie frowned. She hadn't known about it, but it had been

inevitable.

"I didn't know where else to go."

Jamie sighed and opened the driver's side door. "Come on."

Shane followed Jamie into the house.

"Do you want a coffee?" Jamie asked.

"Okay."

In the kitchen, Jamie took out two cups from the cupboard by the sink and glanced back toward the living room. Her stomach took a dive as she thought about Shane in her home for the first time since that first night. Her mind tried to tease her with memories of that intimate encounter and she took a shaky breath trying to calm her nerves and clear her mind so she could think more clearly. *What does she want? What should I say?* Her chaotic thoughts crowded her without giving her any answers until she had no choice but go back and face Shane. She was unnerved by the unsteadiness in her fingers as she poured the coffee and carried the cups into the living room.

They sat facing each other as they drank their coffee. Jamie felt the pull of Shane's presence, but fought against its effect on her body. Shane's scent drifted over her, and she forced her attention to her coffee.

"What are they looking for?" Shane asked. Jamie shot her a look of disbelief and Shane had to smile. "I know. This is awkward."

Jamie laughed without humor. "Awkward? I'm not sure that's how I would describe it. 'Fucked up' is the term I would use."

"I wish..." Shane stopped.

"You wish what?"

"I wish I could be alone with you just for a moment without any of this between us. I wish you could look at me and just see me," Shane said with a faint smile.

"I did. The first night I saw you. Then you lied to me." Jamie shrugged.

Shane opened her mouth, but closed it as she met Jamie's quiet look of rebuke. "This is nuts," she finally said.

"You won't get any arguments from me on that."

"I should go." Shane stood up to leave, half expecting Jamie to stop her, but Jamie continued to study her without moving. Shane let herself out without another word.

When she heard the car drive off, Jamie stood up and pulled a slip of paper from her pocket—a message that Barney wanted to see her. She knew what that meant—he had something. Fear lick at the edges of her soul. Instinct warned her that she wasn't going to like what he had found.

Chapter
Sixteen

DARCY STAYED ANGRY for two days and she didn't even know why.

By the weekend, Madison who had been watching Darcy bang around Murphy's with a scowl on her face, had had enough. "What's got you so twisted, Stretch?"

"Huh?"

"You're going around snapping at everybody and everything. You're not just your usual rude self."

Darcy blew out a breath. "Christ, I have no idea. I feel like I have a permanent case of PMS."

"Menopause?"

"Shut up." Darcy pushed a hand through her thick waves and frowned.

Madison studied Darcy for a while. She looked miserable. "Darcy, what is it?" she asked in a concerned voice.

Darcy paced behind the bar. "Something Jamie did pissed me off."

Jamie is sure getting around upsetting everyone, Madison thought. "What did she do?"

"She had a one night stand, a wild one, in her words. Now she's mooning over this woman."

"A..." When she saw that Darcy was serious, Madison stopped the bubble of laughter that was threatening to erupt. "I see. Why would that bother you? You do that all the time."

"I know, but it's not the same thing."

"How so?"

"It's *Jamie.*" The more she talked, the more ridiculous she knew she sounded. "Fuck, that sounded stupid."

"I won't argue with that," Madison said. Darcy glared at her. "That look stopped working on me years ago." A thought occurred to Madison and she narrowed her eyes. "Listen, Darcy, do you have feelings for her?"

"For who? Jamie? Fuck no."

"Mmm, because if I didn't know better, I would say you're jealous."

"Jealous? That's crazy. We've been friends for a hundred years."

"Yeah. Still, why would it bother you so much?"

"Maybe I'm jealous because I haven't had sex in a while." Darcy stopped pacing. *How long has it been?* She frowned.

"Darcy, it's okay if you have feelings for her. You shouldn't be scared of feeling them once in a while."

Jamie's accusation echoed in Darcy's mind. She spun around to glare at Madison. "What the hell are you talking about? I'm not scared."

Madison rolled her eyes and smiled. "I've known you for twenty years, so I'm entitled to say certain things. And you, my dear, have a fear of attachment. And that fear makes you paranoid about commitments."

"I think you need committing."

"Okay." Madison stood up. "Stay grumpy; most people are used to it. But you might want to think about what I said."

Darcy stared at the door long after Madison had left. She had always been a big believer in living in truth. A part of her acknowledged her ability to toy with others, but it was a thought she rarely ventured to.

A flash of a smile had won her more than her fair share of bed partners, and she had rarely questioned her inability to stay with anyone too long. No one had ever penetrated deep enough below the cool layers to touch her heart. No, she always made it clear at the beginning what she was looking for. Still, it never stopped them from hoping for more.

Perhaps she was too careless with the feelings of others. She rubbed the ache in her chest. These were not pleasant thoughts. *And it's all Jamie's fault*, she thought grumpily, knowing deep down that it wasn't.

Chapter
Seventeen

JAMIE SLIPPED INTO the familiar booth across from Barney. "So, what do you have for me?"

He smiled. "Gee, no 'hello, how are you?'"

"I'm fresh out of pleasantries today. What do you have for me?"

Barney smiled. "I think I hit the mother lode. You might even want to buy me a case of that bourbon you always promise me."

"That good?"

He slid an envelope toward her. "See for yourself."

Jamie slid it over in front of her and left it lying on the table. She had a feeling that the information would be upsetting, to say the least.

Barney studied her. "You didn't tell me you knew the judge."

Jamie started. "Which judge?"

"The dead one."

Jamie's heart raced.

Barney smiled. "Don't worry about it, Saunders. I won't say anything." He took a sip of his drink. "I got an informant that shall remain nameless, someone who works — or should I say — used to work with the Chief Justice. When I started to ask around, my snitch was more than happy to share some stuff — for the right price, of course."

He smiled and she did not like the look of that smile.

"It appears that the Chief was into kinky stuff — taking pictures, that sort of thing. He kept a whole stack of 'em in a safety deposit box." He rubbed his nose. "It was only a quick step from that to finding the deposit box and its contents." He nodded toward the envelope.

Jamie blanched. She couldn't find her voice, couldn't find the nerve to look inside the envelope. She knew now that digging further had been a mistake.

When she made no move to look at his findings, Barney took the envelope and opened it. He pulled out several typewritten sheets and a stack of Polaroids. "It looks like your pretty judge lady was into it as well, or at least posed for him. Those ones are yummy." He handed them to her and relaxed back, satisfied.

Jamie knew she shouldn't look, but with almost macabre interest, took them from him. She swallowed and looked down at the pictures. Her nausea rose quickly and her forehead broke out in sweat. Her fingers trembled and she was thankful that Barney's attention appeared to be on the baseball game on one of the washed out television sets by the bar. She shoved the pictures back into the envelopes, pulled a few bills from her pocket, and threw them on the table. She stood up on shaky legs, knowing she was going to be sick.

"You did good, Barney. Thanks."

He looked at her. "Yeah? Than why do you look so glum?"

She avoided his eyes. "You're not drunk enough for me to tell you." As she picked up the envelope, she tried to smile but failed. "I gotta go. I'll see you around." The smoke seemed thicker, and the gloomy interior of the bar suffocated her. Her stomach clenched. If she didn't leave immediately, she would make a fool of herself.

Barney was disappointed at her reaction. "You were hoping for more? I could continue to dig."

"No. No. This is plenty to move the case forward. If not, I'll be in touch. I'll get you your fee tomorrow."

Barney looked after her departing back, puzzled. He'd thought she would be over the moon with what he'd found. Maybe he would keep digging, just in case.

Outside, Jamie threw up as she leaned a weak hand against the side of her car. She slowly straightened and wiped her mouth with shaky fingers that were as cold as ice.

In the car, she waited for the trembling to stop. She pulled the pictures out. There were about a dozen of them — black and white, color, of different people in various positions. Her heart slammed against her ribcage as she stared at the pictures of a young blonde child with gray eyes, and red bows in her hair. She might have been four. Jamie felt pity for her younger self. The pictures were innocent looking, the child sitting naked on a blanket, playing with her favorite doll. Except Jamie knew they weren't so innocent. She had always loved that doll. The solemn expression on her younger face punched her like a physical blow, the eyes so watchful as if waiting. No child of that age should look so serious. Had she ever seen a picture where she was smiling? Unconcerned? She felt the bile creep up her throat and swallowed it back down with a sob.

She looked at the next picture. It was a picture of her in full dress uniform taken during her police academy graduation ceremony. *The bastard came. How did I miss him? How did he know?* She started to shake again, but forced herself to flip through the rest.

Pain speared her chest when she stopped at two pictures of Shane in bed with her father and another woman. The angle of the picture was such that she could not tell anything about the other woman, except that she had dark hair. But what was clear was that the other two people in the picture were Shane, and her father. The fiery shock and revulsion engulfed her and hot tears filled her eyes. She leaned her head against the steering wheel and closed her eyes. *You sick bastard.*

She looked at the golden haired woman, who had shared her bed only days before. Here was Shane's motive, what she was trying to hide. *Was he blackmailing Shane with these pictures?* She felt a momentary flash of pity for the woman, but anger quickly overtook it. *Shane must have known who I was that night,* she thought, sickened.

She threw the pictures on the seat next to her and grabbed the steering wheel until her knuckles showed white. Then she forced herself to slowly relax her death grip. She wiped the tears from her eyes, felt the bitter aftertaste in the back of her throat as she breathed in deeply through her nostrils. *I have to get hold of myself. I have to get out of here.*

She drove home in a fog. The phone was ringing as she entered the house but she ignored it. She kicked off her shoes and marched straight to the living room bar and pulled a bottle off the shelf. The phone rang again.

She glanced at the call display, and saw that it was Darcy. For one instant she was tempted. *Darcy.* The need for her was so great that it left her weak. She suddenly felt unbearably alone and she slid to the floor and started to cry, her arms tightly wrapped around her knees, face buried in them. She cried for the innocence she had lost, for the wounds that stubbornly remained tender under the skin.

DARCY SLAMMED THE telephone down. This had to stop. She had been trying to get hold of Jamie for the better part of the last two days. She had even left an apology on the answering machine, which she now regretted.

She grabbed her keys and stormed out of the bar. By the time she drove to Jamie's, she was ready to explode. *If Jamie thinks that she can ignore me, she has another think coming.* She stomped on the brakes and got out of the car. *If she thinks I'm going to grovel, she's in for a surprise.* She slammed the car door.

Darcy tried the front door and found it unlocked, so she walked in. "Saunders, where the hell are you? If you think I'm going to put up with being..." She stopped, and then with heart dropping, rushed in. "Honey, what is it? Are you okay?" She knelt down next to Jamie and wiped her tear-stained face with a gentle hand. "What the hell is going on?"

"Darcy?" Jamie didn't think she had telephoned Darcy, but her friend's touch broke through the fog she was in, and she started sobbing.

Darcy wrapped herself around Jamie and held on tight. "Shhh. I'm here. I'm here." Her mind whirled; she felt helpless to ease Jamie's pain. She clenched her fist in fury and narrowed her eyes. *Whoever hurt her is going to pay.*

Darcy lost track of time as they sat on the floor until the latest wave passed and Jamie was calm enough for Darcy to leave her to search for tissues. When she returned, she sat down and automatically pulled Jamie close.

Darcy sat holding Jamie in silence for another hour, stroking her head, her back. Shadows lengthened on the walls as darkness fell around them. The only sound that penetrated the silence was the ticking of a clock in another room.

"Jamie? Honey? I think my ass is asleep. Can we try and get up?"

The grouchy tone pulled a smile from Jamie, and she nodded against Darcy's chest. Darcy stood, then helped Jamie up.

"I need to go wash up," Jamie finally said in a voice shaky with fatigue.

"Good idea. I'll fix us a drink while you do that."

While Jamie showered, Darcy paced the kitchen. Unnerved by Jamie's loss of composure, for a brief moment she was tempted to run away. "Get a grip," she said out loud. She had never before felt so helpless or lost. She of the decisive action didn't have a clue how to handle this.

At a sound, Darcy turned.

Embarrassed by her breakdown and the apparent weakness it conveyed, Jamie averted her eyes.

Needing something to do, Darcy finally poured vodka into a couple of glasses and handed one to Jamie. She sipped hers while looking at Jamie over the rim.

"Don't," Jamie said, going into the living room.

Darcy stared after her. *Should I leave?* She slowly followed Jamie. "Jamie?"

"What?" Now that she was calmer, Jamie wanted to be alone. Alone with her thoughts. Alone with her memories. Alone with her pain. She avoided Darcy's eyes.

"Are you okay?"

"Yes."

Stung by the curtness of Jamie's response, Darcy put her glass down. "I guess I'll go, if you're sure you're okay."

"I'm fine." Jamie stared out of the window, feeling the pain deep in her chest and the tears threatening again.

Darcy hesitated in the doorway. She tried to think of something to say, but words failed her. With a sigh, she turned to leave.

Jamie turned to Darcy. "Stay," she whispered.

Darcy stopped and turned around and met Jamie's eyes.

Jamie pushed a trembling hand through her hair. "I'm sorry. I'm a mess."

Darcy smiled. "Yeah, honey, you are." Somehow it was the right thing to say and pulled a shaky laugh from Jamie. Darcy went to Jamie and wrapped her arms around her.

Jamie leaned her head against the strong shoulder and sighed deeply. *Why is it that I feel so safe with you?* She pressed closer, letting Darcy's strength soothe her.

THEY SAT ON the sofa sipping their vodka. "Do you want to tell me what happened?" Darcy asked.

Jamie tucked her legs up under her and sighed. "I woke up to a nightmare. Except now it's a waking one." When Darcy said nothing, Jamie looked at her. "The woman I picked up the other night?"

Darcy felt a twinge at the mention of the unknown woman but chose to ignore it rather than examine the feelings behind it. She nodded.

"She's a suspect in a case Alex and I are involved in." Jamie took a deep breath as a tremor went through her. "The murder of my father."

Darcy gasped, the only sign that she had heard correctly. After a long moment, she looked squarely at Jamie.

Aware of Darcy's eyes on her, Jamie stared into the distance. "There are pictures."

Darcy was now convinced that she didn't want to hear any more. Her uneasiness increased, but she forced herself to stay focused on Jamie's white face.

Jamie's gray eyes seemed to shift color as she looked at Darcy. "They're in the car."

"Do you want me to get them?" Darcy's voice bespoke her uncertainty. Though Jamie's nod was slight, it was enough. Darcy stood up and left the room.

Jamie sat staring at her hands. *What am I going to do now?* She wrapped her arms around herself, and felt the cold from inside carry goose bumps across her skin.

When Darcy returned with the envelope, she sat beside Jamie and placed the unopened packet on the table in front of them.

Jamie didn't look at Darcy or at the pictures. "Go ahead, you can look at them."

Darcy hesitated, then picked up the envelope and pulled out the pictures. She stared at them in silence, one by one. She recognized Jamie in her police uniform, Jamie as a baby. She felt the fury course through her, but forced herself to go on. When she was done, she set the photos on the table with exaggerated care and looked at Jamie.

Jamie finally met her gaze. "The last two are of my father and the woman I met that night at your place."

Darcy froze and darted a glance at the pictures. "James —"

"I know. Life has a pretty sick sense of humor if you ask me," she said bitterly.

Chapter
Eighteen

THE BELLS HANGING from the door jangled cheerfully as Jamie walked into the bookstore. Megan, Alex's girlfriend, looked up from her invoices and smiled. She immediately noticed the pale, drawn look, the circles under Jamie's eyes. But what really caught her attention was the stillness, as if the energy that was so much a part of Jamie had been wiped clean.

Jamie wasn't in the mood for pleasantries. "Where is she?"

"Upstairs." *Moping and missing you.* Megan watched the tall blonde cross the bookstore to the back, where a door led to two apartments upstairs.

Alex was sitting in the kitchen, elbows on the table, brooding over the forensics reports. The brown hair found at the scene was Shane's. Alex sighed, then turned as she heard the quick knock before the door opened. She wanted to smile, wanted to go to Jamie, but Jamie's stillness and sense of fragility stopped her.

Jamie threw some pictures and a videotape on the table without so much as a word. Alex stared at her but Jamie looked away. Alex picked up the pictures and studied them one by one. There it was, the motive. Instead of feeling elated, she felt disappointed, diminished by the reality behind the pictures.

"Jamie —"

"Do what you need to do, Alex," Jamie finally said. "I don't want to talk about any of this, not right now. But I want to be there when you confront her."

"Jamie, I'm so sorry," Alex offered.

Jamie's gray eyes swirled with emotion as she looked at her friend. "I know." She left without another word.

Alex stared into space for a few minutes, then went through the pictures again. Her stomach knotted for what Jamie was going through. When she picked up the videotape, she knew without looking at the label on the front that it was the Colonnade security tape.

With a heavy sigh, Alex stood up and trudged to the front of the apartment where the VCR was located. She put the tape in, found the remote control next to the television, and pressed play. She recognized the first half as what she had seen days before, but her heart dropped as the tape played through. She rewound it and played the last half in slow motion, pausing it on the image of Shane stepping out of the elevator.

Her eyes closed as the ramifications of what Jamie had done hit her. She hit the eject button and sat down on the soft, leather couch. For the first time in her investigative life, she was unsure of her next move.

James...damn you. How could you do this?

Chapter
Nineteen

WHEN SHE OPENED the door and saw Alex and Jamie standing there, Shane knew that they had found the pictures. There was no other reason they would both show up on her doorstep. The knowing was there in their body language, the sober looks on their faces. She tried to catch Jamie's eyes, but Jamie looked away. Without a word, Shane stepped back and opened the door wider as they passed by her. Taking a deep breath, she closed the door and followed them into her living room, her hands twisting nervously.

Instead of asking Shane to go down to the station for further questioning, the interrogation was going to be done at Shane's house. Jamie knew that Alex was doing it for her protection, to keep the fact that she and Shane knew each other a secret. She was grateful to Alex for that. But knowing her friend as she did, she also knew that Alex would not accept her gratitude. They had barely spoken a word on the drive over from the station.

In the living room, Alex turned to Shane. "We would like to get your reaction to something we discovered in our investigation."

"Should I call my lawyer?" Shane asked.

Alex shrugged. "If you wish."

Shane glanced at Jamie, then back at Alex. "No, that's fine."

She crossed the room, her footsteps muffled by the thick carpet, and sat down on a high back Louis IX chair. When Alex handed her a manila envelope, she took a deep fortifying breath but her face remained composed. She lifted the flap and looked inside. Her face paled as she stared at each picture then pushed them both back into the envelope. She looked up at Alex, who sat in the opposite chair watching her. Jamie was standing by the window, apparently unwilling to get closer.

"There is really no denying that's you in the pictures," Alex said.

Shane sighed, then nodded once.

"We would like to know more about them," Alex added.

Shane gave a short, humorless laugh. "I think the pictures say enough, don't you?"

Alex continued to look at her silently. Shane's faint smile looked tired.

"It all happened a long time ago, Detective."

"Perhaps, but their relevance is stunning, don't you agree?"

"I made some bad choices. The memories are ugly. Years ago, I expunged them from my mind and got on with my life. I tried to make a new life."

"Very good answer. Except for the fact that those pictures give us sufficient grounds to wrap a motive around the rest of the evidence that points to you." Alex thoughtfully steepled her fingers under her chin as she regarded the woman.

"Let me have a crack at what happened," Alex continued. Years ago you found yourself in a compromising position with a woman and the judge. The 'how' is still to be figured out. Pictures are taken. Maybe you don't know that pictures exist. Then years pass and you ironically become a judge in the same court jurisdiction as your youthful indiscretion — we will call it that for lack of a better term — and lo and behold, he has pictures that he uses on you as blackmail after he figures out who you are. Maybe to force you to vote with him on certain cases, maybe for kicks. Finally, you get fed up and decide to confront him and ask for the return of those pictures. When he refuses, you shoot and kill him. How am I doing so far?"

Shane's face was expressionless. "Pretty good except for the last part. I didn't kill him."

Unable to stand still any longer, Jamie started to pace. "Shane, make it easier on yourself. Come clean. What the hell happened in the hotel room that day?"

Shane stared at her, exasperated. "You should know."

Jamie stopped pacing and stared at her. "What? How the hell would I know? You haven't told the truth since I met you."

Shane sprang up angrily. "And you have? Did you tell the detective here that we slept together that night?"

"I did."

Shane narrowed her eyes. "And did you tell her that you were there in the hotel room that night, too?"

"What? Are you crazy?" Jamie exploded. "I was not." She turned to Alex, who was suddenly studying her with a concerned look. Jamie shook her head at the unspoken question.

"I saw you that night. When I came back the second time, I saw you leaving the room. That's why I changed my mind and left," Shane said, heatedly.

Jamie was stunned. "I haven't a clue what you are talking about."

"Maybe you should start at the beginning," Alex suggested quietly.

Shane sat down, glaring at Jamie. She looked away and rubbed her eyes, suddenly tired. "It was years ago. I was at a law conference, just after being told that I was being put up for the state supreme court vacancy. I met a woman in a bar. One thing led to another and I found myself in her room. We had a lot to drink; some of what happened next is a bit blurry." She grimaced.

"I remember that she asked if it would be okay if a friend joined us. I thought she meant another girl." She laughed bitterly. "I passed out and I woke up alone, with the distinct feeling that there had been a man there, too." She stood up, needing to pace.

"Over the next few months, I would start to remember things, but it was all so hazy that I kept thinking I had dreamt it. One year after I joined his court, Judge Reynolds approached me in chambers and gave me a set of pictures. Some of them, of just the woman and me, were pretty graphic. He suggested in a friendly manner that I should go along with his vote and hinted that if I didn't, the pictures would end up in the media. I panicked."

She turned to Jamie with pleading in her eyes. "I had made a name for myself professionally. I was respected. He knew that I would do anything to protect what I had worked so hard for. It was a clever set up right from the beginning, I think." She rubbed her eyes with fingers that trembled slightly.

"He was not above taking kickbacks from interested parties to swing certain votes like they wanted. I had heard a few rumors, but he was so respected in the court, I never believed them. Being a new addition to his panel, I was an unknown entity for him. I guess he wanted to make sure I would be malleable, as my predecessor had been. I don't know how..."

Her look was distant for a moment, the curve of her mouth sad. "So, I voted with him. On this last case we were working on, the judge was pressing me for my vote. This time I refused. His ruling went against everything that I believed in as a judge and as a woman." She pushed an agitated hand through her hair.

"He threatened me with exposure again. I think I snapped. I was obsessed with getting the pictures back. That's why I was trying to get into his hotel room that day, to steal them. But I didn't shoot him." Her hands spread wide, palms up, as if pleading.

Alex regarded her thoughtfully, skeptically. "Quite the story."

"It's the truth." In desperation, she turned to Jamie. "Tell her."

"Me? What do I have to do with it?"

But something had started to niggle at the edges of Jamie's mind, a thought that was making the hair on her arms stand up. She had suspected that Shane had known her that night they had met in Darcy's place, and now she was starting to wonder if she had been right. *But how, from where?*

"You were there. I saw you leaving his room, so I took off."

Dumbly shaking her head, Jamie stared at Shane.

"But it's true," she insisted. "A few hours later, when I entered that bar and saw you there, I was shocked, and a little scared. At first I thought I was mistaken, but you came over to talk to me, so I thought maybe you had seen me too. That's why I talked to you; I wanted to know what you knew."

"For the last time, I was not at his hotel room!"

White faced, eyes filled with panic, Shane stared at Jamie. "I saw you. Why won't you tell the truth?"

Alex stared at the two of them. Part of her believed Shane and that made her wonder about her best friend; then she was shaken that she would wonder.

At Shane's insistent identification, Jamie went very still and the color drained from her face. "When you saw me that night, what exactly did you see?" She stared intently at Shane's face.

Shane sank down further in her chair. "You. You were wearing different clothes, of course, and a hat, but it was you." Shane stared at Jamie as if questioning the evidence of her own eyes. "I know it was you. Either that, or I'm losing my mind." Shaken, she closed her eyes.

The turbulence in Jamie's gray eyes communicated itself to Alex, who frowned, suddenly uneasy. Her mind swirling with questions. Alex turned to Shane. "This changes nothing. This investigation will continue. You are not eliminated from our lists of suspects, Miss Scott."

"But I didn't kill him, I swear. I thought...I thought you did." Shane turned to Jamie. "That's why I wasn't saying anything about seeing you. I didn't want you to be guilty, not after that night," she whispered.

Jamie felt like she was going to be sick. "I wasn't there, Shane. It must have been somebody else."

Shane rubbed her eyes. "It looked like you."

"It wasn't."

Alex stood up. "We'll be in touch." She motioned to Jamie

and they went to the front door.

"Detective?"

Alex turned to see Shane holding out the envelope.

"Don't forget your evidence." Shane's shoulders slumped.

Alex met her eyes and then caught Jamie's shaken look. She turned her attention back to Shane. "Thank you. I can't promise you to not use these pictures if the rest of the evidence continues to point to you as our suspect, but I can promise you that no one else will see these until our investigation is completed. If you are exonerated, the pictures will be returned to you. That is the best I can do."

The grateful light in Shane's eyes made Alex's stomach churn over what she had just done. Disappointment twisted her mouth into a grimace. She wasn't sure if the disappointment was in herself, or in Jamie for putting her in such a no-win position. She left without another word.

Outside, as they stood by the car Alex looked at her friend. "We need to talk, Jamie," she said flatly.

"I know. But not here."

Chapter
Twenty

THEY DROVE TO a park and sat in the car. For a few moments, they watched a cocker spaniel chasing a ball being thrown by a young man in a red coat.

At last, aware of Alex's stare, Jamie sighed and met her gaze. "It's a long story."

"I've got time."

The painful recounting came out in a flat monotone. Jamie stared out of the window as she told Alex of the childhood abuse and the reason why her father had been excised from her life.

When she was done, Alex took her hand. "Why didn't you say anything before, Jamie?"

Jamie regretted the hurt behind the question. "I spent thirty years trying to forget it. It's not an easy thing to talk about. I'm sorry, Alex; I didn't want it to change our friendship." Tears welled in her eyes and she rubbed at them impatiently.

"Did you really believe that I would think any less of you for the actions of a perverted bastard?" Alex was angry. "What kind of friend would I be if I couldn't be there for you, accept what you went through?"

They both felt that something fundamental had shifted between them. The lack of honesty had created a jagged break in the foundation of their friendship and neither of them knew how to repair it as they stared at each other.

Alex knew that what she had to ask would widen the breach. "Jamie, were you in the justice's hotel room that night?"

Jamie couldn't keep a momentary flicker of hurt from her face. "No." She looked out of the window, then back at her friend.

Alex looked thoughtful. "Well, if it wasn't you, but the person looked enough like you for Shane to have mistaken one for the other..."

Jamie sighed. "I think we both know who it must have been."

"AUNT JAMIE!" ASHLEY, a pig-tailed blonde, ran across the lawn and launched herself into Jamie's arms as soon as she stepped out of Alex's car.

Jamie forced a smile as she hugged her niece. "Hey there, brat, you're getting almost as tall as me."

The six-year-old giggled and turned to Alex. "Hi, Auntie Alex. Do you have your gun?"

Alex smiled at her, but her blue eyes remained cool. "Nope. This is my day off." She glanced at her partner.

Jamie avoided Alex's eyes as she smiled at Ashley. "Where's your mom?"

"Out back. She's painting a chair; I'm helping." Ashley grinned and showed off her paint splattered hands and the gap where her two front teeth should have been. "I'll go tell Mom you're here." She turned and ran off toward the back.

Jamie stared at her sister's two-story house with its pretty peak and bright red door. The nausea she had felt on the drive over returned. She took a deep breath then walked around to the back with Alex following silently.

Jamie's sister Emma, alerted by her daughter, was making her way to the front and waved at them as she wiped her paint-splattered hands on a rag. Her eyes, more green than Jamie's deep gray, watched with amusement as her daughter gave a careless wave and ran to the house.

"This is a surprise," Emma said with a light laugh. She turned her attention to Alex. "And you, stranger, haven't seen you in ages."

Alex forced a smile as she looked at the woman who was identical to Jamie in every way, except that she wore her blonde hair longer. "I know. I'm a slave to my work. And your sister over there keeps insisting on driving, so I never make it over here. I think she doesn't want me to get any of your famous brownies."

Emma laughed, but she discerned the worried watchfulness in her sister's eyes. Years of being in tune with her twin's emotions had her suddenly dropping the rag, concerned. "What is it?"

"We need to talk without being interrupted," Jamie said.

Emma gave her a startled glance, then nodded. She led them into the house and went searching for Ashley. After putting on a video and preparing a quick snack for her, Emma returned to the kitchen where Jamie was pacing while Alex slouched in a chair in pretended nonchalance.

"Not here," Emma said as she stopped in the doorway, and they turned to her expectantly.

She led them to the small study off the kitchen. The desk was covered with a pile of essays that Emma, a fourth grade teacher, still needed to mark. There were also colorful, finger-painted pictures of abstract shapes that were clearly animals, if one was conversant with such things. She stepped to the desk and turned, a faint line of worry between her eyes. Her fingers nervously shuffled some of the papers around.

Alex was the last to enter, and she closed the door and leaned against it.

Jamie started to pace, her body thrumming with emotion. Her mind was tangling in too many thoughts, and she could not figure out a way to ask her sister the questions that needed asking.

Emma's face paled and her body took on the same nervous energy. "Jamie, what is it?"

"Emma, I need to ask you something. God knows I don't want to, but I have to." Jamie choked on the admission. She stopped pacing and turned to her sister, gray eyes turbulent and bright with unshed tears.

"James, you're scaring me."

Jamie's whole body tensed as if preparing to ward off a blow. "I need to know if you were in Dad's hotel room the night he was killed." The words came out in a rush. Jamie closed her eyes as she finished and missed Emma's look of horror.

Watching them from the door, Alex felt her heart sink at Emma's reaction. She fought against her sudden need to stop the questioning before suspicion became fact.

For a long tense moment, Emma could only stare at her sister, then she started to cry.

At that, Jamie stepped toward her and urgently grasped her sister's arms. "Emma, honey, did you go there?" She knew the answer before Emma responded and her heart rapped against her ribcage.

Emma nodded as tears streamed down her face.

The mute admission struck Jamie like a blow and the nausea returned. She ignored the tears trickling down her face. "For God's sake, why?"

Emma wiped a shaky hand across her eyes. "To warn him to stay away from Ashley."

Jamie stared at her, horrified.

"He went to see her at school. She came home one day from school and out of the blue told me about meeting her grandpa."

Jamie barely forced out, "Did he touch her?"

Emma shook her head violently. "No. No." She started to cry again. Filled with a mixture of anguish and fear, she sank with shoulders slumped into a nearby chair. "I felt my whole world tilt and turn upside down that day."

Jamie knelt in front of her. "Emma, honey, what happened the night he died?"

Jamie looked at Alex who was obviously transfixed. When their eyes met, Alex looked away. Jamie returned her focus to her twin.

"When she told me about seeing him, I was terrified. I can't describe the shock that went through me. I hadn't thought of him in years. Tried not to. What was past was past, and I had a new life. But knowing he had come so close to my baby drove me crazy. Thinking of the possibilities. Remembering."

When she shuddered, Jamie felt it as if the shudders were her own. She clenched her teeth until her jaw ached from the tension.

"I found out where he was living and went to see him. He was delighted about the visit. He acted as if nothing had ever happened, as if we had seen each other only the day before and not thirty years ago. I stood there looking at him, and the only thought that I had was that he didn't look like a monster at all."

She gave a bitter laugh. "All these years, I had an image in my mind of him as a monster. It shocked me that I could stand in that hotel room that day watching him be all smiles and full of charm, and know that I hated him but no longer feared him. That's when I knew that I was over it, over the fear of him." She stood up to pace, a habit similar to her sister's.

Jamie straightened and glanced at Alex, who stood staring at Emma with eyes narrowed, face unreadable. Jamie couldn't tell what she was thinking and it unnerved her.

She turned her attention back to Emma and gently said, "Then what happened?"

Emma stopped pacing. "I told him I knew he had been at Ashley's school, and I warned him that if he didn't stay away from her, I would kill him." She looked at Jamie, eyes fiery. "I turned and left. As I was closing the door, I heard him groan, almost a choking sound, and heard a thud as if he had fallen, but I didn't turn around to look. I didn't care."

She looked at Alex and their eyes held. "When I heard he was dead, I was relieved that someone else did it, but I'm glad he's dead."

Jamie sighed in defeat. "Oh, Emma, why didn't you tell me this before?"

Emma shook her head and pushed a trembling hand through her blonde hair.

The gesture was so like Jamie's that the poignancy of it was not loss on Alex.

"I don't know. I guess I was afraid of this." Emma gestured at them.

Alex tried to keep a level head as their pain battered her.

"Do I have to go to the station to give my statement and be questioned?" Emma asked.

Alex sighed as her love and loyalty for Jamie was once again in conflict with her responsibility and duty.

"No. Nothing said here today is relevant to the solving of the case. But I would like to return tomorrow with a picture of a potential suspect. You might have seen this person near your..." She couldn't bring herself to call him a father. "Near the justice's suite."

Having compromised her ethics and possibly the investigation, Alex shot a sidelong glance at Jamie, defeated by the demands love brought.

Jamie's eyes filled with tears; she knew that their friendship would never be the same again.

Chapter
Twenty-one

ALEX WALKED INTO the squad room, a coffee in one hand and a stale muffin in the other and was hit by the absence of noise. Everyone appeared to be talking in hushed tones, and even that became muted as her presence was noticed. She looked around uneasily, and the ready quip on her lips died as her fellow officers avoided her eyes.

After dropping her coffee off in her office, Alex walked to Jamie's office and stopped, frozen in the doorway. Inside the tiny room, Jamie was packing a small cardboard box with her personal effects, and didn't look up as Alex cleared her throat.

"James...what's going on? Alex asked her as her pulse raced with apprehension.

Jamie looked at her friend. "I resigned this morning."

"You did what?" Alex shouted. She took a step into the room then stopped, as if unable to move further.

"I handed in my badge."

The color drained from Alex's face, and Jamie's heart twisted at the shock in her eyes. She took a step toward her, but stopped as Alex took a step back. "I need a break. All of this," Jamie spread her hands in entreaty, "it's too much. Shane, my father, my suppressing evidence."

"You want to clear your conscience, go see a priest," Alex replied curtly.

"Alex—"

"No. You didn't think you should talk to me about this before you quit? We're partners. Best friends. You didn't think I deserved to be told what you were thinking?"

"I knew you would try and talk me out of it."

"Goddammit, Jamie! You had me covering for you, and putting my job on the line to protect you. I asked you to stay away from the case. I can't fucking believe you're going to quit on me now. We've got two of the most visible cases still to solve. I can't..." Alex stopped as the sense of betrayal made even breathing difficult.

Jamie's eyes filled at Alex's words. Because she knew her friend so well, she knew that the angry words and the fury in her voice covered the hurt. "I'm sorry," she whispered, shaken by the widening breach between them.

"Well, you know what? Sorry isn't good enough. You're bailing on me. I don't think I'll ever forgive you for that. If you'll excuse me, I have a job to do."

Alex moved to get past but Jamie grabbed Alex's hand. "Alexandra, I love you. I'm sorry this is hurting you, but I need to do this for me."

Weakened, overwhelmed by it all, Alex leaned her head against Jamie's shoulder for a moment as they held hands. "Damn you," she whispered. "I never thought that you of all people would break my heart." She lifted her head with tears in her eyes. "Then do what you have to do, James. I've got to get ready for a press conference."

Jamie watched her go as the tears rolled down her cheeks. *I've just lost my best friend.*

Chapter
Twenty-two

IT TOOK SIX rings of the phone before the signal reached a corner of Jamie's sleeping brain. By the eighth, she managed to slide a hand out from under her blankets and smack the alarm clock, but the noise persisted. With a groan, she reached out and grabbed the offending instrument.

"'Lo."

"Good morning!" The voice was annoyingly cheerful in the stillness of the morning.

Jamie groaned again. "I will hate you forever."

Emma laughed. "Promises, promises."

"What time is it?"

"Six o'clock."

"Six o'... Are you crazy?" Jamie tried to open her eyes, but the brightness coming in the uncovered window was too painful and she closed them again.

"Mom just dropped in for a coffee. *She* made me do it."

"No sane person just drops in anywhere at six o'clock." Jamie could hear her mother talking in the background before Emma responded.

"Well, this is Mom we're talking about. We've always debated the sanity issue. She thinks that you need us, and she wants to come up for a visit today."

"Where?"

"There."

Jamie rubbed her forehead, trying to forestall the imminent headache. "Oh no, she doesn't."

"I suppose you could try this denial thing, but you know that won't work." Emma's voice was amused. Their mother was like a bulldog when she made up her mind about something, especially when she thought it was for their own good. She and Jamie had learned to live with it.

Jamie sat up, the sheet falling to her bare waist. The room spun, and she immediately wanted to lie back down. "Emma, I just moved in," Jamie protested weakly. "I'm living in the middle of chaos. And besides, I still haven't recovered from her last visit."

"Who ever does?"

Jamie sighed, knowing she had lost the battle before it even began.

"If it helps any, I'll be driving her," Emma added.

"It will only help if you promise to lose her at a gas station on the way." Jamie smiled at Emma's soft chuckle.

There was a pause and then Emma said, "Oh, she wants to talk to you."

"No! Don't you dare put her... Hi, Mom!"

"How are you, dear?"

"As well as can be expected at six o'clock in the morning," Jamie replied dryly.

"Oh! Were you sleeping?" Her mother sounded incredulous and she didn't wait for an answer. "Are you settling in okay?"

"I just moved in yesterday. I just –"

"Yes, well, don't you worry," her mother interrupted. "Your sister and I will be over to help out."

"You don't have to, Mom," Jamie tried hopefully.

"Nonsense. Of course we do. Do you need anything?"

Peace and quiet would be a nice start, Jamie thought, swinging her long legs to the floor. "No. I'm fine." Jamie said her goodbyes and hung up.

How many drinks did I have last night? And why the hell did I insist on having the telephone hooked up right away?

She tested the strength in her legs as she stood up. *Not bad.* Ready to proceed, Jamie devised her plan of attack. *First a shower, then a strong cup of coffee. Of course, another three or four hours of sleep would be better.* She grimaced. *That, and a new head to replace the one pounding atop my shoulders.*

She slowly made her way to the bathroom, determining that walking wasn't as complicated as she'd first thought. *One step in front of the other. Yep, so far so good.*

An hour later, Jamie felt almost human as she padded barefoot into the kitchen. The operative word was "almost." She had run out of hot water, and her scream as the icy spray hit her would have done any horror film proud. To top it off, just as she was turning off the water, she had remembered that she had not unpacked any towels and she had stood in the bathroom drip-drying and shivering, coming up with new and inventive ways of saying the same invectives.

She was searching through the empty cupboards in the kitchen, when the thought hit her: *I didn't buy coffee.* She almost whimpered. *People have killed for far less.*

An hour later, sipping a cup of coffee from the neighborhood Starbucks, Jamie sat on the top step of the wraparound porch, long legs stretched in front of her as she savored her first morning at her new house. She watched a cardinal sweep by and perch on a low branch of the magnolia tree that bloomed on her front lawn, and she grinned in delight.

I need a bird feeder to attract more birds, she thought, beginning a mental list of things she wanted to do. The porch required a new coat of paint; the lawn needed tending. Then another bird joined the chorus, and the mental listing stopped. There was something magical and soothing about the chirping of birds, their individual song the only sound that broke the stillness of the morning slowly waking around her.

Are they singing to each other, to themselves, or just to be heard? Jamie wondered happily as she took another sip of her coffee. In the distance, the sharp, hopeful barking of a dog brought a satisfied smile as she felt the warmth of the early sun touch her face.

Reveling in the peace that surrounded her, Jamie was convinced that the move had been a good decision. Here she could recover, forget what had happened, start anew. If she were brutally honest, she would admit that part of her didn't want to find out that it was Shane who had committed the murder, after all. Having been intimate with her father's killer would be too absurd, even for her. She needed time to figure out who she was and what she wanted to do with her life. She sighed, troubled by her thoughts.

As a car turned onto her street, Jamie recognized it and released a deep breath. *There they are.* She looked ruefully at the Starbucks container. One cup of coffee was not enough to help her survive her mother's visit when she was so clearly on a mission.

Jamie felt the familiar jolt as Emma got out of the car, so identical to herself in nearly every way that Jamie was always mildly surprised to look at that mirror image. Jamie grinned at her sister. Emma wore the familiar pinched look of suffering that an hour in the car with their mother always evoked. Emma waved, then Jamie's attention was captured by the form jumping in the back seat. It came flying out of the car, and her eyes widened at the ugliest dog she had ever seen. *At least, I think it's a dog.*

"What the hell is that?" she asked in horror. All she could see was a lot of brown and gray fur flying around.

Her mother laughed in delight. "Surprise!"

"What?"

The dog turned and charged at her, and Jamie instinctively took a step back, but the dog sat down at her feet with a thud that raised a cloud of dust, then pushed its wet nose into her hand by way of introduction. She pulled her hand away, but not quickly enough to avoid the deposit of wet, sticky film.

"Uugh. Gross. What is that?"

Emma peered at Jamie's hand. "Looks like drool to me. Must be love at first sight."

"What?" Jamie looked horrified as understanding dawned. "No...no...no." Ignoring her protests, the dog charged through the open front door.

"It's not right for a single woman to live on her own without any kind of protection." Her mother beamed at her. "The people at the pound said he has gone to training school and is a very good guard dog."

"But—"

A crash followed by a loud yelp came from the house. His tail between his legs, the dog came rushing out of the house and hid behind Mrs. Saunders' legs.

Jamie watched him cowering and shook her head. "Yeah, I feel protected already." She shifted her focus to her sister. Emma shrugged, not quite meeting Jamie's eyes.

Jamie narrowed her eyes at that. She turned back to her mother. "Mom, I'm not home enough to take care of a dog. And I have to go to Vegas in a few weeks for a wedding. I can't have—"

"Nonsense. He'll be good company for you." Mrs. Saunders entered the house.

It makes me crazy when she leaves in the middle of a conversation. "But..." Realizing she was talking to air, Jamie turned to her sister. "You could have warned me."

"What? And miss the look on your face? Never." Emma kissed her. "I've had her for two days; it's your turn. Anyways, James, I think you should have a dog—if not for protection, for company."

"I haven't even had time to get lonely yet." She hated that she was whining, but the six-year-old in her always resurfaced around her mother.

"Jamie Jane!" Her mother came out to the porch, her voice carrying across the peaceful morning like nails across a blackboard. "What kind of packing is this? How do you expect to be able to unpack efficiently if everything is labeled 'general' and has been thrown in one room? What happened to the color-coded labels and the index? Haven't I taught you girls anything?" Not bothering to wait for a response, she went back inside, shaking her head.

Jamie turned to Emma. "Couldn't find one little gas station? I ask you for one lousy favor..."

Emma grinned. "She wouldn't let me stop."

As her sister went in search of the rampaging dog inside, Jamie rested her forehead against the closed door. She was being punished, she knew, for all of her sins, real and imagined. "I should have moved to Canada," she said aloud.

Her mother poked her head out of the kitchen. "What was that, dear?"

"Nothing, Mom." A loud crash came from upstairs and she leaned weakly against the door. *Under the circumstances, I'm certain that the courts would be lenient. Still and all, it's a good thing that all the sharp objects are still packed.*

Chapter
Twenty-three

"DARCY, I NEED a huge favor," Jamie said as soon as she was through the door of the café.

Darcy, behind the dark polished oak bar, threw a glance over her shoulder. "Shoot."

"I need you to look after something for me until I'm back from Las Vegas."

"Sure. What is it?" Distracted, Darcy continued to check her bottle inventory.

"It's in the car; I'll go get it." Jamie hesitated, then seeing that Darcy had turned her attention back to her work, left to retrieve it.

Darcy's back was to the door as Jamie returned, and at the unfamiliar clicking noise, she turned.

Jamie tried not to laugh at the almost comical look on Darcy's face.

Darcy glared down at the dog. "What the fuck is that?"

"It."

Darcy's eyes widened with realization. "What? No. No fucking way."

"You said yes."

"I thought you wanted me to take care of a plant."

"Come on, Darcy. It'll only be for two days. He's gentle and fully trained and very obedient." Jamie felt just a twinge of guilt at the little white lies, but she was desperate. Darcy was the only one she could think of who had enough space to take care of the dog.

"I don't care. I don't do dogs." Darcy crossed her arms, and put on her fiercest face. As intimidating as she knew it to be, it never seemed to have any effect on Jamie. She looked down at the dog beside Jamie and repressed a shudder. "No."

"You owe me."

"How'd you figure that?"

Jamie couldn't fabricate a reason, so she just grinned. "It

was worth a shot." She adopted her best begging demeanor. "I don't have anybody else that can do this. Please, Darcy." She kissed her on the cheek. "I promise I won't tell anyone what a pushover you are."

Damn, it's that smile that always gets to me. Darcy smiled. "Swear?"

"Cross my heart."

Darcy sighed heavily. "Does it have a name?"

"Monster."

"Figures." Darcy shook her head in disgust as she looked at the dog again. *Two days. How bad could it be?*

THREE HOURS LATER, only sheer will stopped Darcy from killing the dog. Two overturned plants, a smashed three hundred dollar bottle of champagne, a ripped sofa cushion and a chewed sneaker later, she locked him upstairs in her apartment, and for a few minutes believed that she had found a solution.

Darcy's hand froze on the beer tap as a blood curdling sound pierced the soothing jazz. *What the hell is that?* When the howling started again, she realized that it was the dog.

She tried to ignore it, hoping that no else heard him, then winced as he started up again. This time she couldn't ignore the curious looks cast in her direction. She sighed as she started toward the back. *Oh yeah, Jamie's going to pay big time for this. Not just a little. Big.*

Darcy entered the apartment and marched to the back room, where Monster had been left, hearing him whimpering behind the door. She swung the door open, ready to blast him, but was almost knocked over as he jumped on her and licked her face, apparently delighted about his rescue. Her heart softened momentarily until she saw that he had relieved himself on her hardwood floor. She lost it. "For God's sake!"

That set off a whole other wave of peeing, and Darcy sank down on a chair, unable to decide what she was going to do next: search for and then kill Jamie, or kill the dog. Oblivious to her thoughts of mayhem, he sat beside her, tail wagging, happy to have her back. When Monster pushed his nose into her hand and left it covered in a wet film, Darcy decided the dog was going to have to go first; she wanted Jamie to suffer.

UPON HER RETURN, Jamie cautiously entered Murphy's. "Any trouble?"

Darcy studied her. Was there worry in Jamie's tone? A hint

of guilt, perhaps?

"Trouble? Mmm. Depends on your definition of trouble, I suppose." She placed a bottle of wine back on a glass shelf. "Trouble would be making sure he is let out at the proper intervals. Maybe trouble would be him barking when a stranger approaches. Yeah, that would be trouble." She turned and smiled.

It was the smile that scared Jamie. That slow smile meant danger. Jamie sat down on one of the stools and glanced at her worriedly. "Uh, Darcy?"

Darcy continued to smile. "Yes?"

"How much do I owe you?" Jamie tried a smile.

Darcy saw through Jamie's attempt at conciliation; she waved the smile away. "Don't even bother. This time it won't work. You owe me so big that I haven't been able to come up with something big enough for repayment. I thought of hunting you down in Vegas, but I couldn't leave the beast behind for fear of what he would do."

Jamie smiled, and despite herself, Darcy found her mouth twitching in response. She waved toward the back. "He's upstairs. Go get him before I *do* succumb and murder him, you, or both."

Jamie went around the bar and wrapped her arms around Darcy, startling her. "Thanks."

When Jamie turned to go upstairs, Darcy almost missed the contact of her body.

Chapter
Twenty-four

THE RAIN WAS *pouring, soaking everything with sheets of water, and Jamie was quickly drenched. She tried to peer through the driving liquid curtain, but couldn't see. Everything around her was unfamiliar, and she felt the first pearls of panic. She was lost. Then she heard it, the soft whisper coming from behind her. "Did you really want me dead, sweet pea?"*

"What?"

Jamie's eyes flew open and she found herself in her bed, a scream lodged in her throat. *It was a dream, just a dream.* Then she felt the dampness against her legs and a flash of panic. "What the hell?"

Heart thudding, she sat up, trying to will her mind to re-engage. She peered into the dark. She registered the rain driving against the windows and the slow rumble of thunder, then she felt it — the drop of wet. *Good God, is it raining in the bedroom?*

Still suspended between her dreams and full wakefulness, Jamie could only stare dumbfounded at the ceiling. She stood up on trembling legs and finally came fully awake. The roof was leaking — right over her bed.

"Jesus, that was weird," she told Monster as she brushed a not quite steady hand through her hair. She looked at the clock beside her bed. *Two o'clock.*

Nerves still jangling, she forced a breath through her body, then shoved her bed against the wall to avoid the leak. She went in search of a pail, though she knew she wouldn't sleep again that night. The dream still danced around in her mind. She turned the radio up loud to try and block out the images.

Might as well get some work done, she thought suddenly.

"YEP, YOU GOT a leak all right."

"Really?"

The sarcasm was lost on the repairman, who was scratching

his head. The movement stretched his faded blue work shirt over his inflated stomach, and Jamie marveled that the buttons held. He flashed a smile meant to convey charm. "Figure they put a coat of paint over it to hide the stains."

"How much to fix it?"

"Well, now..." There was more scratching. "We've got to rip the hole and then take a look-see under. See what's rotten. We might –"

"How much?" Jamie interrupted, unable to find her patience.

He glanced at the roof, then back at her. "2Gs if we have to replace the whole thing."

Two thousand, Jamie thought, wincing internally. *I'm going to have to tap into the trust.*

Jamie's trust fund had been set up by her mother after the divorce. The settlement, painfully arrived at under threats of exposure, had been put aside for Jamie and Emma's futures. Jamie had refused to touch the money; to touch it would have been to accept it as reparations for the wrongs done by her father. Now, after all that had happened, all that she had found out, she knew it was the least the bastard could have done.

As Jamie decided she had no choice but to use some of the money, she tried not to think about the fact that some of it might have been garnered from her father's illicit activities. She nodded. "Fine. When can you start?"

"Well now..." He clued in that she wasn't willing to wait around. "Tomorrow?"

"Fine." Jamie walked away, waves of tiredness battering at her.

She felt unsettled, the previous night tugging at her subconscious. As she was about to enter the house, she heard a car pull into the driveway and she turned. Surprised, she smiled uncertainly at her best friend. She hadn't seen Alex in weeks. Things had been awkward between them since Jamie's resignation. They had only seen each other when their group got together.

"Is this what a four year university education gets you?" Alex asked, looking at the house as she stepped out. Lips pursed, she looked at the faded façade.

Jamie heard the puzzlement in Alex's voice. She stood at the top of the steps, fighting against the urge to rub her hands on the front of her jeans. That would be recognized for what it was — a sign of nervousness.

Looking through Alex's eyes, Jamie took in the peeling plaster, the cracks, the worn hardwood, the missing planks on the wraparound porch, and she hunched her shoulders at Alex's baffled look. Alex obviously couldn't figure out why she would leave the force to play house.

Jamie gave her the tour, explaining her vision, her plan as they went, but Alex remained silent throughout. When the silence stretched, Jamie knew Alex thought she was crazy.

When they returned to the living room, Alex eyed the chipped fireplace. "When are you coming back to work?"

Jamie stiffened but kept her tone mild. "I'm not."

Alex whipped her attention to Jamie and she frowned. "Seriously?"

"We've gone through this. I'm not."

"Jamie, you needed a break and I understand that. I've done the same thing. It is a tough case and you got hurt. But this..." She waved at the house. "Giving up a promising career just so you can use power tools..."

Alex was hurt by the distance between them, hurt and angry that Jamie had not confided in her and been honest about her father, about her past. What she would not admit even to herself was the resentment she felt at having compromised her principles and then being left to deal with the aftermath of the case alone.

They went out to the porch and stood uncertainly, unable to find the words that would bridge the gap. The chasm between them seemed to grow wider as they stood in silence.

Alex tried to think of something else to add. Inside, her heart was breaking for their friendship, and more than anything she wanted to tell Jamie she missed her. Pride held her back.

"I should go; Megan is expecting me. I just wanted to say hi and see how you are."

Jamie softened. "Alex, I'm fine. I just need some time, that's all." In a move reminiscent of their past, she kissed her friend on the cheek. "Thanks for caring."

They stared at each other, and then Alex nodded once and turned to leave.

Jamie turned away and stared at the house. *Am I crazy? It does run in the family, after all. On Mother's side.* She shook her head and slowly went up the stairs.

She'd known the house was for her the moment she saw it. She could picture it as it would have been a century before, could imagine what it would look like when she was done with it: the long curving staircase, the polished oak floors, the delicate French doors that opened to the garden, the elegant balls that would have been held in the enormous living room.

Like Alex, everyone else would only see the peeling plaster, the cobwebs, the cracks in the ceiling, the dull marked floors, the wobbling balustrade. Everyone but Darcy, who had been the only one who seemed to understand her need for a fresh start. Darcy was also able to see the beauty beneath the paint and neglect. Without thinking twice about it, Jamie had sold her previous house and bought this one in a single day.

Jamie had always done what was expected of her and maybe that was part of the problem, but now — this was for her. She was going to disappoint a bunch of people, but at least she would stop disappointing herself. She was burnt out, no question, hollowed out so that she felt empty from too many days and weekends spent working.

As far as Jamie was concerned, the Reynolds case had been the last straw. The thing with Shane — she couldn't call it anything else but that — had completely sideswiped her, and she needed to lick her wounds in solitude. Dealing with the doubt and fear she had felt standing in her sister's study and hoping that Emma had had nothing to do with the death of their father had left her reeling, uncertain. Until she was certain of her footing again, she would work on her house.

Back inside, she strode to the living room and threw open the French doors to reflect on the view. This was her house. The neglected, tumbled, jungle of garden spread out before her, snaked through with overgrown and broken bricked paths. There was likely a treasure of planting out there. She'd need a landscaper, but an eager little voice insisted she could do it herself, even if she didn't know the difference between an annual and a perennial.

Chapter
Twenty-five

JAMIE WORKED SOLIDLY, ceaselessly, for three days. She kept an eye on the workers as her roof was repaired. She could admit privately that she had no idea what they were doing, but walking around frowning at their efforts seemed to have the desired effect, and there was little time wasted. She steamed off yellowed wallpaper and stripped bare the hardwood floors. In the evenings, she nursed her blisters and aching muscles while poring through house and home magazines. At night she slept little, fighting off too many recurring nightmares, but the lack of sleep seemed not to affect her as she woke with the dawn, ready to tackle yet one more project.

On day four, Jamie woke with a jolt, and in the dark, felt the hard wood of the floor under her, felt the damp coldness of a closed in room.

What the hell?

Groggy, she stretched out a hand...and hit a wall. Her heart slammed in her chest. Slowly she got to her feet, feeling along, searching for the door. She realized that she was on the third floor.

How did I get here?

There were cobwebs in her hair; her hands and her feet were dirty, so she went to the washroom to wash up and to gulp down water, then locked herself in the bedroom.

I was sleepwalking again. I haven't done that since I was a kid. "I'm okay, dammit. And I'm going back to bed."

But the face in the mirror staring back at her looked scared.

Chapter
Twenty-six

"If I hear one more Carpenters' song, I'll—"

"You'll what?" Jamie's eyebrows lifted, a challenge in her tone.

Darcy narrowed her eyes. "Play one and you'll see."

Darcy had stopped in to offer her help in painting the living room. They had split the room in two and had worked for the better part of the morning. Drop sheets protected the hardwood floor from the splatter, and they went quietly about their work, occasionally stopping to chase the dog out of the room.

Monster, it seemed, had discovered a talent for stepping into whatever fresh paint splatter could be found. His blue paw prints were everywhere. It didn't seem to worry Jamie, but it was starting to irritate Darcy.

To top it off, for the better part of the morning, the music-to-paint-by had been a journey through the 1970's. Darcy didn't have any particular fondness for that period and was now pretty much at the end of her patience.

Jamie stood up in one graceful motion. It was like watching a dancer move. Darcy flashed on that thought, then focused on what Jamie was doing. "Don't do it, Jamie," she warned.

"Don't do what?" Jamie hit the replay on the stereo remote and the husky voice of Karen Carpenter floated through the house. "Do this?" She waved the remote control and had only a split second to react as Darcy threw her paintbrush aside and charged her with a snarl.

Jamie danced away from her with a laugh. Giggles escaped Jamie as Darcy chased her around the living room, and Monster joined in, thinking it a new game. The air was punctuated with squeals, muffled laughter, and wild barking. Jamie tried to catch her breath, half holding a chair in front of her for protection as another giggle surfaced.

Was that a giggle? she thought, mortified.

Darcy abandoned the chase, her smile wide as she quickly

surveyed the area. She deliberately relaxed her stance and saw Jamie do the same. Jamie's mistake. Darcy lunged, but her aim was off slightly and as her hand caught Jamie's shirt, she took a quick step back, nudging the chair that was beside her. In a wild heap, they fell to the floor, toppling the chair along with them. Unfortunately, the paint tray that had been setting on the chair followed right along with them, splattering them with paint.

"Fuck!"

"Oh my God!" Jamie tried to speak, tried to apologize, but was laughing too hard. "Darcy...I..." She wiped Darcy's face, forgetting for a moment that her fingers were covered in blue paint, as well. "Oops." She choked on her laughter as she left a wide streak of blue on Darcy's forehead.

Darcy lay atop her, trying to catch her breath as paint dripped from her chin and onto Jamie. She felt her body clench and react to the feel of Jamie's body sprawled out underneath hers, and couldn't figure out how to make herself move.

"Darcy?" Jamie's grin faded slowly. Her pulse kicked as the laughter died out of Darcy's eyes. Worried that her friend was upset, she tried to apologize. "I'm so –"

"Shut up a minute," Darcy snarled. Then her mind went blank as she looked at Jamie. *Well, hell.* Her mouth closed on Jamie's with a force that was stunning.

The heat slammed into Jamie, and she parted her lips as Darcy's urgency stirred a gaping need deep within. As their mouths moved with piercing urgency, a quiet moan ripped from Jamie's throat.

The soft sound penetrated the haze and Darcy froze. Heart thudding, she stared down at Jamie, shocked. "Oh God, Jamie, I...I'm sorry."

"Don't be."

"I'm sorry." Darcy jumped up, and for the first time in her life, ran, leaving a stunned, aroused Jamie behind.

As she sat up, Jamie felt her heart rate slowly return to normal.

What the hell was that?

Chapter
Twenty-seven

"SHE KISSED ME."

"Who did?"

"I mean, I kissed her."

"Who?"

"Jamie."

"So?"

Darcy turned to glare at Lauren who stared back, puzzled. Their group of friends kissed each other all the time.

"*So*? *So!*" Darcy started to pace again. "So it's *Jamie.*"

Still confused, Lauren looked at her, then something clicked. "Darcy, what do you mean you *kissed* her? What kind of kiss was it?"

"Fuck, you want details?"

Lauren smiled. "Sure, if you have them." Her smile widened at the look on Darcy's face. "What I meant was, was it a friendly kiss on the cheek, or something more?"

"More," Darcy mumbled. "The blood drained out of my head."

Lauren narrowed her eyes in speculation. "I see."

"Do you? Because I sure as hell don't. Jesus, it's Jamie."

"So you keep saying."

Darcy started to pace. "How can I suddenly turn around after all of these years and think 'wow'?"

How indeed? Lauren thought. "What does Jamie say about it?"

"She doesn't."

Lauren raised an eyebrow. "You haven't talked to her about it?"

Darcy hunched her shoulders. "No."

"Why not? What happened after you kissed?"

"I ran away," Darcy mumbled.

Lauren looked at her, swallowing a laugh. "You what?"

"I-said-I-ran-away." Darcy snarled out each word. She

pushed a hand through her hair. "I panicked, and I haven't talk to her since." She glanced at Lauren who was staring at her, apparently amused. "I know, I know. I just didn't know how to handle it."

"Well, running away is probably not the ideal way," Lauren commented dryly.

There was a pause. "I should talk to her."

Lauren smiled. "Yep. And, Darcy, if you kiss her again and the blood drains out of your head, this time jump her bones."

"Jump her bones? Christ, that's your advice?"

Lauren had to smile at the look on Darcy's face. "Well...yeah." A thought suddenly occurred to her. "Did she kiss you back?"

THE NEXT DAY, Darcy finally worked up the nerve to talk to Jamie. On the drive over, she felt the dampness on her palms, the quickening of her pulse, and had to pull over once to calm herself. *Get a grip, it's just Jamie. We'll probably laugh about it.* When she got to Jamie's house, she sat in her car for another ten minutes. *What if she slams the door in my face?*

Out of delays, Darcy finally strode to the door and knocked once. When she got no answer, she tried the door, found it unlocked, and stepped inside. She heard the blast of music coming from the back of the house, punctuated by the unmistakable sounds of hammering. She wiped her hands on her jeans and went to the kitchen, where she froze in the doorway. The blood drained out of her head again, the sight of Jamie almost brought her to her knees.

Jamie was dressed in a black sports bra and faded, ripped jeans that hung low over lean hips. And each time she swung the mallet, the muscles in her back and shoulders flexed.

Darcy was unnerved to feel the weakness in her knees. *Good God, how did I miss seeing that all these years?*

Jamie turned, and time stopped for Darcy. Something flared in Jamie's eyes, but was quickly banked.

"Hey," Darcy said, "I hope you're not going to use that on me."

Jamie studied her for a moment, trembling inside as she remembered their kiss. "I'm thinking about it."

Darcy tried not to look at Jamie, fearing that if she did she might do something stupid, like drooling or becoming incoherent. Instead, she looked around the kitchen. Jamie had ripped out the center island, the counters and cabinets, and was now halfway into tearing down the wall that separated the kitchen from the dining room.

"I see you're opening things up."

Jamie dropped the hammer and bent down to grab a bottle of water from the floor, a fine sheen of perspiration glistening on her skin.

Darcy turned and caught Jamie drinking thirstily, swallowed, and forced herself to look away. *What the hell is wrong with me? I haven't had sex in way too long. That must be it.* She felt the twitching pulsations gathering between her legs and, unsettled by her body's reaction, she pushed a frustrated hand into the front pockets of her jeans. It was unnerving to know that her fingers were not quite steady.

"I'm sorry about the other day," Darcy offered.

Jamie lowered the water bottle. "You are?"

"I mean...the kiss. It just happened. It didn't mean anything."

Jamie felt a quick, sharp stab of hurt. "It didn't?" That kiss had kept her awake for more than one night. She studied Darcy's face for a moment, seeing the misery on it. Forcing herself to play it cool, she shrugged. "Okay."

Darcy frowned at Jamie's easy acceptance of her apology. *Wasn't this what I wanted?*

"Want to see what I've done?" Jamie asked.

"Sure."

Jamie turned to go, then the room spun. She heard a scream, saw Darcy's face, the alarm that leapt over it. She thought she saw Darcy's mouth move before her vision grayed, white spots dancing through the mist.

"Jamie, Jamie."

Someone was stroking her head, her face. Jamie opened her eyes to a blur, so she simply closed them again.

"No you don't." Darcy tapped her cheeks with fingers that trembled slightly. "Open your eyes now."

"What the hell happened?"

"You fainted."

"What?"

"Passed out. Dropped like a sack to the floor. You do that a lot?"

"Nope. Not even when I drink myself into oblivion, which I haven't done since college."

"Can you sit up?"

"Yeah." Jamie sat up, felt a wave of nausea pass, and leaned into Darcy's arms. "I'm okay. I'll be okay." She said it mostly to calm her own jangling nerves. When she saw the concern darkening Darcy's eyes, it filled Jamie with warmth—liquid and soft. Jamie smiled at her. "I'm really okay."

"Did you eat today?"

"Yeah. I had cereal. I think."

"Jesus. I'm going to fix you something. Come on. Can you stand up?" Darcy wrapped her arm around Jamie's waist, taking most of her weight, and helped her stagger to her feet. "Let's get you to bed."

"I bet you say that to all your girls."

Too shaken to banter back, Darcy ignored the joke. Her mind replayed the moment when Jamie had dropped in front of her. Jamie had gone down like a stone, right after her face had drained of color and her eyes had rolled back, white. A white flash of fear dried Darcy's throat. Maybe she should call Madison. Being a doctor, Madison could check Jamie out without appearing to.

They went up the stairs and Darcy helped Jamie into bed, shoving the dog aside to get at the covers. "I'll fix you something to eat. Maybe you should try and get some sleep. Have you been sleeping lately?"

Jamie looked sheepish. "No. I've had a few nightmares."

Darcy's anger flared. "Why didn't you call?"

"I thought you were avoiding me." Suddenly Jamie was overwhelmed with fatigue and her eyelids drooped.

Darcy shook her head, silently cursing her own stubbornness. "Even if I was pissed at you, which I wasn't, I would drop everything if you needed me. You should know that by now."

"I thought you were disappointed in me."

Her thoughts suddenly frozen, Darcy scrambled for an answer as their eyes met. She lightly touched Jamie's shoulder. "Disappointed? No, never that."

Jamie closed her eyes and she smiled. "Good to know."

"SHE FAINTED."

"Darcy? Whatever happened to people saying 'Hello, how are you?'" Madison asked.

Darcy sighed heavily into the phone. "Hi, how are you, she fainted."

"Who did?"

"Jamie. One minute she's talking to me, the next her eyes are rolling back into her head." It had taken years off her life, she was sure.

"How is she now?"

"Okay, I think. I put her to bed. I don't think she's been

sleeping or eating or — "

"Darcy?" Madison interrupted.

"What?"

"I'm sure she's fine. I'll drop by to check on her, though."

Darcy had never felt so rattled. "All right." After hanging up, she lifted her eyes to the ceiling and debated whether or not to go up and check on Jamie. Afraid, she stayed put. For the life of her, she couldn't figure out what she was afraid of.

MADISON AND LAUREN showed up at Jamie's house a couple of hours later. While Madison went upstairs to check on Jamie, Lauren stayed downstairs with Darcy.

"She scared me," Darcy said quietly. "I've never been scared like that before."

"I'm sure she's fine, Darcy."

"She dropped to the floor just like that. Jesus."

As Darcy started to pace, Lauren watched her thoughtfully. "Did you guys get a chance to talk?"

"Yeah. I told her I was sorry and that the kiss didn't mean anything. She said okay."

"I see." Lauren tilted her head. "You never did answer me. Did she kiss you back?"

"What does that have to do with anything?"

"Just curious."

"Yeah. She kissed me back," Darcy replied reluctantly.

Lauren worried her lower lip with her bottom teeth while she thought. There definitely was something there. Why hadn't any of them noticed it before? She finally took Darcy by the arm. "Stop pacing. You're making me dizzy." Darcy stopped and looked at her. "I'm going to give you just one piece of advice – don't run away from this."

Darcy frowned. "From what?"

"This thing with Jamie. Don't run away from it."

Darcy felt a flicker of panic dance down her spine. "What thing? There's nothing there."

"If you say so." They stared at each other. "But, Stretch, just try and ignore most of your typical impulses. You might surprise yourself."

"I think I woke up in a parallel universe this morning, because nothing is making sense," Darcy grumbled.

"I know. Isn't it grand?" Lauren smiled. "Not to change the subject, but how was it?"

"How was what?"

"Kissing Jamie."

"Who kissed Jamie?" Madison asked as she entered the living room.

"Darcy did."

Madison stared at Darcy. "You kissed Jamie? When? Is that why she fainted?"

Darcy could feel the blush creep up her neck and couldn't do anything to stop it. "No, that's not why she fainted." She glared at Lauren, who smiled innocently at her. "I'm dreaming; I must be. I'm going to wake up now," she muttered to herself.

Madison grinned, wiggling her eyebrows. "So, Stretch, was it any good? Don't skip any of the details, however small. Was there any tongue action?"

Darcy felt her face flame. She opened her mouth, but nothing came out. She glared at her friends, who continued to grin back at her. With a huff, she shook her head in frustration. "That does it. I disown both of you. You are no longer my friends. I'm leaving now." She turned to stalk out.

Madison put her tongue firmly in her cheek and winked at her girlfriend. "Hey, Stretch, don't you want to know how she is?"

Darcy stopped in the doorway. "How is she?" she threw back over her shoulder.

"I think she'll be fine. Too much work, too little food or sleep would be my guess. But someone should probably stay with her tonight, just in case."

Concern flashed in Darcy's eyes as she turned to look at her friend.

"But I can stay with her," Madison added with a quick grin at Lauren.

Darcy clenched her hands. She was being tested, she knew. "No, I'll stay."

"If she wakes, get her to eat something. I wouldn't kiss her right away, though."

"Fuck off."

Chapter
Twenty-eight

DARCY WASN'T SURE what woke her. She lay in the darkness, her mind slowly transitioning into wakefulness. Then she heard the sound, like a screen door slamming, and she sat up as it registered that it was the front door. She grabbed at the clothes she'd thrown on the chair and pulled on her shirt as she went to the landing.

At the foot of the staircase, light from the outside spilled into the entryway. The door was open, and as Darcy trotted down the stairs, she caught a glimpse of Jamie walking down the drive, and hurried after her.

"Jamie!" she called. When Jamie turned, Darcy's heart lurched as Jamie stared at her, eyes blank. "Jamie?" she whispered as she got closer.

Jamie turned away and started walking. "Daddy, I'm going to the pond."

"What pond?" Darcy asked, puzzled. "Jamie, wake up. You're sleepwalking."

When Jamie simply continued to walk away, Darcy ran after her, afraid. *What was that I've heard about not interfering with sleepwalkers?* She put her hand gently on Jamie's arm.

She tried desperately to think of a way to wake Jamie. Frantic, afraid, going with instinct, Darcy slipped close to her and gently closed her mouth on Jamie's. She felt Jamie respond, soft and dreamlike, but then knew the moment Jamie woke up as she felt Jamie's body stiffen against hers, and the texture of the kiss changed, became deeper. Darcy forced herself to pull away, though her body cried out for more.

"Hey."

"Darcy?" Jamie looked around and shuddered. *I'm sleepwalking again.* "How did you...?" She met the intent look in Darcy's eyes.

"The front door woke me up. Have you been doing this a lot?"

Jamie rubbed her face with a trembling hand. "I haven't done this since I was kid. It started again after I moved into this house."

"You were talking in your sleep, too."

"I was?"

"Yeah. You called me 'dad.'"

Jamie started to shake. "I'm sorry. I must be having those nightmares again. I don't remember."

Jamie suddenly looked so lost that Darcy's heart clenched and she gentled her hands on Jamie's shoulders. "It's okay. Let's get you inside." She wrapped a hand around Jamie's and led her back inside. She followed Jamie upstairs and watched her slip back into bed. Unsure about what to do, Darcy hesitated.

Jamie snuggled under the covers, then looked at her friend in the doorway. "I'm fine. I don't usually do it twice in one night." But her tone belied her uncertainty.

Darcy stared at Jamie. *To hell with it*. She strode into the room and grabbed the comforter cover. "Move over."

Jamie looked at her in surprise, but then simply shifted, making room.

Darcy pulled the covers over herself and briefly debated whether or not to take off her shirt. Though she never slept with clothes on, unexpectedly nervous, she decided against its removal and settled beside Jamie. "You don't snore too, do you?"

Jamie chuckled. "I don't think so, but I do kick occasionally."

Darcy raised her eyes to the ceiling. *Figures*. She turned on her side, her back to Jamie, and tried to relax. "Good night, James."

Jamie stared at the broad back and the auburn hair spilling over the pillow, and instinctively knew she would sleep all night. She moved closer and fitted herself against the long form.

Darcy stiffened at the first feel of Jamie's body, but forced herself to relax.

"Good night, Darcy." Pressed tightly against Darcy's back, she was soon asleep.

It took some time for Darcy to follow suit but finally, with Jamie's scent wrapped around her, she succumbed to her exhaustion.

The noise pulled at her, persistent, close by. Darcy stubbornly tried to hold on to sleep but the noise seemed to be getting louder. She struggled awake and lay confused, trying to remember where she was.

Jamie. I'm in Jamie's bed. And Jamie was snoring beside her.

I've heard of snoring, but this is ridiculous, Darcy thought as the buzzsaw started up again.

She flipped onto her back and ventured a look beside her. Nestled against the pillow, facing her, was Monster. Sound asleep. There was the guilty party. When he started snoring again, Darcy raised her eyes to the ceiling. *For God's sake, how the hell does she sleep through that racket?* She shoved at him but could not budge him. She tried a second time, and he opened one eye and bared his teeth in a very efficient doggie snarl.

"Stop moving," a grumpy voice called out from the other side of the canine.

"I'm trying to move this tank." Darcy shoved at him again. "How the hell do you sleep with his snoring?"

Jamie chuckled. "I'm usually not sleeping." She sat up and pushed a hand through her tousled blond hair, blinking at Darcy in the darkness. She had to smile at Darcy's fierce frown. *Damn, she's cute when she's all sleepy and grumpy.* "Monster, off."

He waited a beat but when it looked like she meant it, he stood up very slowly and, with a forlorn look at her, jumped off the bed.

Jamie smiled after him affectionately. "There you go. The tank is gone."

Darcy watched as the dog slouched out of the room. Satisfied, she turned and caught Jamie's intent look.

"What?"

Jamie blinked slowly. For a moment, she had had a flash of what her future could look like. And with that flash, something very close to yearning settled in her stomach and tightened her chest. She closed her eyes. "Nothing. Go back to sleep."

Darcy lay back down. "Easy for you to say. That dog hates me."

Jamie pulled Darcy close, wrapped an arm around her middle, and settled her head into the curve of Darcy's neck. "I'll protect you. Now be quiet; I still have some sleep left in me."

Darcy's body tensed at the feel of Jamie pressing close. She closed her eyes at Jamie's scent, assailed by images and needs that left her anxious, unsettled. She felt the twinge of arousal pull at her, the heat flow through her. She recognized the feelings for what they were. It was just biology after all, a chemical reaction to being close to a partially nude woman. Anyone else triggering those emotions would have had her seeking relief. Instead, she trembled and tried to clear her mind of the memory of what Jamie's body looked like.

"Relax."

The whisper caressed her neck and sent shivers dancing

down her skin. Darcy felt her heart pound under her skin and was afraid that Jamie would be able to feel it too. "James–"

"Darcy, I want to hold you. Let me."

Darcy's hand drifted down Jamie's back and she pulled her closer, one leg shifting away slightly as she forced herself to relax at the quiet words. *This is Jamie. I shouldn't be feeling this way.* It was the last thought she had as sleep overtook her.

Chapter
Twenty-Nine

WITHOUT TALKING ABOUT it, without acknowledging it in any way, something had shifted between them, and Darcy began to spend more time at Jamie's, helping with the renovations. The rest of the walls downstairs were stripped, repaired and prepped for paint. In the evenings, they pored over paint chips and argued about each one. The old pine flooring upstairs was also exposed and protected now with drop cloths. They spent countless hours in the garden, digging and cutting and planning. Darcy would leave the café early and drive to Jamie's, usually with some leftovers from the kitchen. They would sit on the floor and share a meal while planning the changes to the house.

"IT'S BROWN," DARCY said.

"It is not brown, it's mushroom," Jamie replied. She could not mask the exasperation in her tone.

"Mushroom? What the hell kind of color is that? Since when has a vegetable become a color?"

Jamie stared at her, then smiled. Darcy was glowering at her with puzzled aggravation, and Jamie couldn't help but be amused. She had become so accustomed to their arguments, that if an evening went without one, she felt at a loss, almost missed them. "Stretch, all of your apartment is painted white. You of all people cannot claim to understand the delicate nuances of choosing the right shade."

As on most nights, Jamie felt Darcy studying her, felt the heat of her stare. And as was becoming too common for her peace of mind, Jamie felt her body respond to the look, and the surprising ache for Darcy increased. She shook free of her thoughts and waved the paint chip at Darcy. "Mushroom."

"Delicate nuances, my ass. It's brown. And an ugly brown at that."

Jamie fought down the urge to crush her mouth against Darcy's, fought against the itch in her fingers to touch her. *What the hell is going on with me? This is Darcy. We're friends, for crying out loud. How can I be attracted to her after all these years?*

Instead, she shrugged and picked up another paint chip. "Well then, what do you think about eggplant?"

"Fuck."

JAMIE GAVE UP on worrying about the fact that she was lusting after one of her closest friends. She couldn't begin to understand when or why their relationship had changed. Had it been when Darcy kissed her? Had that kiss been the flashpoint in her starting to think about Darcy in a different way? Whatever the start of it, the change had been subtle at first, but somehow over the past few months, what she felt for Darcy had altered.

When the throbbing in her body became unbearable as she lay in bed later that night, Jamie let her hand drift down to try and ease the ache. As she touched herself, she imagined it was Darcy who was touching her. And the instant Darcy's face appeared behind her eyelids, the orgasm rolled through her in slow waves. The fingers touching her were Darcy's long fingers; Darcy's voice was the one whispering her need in her ear.

Still shuddering, she lay in bed and closed her eyes and felt the want for Darcy throb through her pores. *Maybe I've always felt this way about her. There has to be a reason why she's the only one I've run to. God, I can't keep going through life pining after my friends. That's so pathetic.*

AS SHE HAD over the past few weeks, Darcy showed up at Jamie's with food—a tin foil packet of leftover chicken. She let herself in and followed the sound of music. She always knew where Jamie was by the music that was always blaring somewhere. This time it came from the second floor, and after putting the containers on the kitchen counter, Darcy followed it up the stairs. She peeked into the second room and her breath left her with a rush.

Jamie was standing on a ladder, arms extended above her as she painted the ceiling. Dressed in cutoff shorts and little else, she was humming to an old tune from the seventies.

Monster, who was happily chewing on a corner of the drop cloth, lifted his head, saw Darcy, and jumped up barking and pranced to Darcy.

Jamie dropped the brush in surprise as she turned toward

the doorway.

Darcy bent down to rub Monster's ears to stop him from jumping on her with his paint-covered paws, then she lifted her eyes and locked her gaze on Jamie.

The hunger in Darcy's eyes, for a moment unchecked, slammed into Jamie and she pressed her hand against her suddenly churning stomach. *This can't go on much longer. I'll lose it.* She climbed down the ladder and smiled at the auburn beauty. "Hi."

"I brought food. It's downstairs," Darcy said, unable to look away.

Jamie studied her. *I can't take this anymore.* "Great."

Something in Jamie's eyes made Darcy's nerves jump. "I...I should go heat it up." She started to back out of the room.

"Darcy?"

"What?" Her tone was wary.

Acting on impulse, Jamie went to Darcy and closed her mouth on her's. Her passion exploded in one blinding white flash of heat that came from nowhere.

Shaken, Darcy drew back, trying to gauge her own reaction, fighting to keep her own needs in perspective.

Jamie stared up at Darcy, her breath coming in jerks. Her mind was reeling and she shook her head as if to clear it. Just as she began to draw her first coherent thought, Darcy swore and crushed her mouth to hers.

A thousand warnings jangled in Darcy's brain...and were ignored. For one reckless moment she gave herself over to the heat, to the need, to the yearning. She changed the angle of the kiss, deepened it.

"That's something to think about, all right," Jamie commented quietly as they pulled away slowly. "Let's go eat." She was pleased that her legs were still supporting her as she walked out of the room.

Darcy stared after the departing back and knew that she was in trouble—Jamie was killing her by inches. She knew what it was to want a woman, to have one stir blood and spin images in the mind. It could be a kind of hunger that slowly churned in the stomach, gnawing there until it was finally satisfied. But now she carried Jamie's taste inside, and knew, watching Jamie go, that she wouldn't rid herself of it. That alone was infuriating, not to mention scary.

Chapter
Thirty

THE RAIN CONTINUED all morning—soft, slow, steady. It brought a chill, and a gloom that spread over the day. Clouds hung low, turning everything to different shades of gray. Darcy sat on the covered porch watching Jamie, bundled in a windbreaker, return from taking Monster for his morning run.

The rain had darkened Jamie's hair, and the dark blue sweats she wore stuck to her like a second skin. As she jogged lightly up to the porch, dripping wet, cheeks pink from her run, Darcy thought she couldn't possibly look more seductive. It annoyed her. Just remembering her response to Jamie's kiss infuriated her. It felt too much like weakness. She had left Jamie's the night before, unsettled, stomach in knots, trying to pretend she didn't want to feel Jamie's mouth on hers again. To top off her mad, Jamie had been nonchalant the rest of the evening, as if she wasn't bothered by their kiss at all. As Jamie climbed up the steps, Darcy sat scowling at her.

"Hi." Jamie smiled as she pushed wet hair back from her face. If she was surprised to see Darcy out and about so early in the morning, it didn't show. She was holding tight to Monster's leash, trying to stop him from jumping on Darcy.

Monster shook himself free and was inches away from welcoming Darcy by putting his wet, muddy paws on her when she growled at him. He sat down at her feet with a whine, his whole back end shaking uncertainly.

Jamie raised an amused eyebrow. "Very effective. Do you practice that?" When Darcy just frowned at her, she shrugged, unperturbed, too accustomed to Darcy's moods to take offense. She took her keys from a pocket and unlocked the front door, then stepped inside.

Monster followed her in, making a beeline for the kitchen where he knew breakfast would be waiting.

Darcy remained on the porch, undecided. For the life of her, she couldn't remember why she had come over. She tried to dissect the reasons for her confusion, her indecision. *Was it the kiss?* She wouldn't call the kiss they'd shared uncomplicated. There had been layers to it, and she for one was in no mood to peel away at them.

Raindrops hissed on the roof and at the windows, and Darcy felt the dampness against her skin. Jamie's sudden reappearance in the doorway had her staring, without the ability to marshal a thought in her head. All she could do was stand there on the covered porch looking cold and miserable.

Jamie smiled at the sudden fierce look in Darcy's eyes. "Are you going to come in?"

Darcy frowned. It seemed almost contradictory that such a calm-eyed, smooth-voiced woman could explode with passion. Yet she had. Except now she acted as if nothing had happened. Did that mean that the kiss had meant nothing to her—so that Jamie could calmly ask her in without a worry? *Maybe it's best if I avoid Jamie, keep some distance. For the time being.*

Darcy turned to leave and Jamie frowned. "Stretch? Where are you going?"

Darcy stopped at the top step. She glanced at Jamie, then away. "Home, I guess."

"I just put some coffee on. Why don't you stay and warm up first." When Darcy hesitated, Jamie stepped onto the porch, her eyes fixed questioningly on her friend.

Blushing under the cool, gray stare, Darcy suddenly felt foolish. *Hell, if Jamie can handle it, so can I.* She gave up. "Okay."

When Darcy turned to go inside, Jamie stopped her with a hand on her arm. "Things have changed between us."

"Yes. Yes, they have."

"Right or wrong, we'll finish it," Jamie added quietly.

"No." Darcy was far from calm. "*If* it's right, we'll finish it. I'm not going to pretend I don't want you, but right now I'm not ready to deal with this, whatever *this* is."

Jamie gave her a quick, unsmiling look before she turned away to go inside. "Apparently it's something we both have to get used to."

Chapter
Thirty-one

TWO WEEKS LATER, to celebrate Alex's birthday, their group unanimously decided that it was high time for a night of dancing, of letting the tensions burn away under throbbing lights and loud music. It happened rarely, but when the mood struck they knew to grab the moment. On the night in question, they made plans to gather at a dance club, and a little after nine that evening, four of them were settled in a booth in the back with a view of the dance floor.

Alex, her arm slung casually around Megan, was laughing at Madison when a stillness came over the group and she tensed, as if in anticipation of an impending confrontation. The discomfort of the moment was dispelled as Lauren's face split into a wide smile and she hurried to the door where Jamie stood hesitating.

"I'm so glad you decided to come."

Alex turned slowly, her smile tentative as Jamie walked toward them. "Hi."

"Hi, yourself." Jamie bent down to hug her. "Happy birthday."

Alex's grasp was tight, then she pulled away and looked into Jamie's eyes. *I've missed you*, she thought, but couldn't bring herself to say it out loud.

Their eyes met as the rest of the group tried hard to pretend they weren't staring at the encounter between the former partners. The awkwardness between them was still there; the change in their friendship still hurt, but for one night it would be pushed aside. Then they were past the moment as someone ordered a round of drinks and the party took on a giddy feel.

Jamie searched the room. "Where's Darcy?"

Madison shrugged. "I think something blew up in the kitchen. She's running late and... Well, speak of the devil."

Something almost electric surged through the bar as Darcy stood framed in the doorway. She wore her hair loose, and it flowed down her back in a wild auburn mass; the crisp white shirt, faded jeans and tan suede boots were casually elegant. But there was something more, a sexual energy that emanated from her as she strode to them, oblivious to — or not caring about — the interest she was generating.

Jamie caught her breath at the effect and she blinked once.

Darcy glanced restlessly over her group of friends until she settled on Jamie.

When their eyes met, Jamie felt as if her entire body liquefied under the stare. "Jesus," she whispered, forcing herself to look away. She grabbed her beer with a trembling hand and took a long swallow.

Her agitation was not lost on Lauren, who sat beside her, watching them both thoughtfully.

THE ENTIRE NIGHT, Darcy danced with everyone except Jamie, who was trying hard to ignore her. But that was a difficult thing to do. Darcy danced with a wild, erotic abandon that made everyone who saw her want to get closer to the flame.

When Darcy approached the table after another dance, Madison grinned at her. "You know, Stretch, you should try and bottle that stuff. It has the potency of Viagra."

Darcy shook her head. "Moron." She tried to catch Jamie's eye, but again wasn't unable to. Jamie was, it seemed, particularly interested in her beer label. "Anyone need a drink?"

When they all declined, Darcy turned and made her way through the crowd. As she leaned casually against the bar and placed her order, a young, androgynous brunette with a superbly toned body shifted closer to her. Their eyes met and Darcy smiled automatically.

Watching from the table, Jamie saw the interaction and was vaguely irritated by it. She finished her drink with a gulp and stood up abruptly. "I need another." No one paid any attention to her and she crossed the dance floor, elbowing through the crowd until she got to the bar. She got there just in time to see the brunette put her hand on Darcy's arm and lean in close to whisper something.

Darcy smiled and was about to decline the offer, when her eyes caught Jamie's glare. She raised an eyebrow in question, but Jamie looked away. Darcy turned to the young woman and smiled again. "Thanks for the offer; perhaps some other time." Thus dismissing the brunette, Darcy grabbed her glass and went to where Jamie waited for her drink.

Jamie tried to ignore her, but Darcy bracketed her on either side with her arms, effectively trapping her.

"Problem?" Darcy asked.

Jamie shifted away from Darcy's lean body. "No. You?"

"No." Darcy shifted closer, testing them both. She grinned when Jamie moved away again. The bartender placed the beer bottle in front of Jamie. Just as Jamie's hand closed on it, Darcy encircled her wrist with her hand. Under her thumb, Jamie's pulse raced.

"Come dance with me. You're the only one I haven't danced with."

Jamie resisted. "No, thanks. I'm not in the mood. Why don't you ask your young friend?" She nodded toward the brunette who was still staring at Darcy.

"Who?" Darcy followed Jamie's nod. "I'd rather dance with you. Why won't you? Are you afraid?"

"What? Don't be ridiculous." There was a challenge in Darcy's look that had Jamie wanting to grab a fistful of clothing, drag her close, and assuage her craving. "Oh, for crying out loud! Have it your way."

Jamie marched to the dance floor ahead of Darcy. The gods did not cooperate, and as soon as she hit the middle of the floor, the tempo slowed, the lights dimmed, and the dancers quickly paired off. Darcy looked at her, an arrogance in the way her eyebrow rose that set Jamie's teeth on edge. She would not back down.

They moved closer, arms holding each other loosely, and started to slowly shift with the music. Jamie could smell the light fragrance that seemed so much a part of Darcy. Seduced by it, she leaned in closer. She felt rather than saw Darcy's swift intake of breath. *So, she's not as cool and calm as she pretends to be.*

That pleased Jamie. In a way, testing herself as much as Darcy, she pressed closer until they were hip to hip, until a hard thigh rubbed against a muscled leg. Their feet now barely moving, they swayed in place.

Darcy's long fingers reflexively pressed Jamie closer, and she felt her nipples harden at the feel of Jamie's body against hers. She was sure that Jamie must be aware of the effect she was having.

Jamie could feel Darcy's heart beating against her, quick now, and not too steady. She closed her eyes, and for a moment let herself enjoy the sensations coursing along her spine as Darcy pulled her closer. She had held Darcy that close before, but this night everything felt different. Where before there had been comfort in the closeness, now there was heat. She wanted to smile, to make some light, easy comment. But she couldn't push the words out; her throat was locked. The way Darcy was looking at her—as if she was the only woman she had ever seen or ever wanted to see—made her forget that the dance was supposed to be an expression of friendship.

Jamie curled her hand against Darcy's neck, and Darcy groaned. Jamie smiled, pleased.

Madison, watching from the table, turned back to the group. "Weird as this all is, ten bucks says they do it tonight."

Alex turned with a frown and studied the swaying couple. She shook her head. "I say they don't make it out of the parking lot. I say they do it in the car."

Lauren, who had been watching Jamie and Darcy for a while, grinned. "They're both stubborn ladies. I say it won't happen tonight."

Megan frowned at them and wondered briefly if that was why things had been awkward between Alex and Jamie. "I can't believe you're betting on them doing it or not. Since when is this even a possibility? What have I been missing?"

Madison shrugged and grinned. "Look at them. They're practically engulfed in flames. It's bizarre to see it between the two of them, but there it is. One can't ignore the scientific evidence." She gave Lauren a slow and easy smile. "Besides, anything is possible."

Megan turned and looked. Sure enough, the way the two were dancing had even her feeling the heat. She shifted with a sigh and then slapped a twenty on the table. "I say they kiss here tonight."

Unaware of the interest they were garnering, Jamie and Darcy continued to torture themselves as they moved against each other. Maybe it was wrong, but it didn't seem to matter as they glided across the floor.

Jamie didn't even try to think, never attempted to reason as she pressed her mouth along the curve of Darcy's neck.

Darcy almost whimpered at the feel of Jamie's mouth on her skin, her control threatening to slip. She leaned back slightly and she and Jamie stared at each other, oblivious to the couples bumping into them as they stopped dancing. "James, I..."

The tempo of the music changed, the lights brightened, and the mood was shattered. Reluctantly, they pulled apart, eyes still locked.

Something shifted inside of Darcy. A yearning so huge that it left her trembling as she stared at Jamie. *I have to get out of here or I'll make a fool of myself.* Without another word, she left the dance floor. She returned to the table and grabbed her jacket, hoping to sneak away without anyone noticing.

Alex smirked. "Going somewhere?"

Darcy frowned. "Yeah. I got to go close up the bar." It was a lie, but the only thing she could think of at the moment.

Madison broke away from nibbling on Lauren's neck. "What's this about you leaving?"

Now everyone at the table was staring at her. Darcy almost snarled. "I've got to go, you guys. I'll catch you later." She could sense their amusement and had a sneaking suspicion that it was at her expense. She fled, leaving Jamie staring after her.

Jamie met Lauren's eyes, who smiled encouragingly. She shrugged and took a sip of her drink. Inside, she was angry, frustrated, hot and bothered. *The damn fool.*

Chapter
Thirty-two

A COUPLE OF hours later, Jamie walked into the café, and, as if she sensed her, Darcy turned and locked eyes with her.

Darcy felt her heart stutter at the look in Jamie's eyes. The gray eyes had shifted to slate, and her look was smoldering.

Jamie slowly walked to her without breaking eye contact. "Why is it that you always seem to run away from me?"

"What? You're crazy. I don't run away." Darcy forced herself to look away.

"No? Then why didn't you say goodbye tonight?"

"I was running late." Even to her ears, it sounded lame.

Jamie studied her with a faint smile. "You know, I think I just figured it all out tonight. You're afraid."

"Give me a fucking break." Darcy ignored Jamie's presence as she continued to count the receipts. Inside she was shaking.

Jamie smiled. "Yeah, that's your answer for everything. And yet, you were watching me tonight, the way I was watching you."

Darcy slammed the cash register shut. "I don't know what you're talking about. I might have looked at you once or twice."

"Wanting me. The way I was wanting you. And more. There's more than the wanting between us."

"Please. You'll embarrass yourself. There's nothing—"Darcy gasped when Jamie's mouth crushed down on hers. Hungrily their mouths moved together, and she groaned as she felt the tip of Jamie's tongue savor her lips. Emotions funneled from one to the other, then merged in a torrent of need.

"If it was just this, just the heat, you wouldn't be so scared," Jamie said as she pulled away out of breath.

"I'm not afraid." *If only it were so simple,* Darcy thought as her desire grew. But she knew instinctively that once begun it wouldn't be simple, not for either of them.

"Sooner or later, we'll have to deal with it." Satisfied that she had made her point, Jamie turned and started toward the door.

Darcy stared at her, stung by her words. Her control, too
long held, snapped with a very loud crack. She tossed the
receipts aside and with long strides ate up the space between
them. She slapped her hand against the door Jamie was opening,
slamming it shut.

Startled, Jamie turned and met Darcy's suddenly fierce blue
eyes. She knew to be momentarily alarmed. Darcy's mouth
closed on hers, her tongue stroking deep, tasting the wet heat
within. Earlier, when they'd first kissed, Jamie had sensed the
volcano inside of Darcy. Now, as it erupted around her, she was
rocked by the power, the dark violence of it. She grabbed at
Darcy, pulling the long length of her close. The heat, the scent of
the woman swam into her senses until she was steeped in the
sensations, and she knew that she had lost control. *So this is what
drives people to mad, desperate acts,* she thought as their tongues
tangled.

Darcy forced herself to pull away. "Are you sure?" she
whispered.

"No. But if we don't do something soon, I'll combust on the
spot and my head will explode."

That pulled a smile from Darcy. They intertwined their
fingers and silently walked upstairs. Inside the apartment, Darcy
turned to Jamie and gave a shaky laugh. "Fuck, I'm nervous."

Jamie smiled. "You too? My legs are shaking."

"If you want to change your mind," Darcy offered, suddenly
shy.

Jamie studied her, then had to smile again. *What a pair we
are.* "I can honestly say that I've never wanted anyone so badly
in my entire life. I'm weak with wanting you. I have no idea
where it came from, but if you don't touch me soon I won't be
responsible for my actions."

"What if it alters our friendship?" Darcy asked as she
stepped closer. "Maybe neither of us is ready for that."

"It already has. I look at you and want to tear off your
clothes. Not necessarily a feeling that should exist between
friends, you think?"

Darcy might have chuckled, if she could have found the
breath for it. But her lungs were clogged and her head had
already started to reel. *Where has this feeling been all of my life?
How much more have I missed?*

She cupped the back of Jamie's head and pulled it close.
They stared at each other for what seemed like forever, noses
almost touching. Then she bridged the gap and softly pressed
her mouth against Jamie's.

"Oh my God, your mouth drives me insane." Jamie groaned

as she parted her lips and pressed harder against Darcy. She swallowed Darcy's smile as she took the lead, and their mouths toyed and savored the sensations of lips against lips. Darcy's hand brushed against the soft curve of her breast and the nipple strain against the material. Her breath caught in her throat. *This is Darcy kissing me, touching me,* she thought with wonder, then her mind emptied as Darcy pulled her shirt from her jeans, and ripped it free from the buttons in her haste for her hands to finally touch skin. When Darcy's thumb stroked the hardening bud of her nipple, she almost cried out. She had never felt such want, almost a physical ache.

"Darcy...Darcy I need to feel you," she whispered urgently.

Darcy stared at her and then with a low growl, so quickly that Jamie had no time to react, she lifted her into her arms.

Jamie wrapped her long legs around Darcy's waist, and her mouth was hot and urgent as it closed on Darcy's. "Hurry," she whispered, as Darcy stumbled down the hallway to her bedroom and to the bed, and threw her down. She laughed at the crazed, wild look in the blue eyes, her body already ready, tugging off her shirt as Darcy removed her own. Divested of their clothing, breath ragged, they stared at each other. Whatever shock there was, was on both sides.

Darcy, feeling suddenly sober, stood looking down at Jamie. "You are breathtaking."

Jamie smiled as she took in the vision in front of her. The tall, auburn haired Darcy was stunning, her toned body awe-inspiring. "And you look like all of the fantasies I've ever had."

Darcy knelt above her and slowly fitted her lean hips snugly between Jamie's accepting legs. As they rocked against each other, their eyes locked. The heat was now a slowly spreading flame, the earlier frenzy simmering to a gentle pulsing. Their mouths met again and again. Darcy gently bit down on Jamie's lower lip, sucking on it, drawing a quiet moan from Jamie.

Jamie greedily stroked Darcy's back and gripped her butt, pulling her closer. She gently nudged Darcy's legs apart with her knee and gasped when she felt Darcy's wetness against her thigh. She caressed and stroked and heated the skin above her, then slipped her index finger in the silky wetness.

Shuddering at the soft touch, Darcy groaned. "Feel what you do to me."

Jamie gathered more of the wetness with her finger. "I did this? Christ, you feel so good."

Darcy shifted slightly so that her mouth could savor the tender skin of Jamie's shoulders. She was at once familiar and not. Jamie's scent was familiar, but the taste and texture of her

skin was different, unknown. When she swirled her tongue
around a hard nipple, she heard Jamie's quiet moan bubble up
from deep inside. The sound was new and sent need coursing
through her — a need to hear more, to feel and taste more.

Moved by that need, she reverently caressed Jamie's body
with her mouth and hands. Finding with her mouth what
pleased Jamie, she was attuned to every change of breath — the
quiet catch when she nibbled, the low moan when she stroked
her fingers. When she finally closed her mouth — wet and hot —
on a nipple, Jamie arched into the touch.

"Darcy," Jamie groaned, an urgent whisper in her head. *Not
yet. Not yet.* She'd never been more aware of herself, nor more
distanced from rational thought.

Forcing herself to go slowly, Darcy sat back and looked
down at Jamie as she trailed her fingers along the curve of a
perfect breast. "Jesus, James, you're absolutely beautiful."

The hunger in Darcy's eyes sent a fresh wave of arousal
spinning through Jamie. She traced her fingertip along the tattoo
on Darcy's hipbone, just above the panty line. "What's this?"

"That's my dragon; he guards the gates." She closed her eyes
as Jamie's thumb stroked her tattoo, the touch tantalizing.

"Will I be allowed through?" Jamie whispered as she traced
soft circles that inched closer to the heat.

Darcy was trembling, and wasn't ready to tremble. "Jamie, I
need to taste you. I need to see you come."

Jamie groaned at the words, unbelievably aroused. She
grabbed Darcy's shoulders and pulled her back down.

Darcy traced a finger over Jamie, watching her face in the
moonlight as her eyes closed and her lips trembled on a groan.
She slid her tongue into the hot, wet velvet of Jamie who arched
up, cried out.

"Oh my God, Darcy. Oh my God."

Jamie's cries drove Darcy mad. Pressing her face into the
wet silk, she flattened her tongue and felt the muscles contract
against it. She held it there and watched Jamie shatter. It was the
most beautiful thing she had ever seen.

Unable to stop the tremors that coursed through her, Jamie
gulped once, twice, trying to stop herself from completely falling
apart. Because as she peaked, she knew with absolute clarity that
she was in love with Darcy. Her body was a mass of aching, of
joy, with the sharp edge of her discovery slicing through her like
a bolt of light. She pulled Darcy close. "Come here. Jesus, come
here."

Darcy settled her long frame over Jamie and softly kissed
Jamie's jaw line, her mouth. The ripe scent of passion covered

both of them so that their skin was slick and hot. When Jamie started to move beneath her, Darcy followed her lead as their eyes met.

They tumbled to the edge together, unhurried as their mouths met then retreated and their bodies set the tempo. *Have I ever been affected by anyone like this before?* Darcy wondered as she clung to that slippery line of control. That wild, painful pleasure, once tasted would never be forgotten, would always be craved.

Jamie wrapped her legs around Darcy and pushed up against her. At the same time, she slid her fingers deep into Darcy. Darcy gasped.

They kept their eyes on each other as they moved at an almost lazy pace that generated ever-widening ripples of pleasure. Darcy buried her face against Jamie's throat as the heat spread.

Jamie couldn't say how long they moved together—minutes, hours. But she would never forget how Darcy opened her eyes and stared into hers as Darcy tumbled over.

"Jamie," Darcy said helplessly, on a half sob, as she let herself fly.

THE BUZZING PERSISTED, and with a groan Jamie grabbed at the noise. "'Lo."

"Darcy?" Lauren's voice was uncertain.

"No."

"Jamie?"

"Yeah."

"Oh, hi. It's Lauren. Is Darcy there?"

"Mmmhmm." Jamie passed the phone to Darcy, who lay sprawled next to her.

"Yeah?"

"Darcy, is everything okay? You left so quickly last night."

"I'm fine. Everything's fine." She hissed when she felt Jamie's fingers stroke her. "I...I gotta go, Lauren. I'll call you later." Darcy hung up, then threw the telephone on the floor and turned to Jamie.

At the look on Darcy's face, Jamie laughed. "Problem?"

"You drive me crazy, Jamie. Absolutely, mind blowing crazy."

"Good." Jamie smiled, feeling smug. She widened her eyes in shock when with one quick move Darcy had her tongue buried so deep inside of her that she thought Darcy could touch her heart. Her orgasm slammed into her with such force she screamed out. When she was finally able to focus, she whispered shakily, "My God. What the hell are you doing to me?"

Darcy took Jamie's hand and placed it between her legs where her wetness coated Jamie's fingers. "Same thing you do to me," she whispered hoarsely.

BEMUSED, LAUREN HUNG up the telephone after Darcy disconnected her.

Madison looked up from the newspaper as the silence stretched. "Everything okay?"

"I think I owe you ten dollars."

A FEW HOURS later, leaving a sleeping Jamie behind, Darcy went downstairs to check on the bar. She was also hoping to sweet talk her chef into making a special breakfast order for her and Jamie. She opened the door that led into the café...and stepped into her past.

"Baby!" Nicole Murphy threw open her arms.

Sluggish with shock, Darcy was unable to move before they wrapped around her like chains. Trapped, she was assaulted with impressions: too much perfume that didn't quite cover the smell of stale smoke and vodka; a bony form honed down by years of hard living. And through it all seeped her own dark dread.

"I was just on my way up to your apartment. The nice man at the bar said I might still find you there. Why, I'm so glad to catch you." The voice was a bright bubble that bounced and jerked in the air. "Let me just look at you. You look just like me. I swear you get prettier every time I see you. Honey, I just have to sit down a minute and catch my breath. I'm just so excited to see you, I can hardly stand it."

She talks too fast, Darcy noted. *Her eyes and smile are too bright. She's drunk or high again.*

"Look what you have done with this place!" Nicole dropped into a chair. "I just love it. Suits you. It sure does suit you."

At fifty-four, Nicole's faced showed the wear from too much liquor, too many pills, and too many of life's disappointments.

Darcy stepped around her and took refuge behind the bar. "What do you want?"

"Why, to see you, of course." Nicole trilled out a small laugh that grated. "What a thing to ask. Can't a mother want to see her only child every once in a while?"

Disgust rolled through Darcy and she clung to it. Better disgust than the despair that crept along just beneath it. "Sorry. I have things to do."

"Oh now, you can take a little while for your own mother. After all, you own the place. I'm so proud of you, honey—all grown up and running your own business. Doing so well for yourself, too," she continued as she looked around the restaurant.

Darcy caught the look and the calculation in it. It tightened her chest and stiffened her spine. Her heart still bled a little whenever she thought back to a call that wished her a happy birthday, then in the same breath asked for money. Again. It had always been the only reason Nicole ever communicated with her—when she was strapped for money. "I told you the last time you called it was the last time. You won't get any more money from me."

"Why do you want to hurt my feelings like that?" Nicole widened her eyes as they filled with tears. "I just want to visit my little girl."

"I'm no one's little girl," Darcy said dully. "Especially not yours."

"Don't be mean, honey, after I've come all this way from New York to see you. I know I haven't been a good mother to you, baby, but I'm going to make it up. I've changed."

Nicole stood up and hurried to the bar. She was not quite able to mask her desperation. "I made some mistakes, I know I did." Her voice rang with apology, with regret, but the tone was flat, off key. Practiced tears flowed. "You got to understand, I was just so young when you came along."

The words were old but it didn't stop Darcy from feeling the ache run through her. "You've used that one up."

Nicole dug into her black purse and pulled out a tissue. "Why do you want to be so hard on your mother? Why you wanna hurt my heart like that?"

"You don't have a heart. And you're not my mother. You just gave birth to me, that's all. The day you dropped me off at the orphanage was the day you gave up any claims to calling yourself my mother."

Nicole's sorrow drained away as fast as it had been summoned. "Carried you inside of me for nine months, didn't I?"

"And left me within a year."

"I was seventeen."

It was that, the sad fact of it, which had caused Darcy to make room, time and time again, in her heart. Until her heart had simply calcified from the blows. "You haven't been seventeen in quite a while. Neither have I. I'm not going to waste my time arguing about it. I have things to do, and you have to go."

"But, baby." Panicked, Nicole shifted back to the teary, choked voice. "You've got to give me a chance to make things right. I'm going to get me a job. I could work for you a while, wouldn't that be fun? It would give us a chance to catch up."

"No, you won't work for me, and no, you can't stay here. I made that mistake four years ago and you stole from me. Emptied my cash register, and if that wasn't bad enough, you tried to break into my safe. Unlike you, I don't repeat my mistakes."

"I had a problem back then; I'm clean now. I don't drink anymore, I swear. You can't just turn me out." She held her hands out, palms up, in a gesture of pleading. "I've been sick, real sick, and had to get me some medicine. Those damn doctors cost a lot. I can't afford health insurance. I'm broke."

Darcy looked at her mother, seeing in the bloated features a resemblance to herself that fed her disgust. Nicole had been pretty once; now she had the look, like countless others, of someone who had fallen on hard times. Resigned, she walked to the cash register and counted out fifty dollars. She tried to ignore the tugging at her heart. "Here." She stuffed the bills into Nicole's hand. "Take this, get on a bus back to New York or ride it as far as this takes you. Don't come back here again. There's no place for you here."

"You can't be so mean to me, baby. You can't be so cold."

"Yes, I can." Darcy walked to the door, opened it and stepped aside, then turned to her mother. "It's in the blood. Take the fifty, Nicole. It's all you're going to get. Now leave."

Nicole marched to the door. The money had already disappeared into her purse. She stopped, gave Darcy one last look. "I never wanted you, you know."

Darcy knew. "Then we're even. I never wanted you, either." She shut the door in her mother's face, then flipped the locks, sat down on the floor, and started to cry.

Chapter
Thirty-three

JAMIE BECAME AWARE of the silence, and for a moment puzzled over it. It slowly registered in her sleepy brain that the morning quiet had not been interrupted either by barking or a wet nose pressed against her bare back. Startled by that realization, she sat up, and the previous night and earlier morning came flooding back. *Darcy.* She was at Darcy's.

Feeling the pleasant lethargy in her legs, she leaned back against the pillow and couldn't stop the smile that drifted across her face. She looked at the sheets tossed at the foot of the bed, their clothing carelessly dropped on the floor, and felt the heat return as vivid images of their night together flooded back. Then her heart stuttered as she also remembered the truth that had been discovered: *I'm in love with Darcy. It's not supposed to be that way.* She pounded the pillow, then hugged it against her as her stomach took a deep, diving dip. She frowned with worry. *How am I going to handle that?* The thought squeezed her heart with a mixture of wild pleasure, hope and fear.

But where was Darcy? How could she leave without a word? Had she left in order to avoid dealing with what had happened? She wouldn't be surprised if Darcy had. Darcy had never been particularly good at sticking around when the moment got too touchy-feely.

Jamie pondered the change in their relationship with nervous uncertainty. Maybe Darcy was regretting everything and was now hiding downstairs, hoping Jamie would leave without confronting her. She pursed her lips with embarrassment. She hated feeling insecure and vulnerable.

She swung her legs around and looked for something to put on, then grabbed the blue bathrobe that was thrown over the back of a chair in the corner and padded out of the bedroom. The robe smelled like Darcy, and she felt the want for her tangle with her annoyance.

She was about to go to the kitchen to try and scrounge up a cup of coffee when she heard the key jingle against the lock. Her heart jumped and she was unable to stop the relief and the sheer joy of the moment from spreading.

When she caught sight of Jamie, Darcy froze in the doorway, and for a moment felt awkward. She wasn't so certain she'd smoothed away the tattered edges from the encounter with her mother by the time she made her way back upstairs. She had taken extra time to recover by going for a short drive, determined not to acknowledge the grief that had slashed its way into her heart despite the locks she thought she had securely in place.

"You're up," Darcy interjected into the strained silence, then cursed silently as she felt a blush crept over her face.

"Yeah. I was about to go search for coffee."

Darcy stepped in and closed the door behind her. With a wry grin, she lifted a white paper bag. "Already ahead of you. I also got you some fresh croissants."

She had given up on the idea of trying to cajole her chef into feeding her and Jamie, the confrontation with her mother having made her lose her appetite. Seeing Nicole was a hard reminder of the promise she had made to herself: to succeed, on her own terms; to live precisely how she chose to live, and never, never to place her hopes, her needs, her wants in the hands of another.

Darcy sighed. It was hard to remember her promises when Jamie looked like she belonged there in her home. She fought to hide her misery from Jamie's searching gray eyes, and instead sidestepped having to deal with it by going to the kitchen.

Uncertain, Jamie stood watching her retreat, feeling disappointment spread, convinced that Darcy regretted everything. *She can't even look me in the face.*

Darcy returned and caught the worried look on Jamie's face. Suddenly feeling shy, she handed her a coffee. She cleared her throat, then hunched her shoulders and said softly, "I went out this morning and grabbed your beast."

The soft admission startled Jamie and she stared at Darcy. "You did?"

The look of tenderness that crossed Jamie's face had Darcy shifting from foot to foot. "I figured you might worry about him." She shrugged, embarrassed. "He's downstairs getting a treat."

Jamie smiled, touched by the thoughtful gesture.

Darcy fiddled with the collar of her shirt.

After placing her cup on the small table, Jamie went to Darcy and wrapped her arms tightly around her.

Darcy automatically circled her arms around Jamie.

Their eyes met and Jamie softly traced Darcy's jaw line with her thumb. "Are you sorry?" She held her breath, waiting for the answer.

Darcy didn't pretend she didn't understand the question. She stared into Jamie's warm gray eyes for a moment. "No. You?"

Jamie shook her head. "No."

They continued to gaze at each other. Darcy closed the gap between them. They kissed — eyes open, watching each other — until the kiss deepened and changed, the texture of it becoming more urgent. They pulled away, reluctant to break the moment.

"It's still there," Darcy whispered.

"Oh, yeah. I'm not over it yet." Jamie grinned as she felt the arousal triggered by the kiss warm her. *I'll worry about my heart later, but not now.*

"Me either. Listen, James, I do have to work this afternoon but maybe later, if you're free, we could..."

Her uncompleted invitation warmed Jamie. "I have some work to do around the house, but why don't you come by later?" They smiled at each other, then Jamie watched Darcy's eyes deepen and change as they raked over her.

"You look good in my robe."

"It smells like you."

"Does it?" Darcy grabbed the front of the robe and pulled Jamie closer. She kissed her, but because of the time had to be satisfied with a mind-numbing kiss.

Jamie weakly held on to Darcy. "Jesus, Darcy, where in the world did you learn to kiss like that?"

"Little Timmy McAllister, fourth grade," Darcy replied with a soft laugh. "The rest is sheer inspiration. I guess you inspire me, James."

Jamie smiled. "Good to know."

JAMIE, WEARING JEANS faded to white at the stress points and a bright blue sweater with the sleeves rolled up to her elbows, sanded the steps of her front porch. She had kept busy all day, trying to keep her mind from venturing too often to Darcy. It worried her, this sudden certainty about her feelings for her long-time friend. It bothered her that her day — as full as it was — had been taken up with thoughts of their night together, of the way Darcy had looked at her when she'd left for home. It scared her that she had no idea how Darcy felt or how long she would stick around. More terrifying was the thought of losing their friendship if their new-found relationship didn't work out.

Frustrated with the direction her thoughts had taken, Jamie

stood up and threw the sandpaper down. She blew out a breath and narrowed her eyes against the setting sun as she saw the familiar red car turn onto her street. She didn't like the way her heart stuttered and started to race either. She frowned in annoyance. *Damn it, I'm completely losing control.* Then Darcy stepped out of the car and flashed her that familiar wicked grin, and she forgot about being worried or annoyed.

Darcy went to her, and slowly took a survey of Jamie's body.

Jamie trembled under Darcy's scrutiny. "You keep looking at me like that and I swear I won't be responsible for my actions."

Darcy continued to look at her. "Like what?"

Jamie smiled, pulled off her sweater, and threw it on the porch.

As Jamie reached for the top button of her jeans, Darcy felt the muscles in her stomach clench. Jamie continued to smile as she loosened the button. Darcy heard the blood roaring in her ears. She crossed the driveway with her eyes locked on Jamie's fingers.

"I want to do that," Darcy said hoarsely as she stepped onto the porch, and stopped Jamie's fingers with her hands.

After giving her one long look, Jamie turned and stepped into the house. "Coming?" she asked Darcy over her shoulder.

"Almost there," Darcy muttered.

"WHAT'S GOING ON with you and Jamie?"

"What? Nothing. Just hanging out. Having fun," Darcy answered, immediately on the defensive.

Lauren, who had stopped in at the café with the intention of obtaining as many of the details from Darcy as she could pull out of her, continued eyeing her intently. "Mmmhmm."

"What? What are you thinking?"

Lauren smiled blandly. "Nothing. Friends often have sex together."

Anger flashed through Darcy. "It's not like that, Lauren."

Darcy's anger pleased Lauren, but she kept her face carefully blank. "No? How is it then? You *are* having sex, right?"

"Yes. No." Darcy frowned as she felt a blush warm her cheeks. "We're enjoying each other, and I don't want to jinx it by talking about it." She tried to avoid Lauren's steady gaze, but after a moment she met her eyes with a sigh.

Lauren smiled, seeing more in those blue eyes than she'd ever thought possible. She touched Darcy's hand. "I'm glad, Darcy."

Chapter
Thirty-four

AS SOON AS Darcy opened the door, she heard it and winced. This time Abba was blasting through Jamie's house. For a moment, standing in the dark in the doorway, she thought of turning right around and leaving, unable and unwilling to cope with any more of the 1970's. The need to see Jamie overruled her abhorrence. Frustrated that Jamie seemed to have control of her thoughts and needs, she sighed heavily as she followed the music up to the second floor.

"You have got to change decades, Saunders, I beg of you."

Jamie, busily painting baseboards in the spare room, turned with a grin. "Never. My house, my music." She brandished a paint brush, her smile teasing. "Do you want to fight about it again?"

Darcy smiled, tempted. The idea was appealing, but she was wearing her favorite jeans. "Not particularly. I just don't understand this strange affinity you have with that decade. It boggles the mind."

Jamie stepped over a slumbering Monster to get to Darcy. "I looked good in platform shoes."

She crinkled her eyes in amusement as she studied Darcy's disgusted pout. Just as quickly, her amusement faded. Something was happening inside of her—a quivering, but not that lustful shiver in the belly. This was around her heart, and more ache than pleasure.

With sudden certainty about what she wanted, she took the plunge. "You know what I think?"

"What?"

"You should move in with me. Then *maybe* I'll let you choose the music."

"Move...move in with you? Have you lost your mind?"

"Anyway, there's plenty of room for your stuff here."

Darcy frowned in bafflement. "I'm not moving in with you."

Now that it was out, Jamie felt almost giddy. "Yes, you are."

"James, I can recommend a good therapist. There's absolutely no shame in seeking help for mental instability."

"I'll keep that in mind. God knows I haven't been clear in the head since I got tangled up with you, Stretch. We can make an appointment together, after you move in."

"I'm not moving in with you." Darcy snarled. She felt panic now, little slivers of it dancing down her spine.

Jamie recognized the panic, but it was too late to back down. "Yes, you are. Because it's what I want, and I always get what I want."

Darcy's panic turned to anger to mask the terror she was now feeling. "If you think I give a single damn about what you want right now —"

"Because," Jamie continued unperturbed, "I'm as crazy about you as you are about me."

The certainty behind the words left Darcy speechless.

"That shut you up, didn't it? It's time. Time we started dealing with it instead of dancing around it."

"I'm sorry." Darcy's voice shook. "I don't want this."

The hurt stabbed quick and sharp to Jamie's heart. "I'm sorry you don't want it, too, because it's the way it is. Look at me." She framed Darcy's face with fingers that shook slightly. "I wasn't looking for it either, but it's been there for a long time. Let's see where it takes us." She lowered her mouth, inching closer. "Just us."

Just us, Darcy thought. She wanted to believe it, wanted to trust all the soft and liquid feelings that were flowing through her. To love someone and have it be strong and true; to be capable of it; to be worthy of it: she wanted to believe it all.

Jamie sensed the struggle and took Darcy's hand and pulled her to the bedroom.

This, Darcy could understand. They undressed slowly as the moonlight shimmered over their skin. Her breath caught, released, caught again when Jamie touched her. When Jamie pressed her lips to her heart, she wanted to weep.

Jamie took her hand, holding tight. *No one else*, Jamie thought, *has ever unlocked me this way*. "This is different." She pressed her mouth down as Darcy shook her head. "This *is* different. I love you, Darcy."

Darcy's vision blurred with tears. Her lips trembled with words she didn't know how to say.

"I love you," Jamie repeated.

Darcy's breath caught again as sensation swamped her, tore at her breath, fear and joy bursting. "Don't."

Jamie gently pressed her lips to Darcy's. "I love you." She

kept her eyes open and on Darcy's, watched tears swim and shimmer.

"Jamie," Darcy said helplessly. She felt her heart quake, seem to spill over, then her lips clung as she opened her mouth under Jamie's. "I love you back."

"Say it again."

Darcy shook her head.

"I like the way it sounds. I want to hear it again." Jamie felt the tension in Darcy's body and hid a smile. "There's no point in trying to take it back. You won't get away with it."

Full-fledged panic returning, Darcy scooted away and nearly made it off the bed. "People say all kinds of things in the heat of passion."

"Heat of passion? When you start using clichés like that, I know you're fumbling."

In one easy move Jamie flipped Darcy back on the bed and stretched over her, pinning her. She saw Darcy's eyes darken, the pupils dilating—sure signs of her arousal. "Say it again, Stretch. It's not as hard the second time." She nipped at a bare shoulder, teased a hard nipple with her fingers.

Darcy shifted, trying to move from under her, and was taken aback by Jamie's strength. For the first time she could remember, her own nudity left her feeling uneasy and exposed.

"Whatever I might be feeling at the moment doesn't mean—" She gasped when Jamie's finger found her wet. "God! I hate when you look at me like that—all amused smugness. It's insulting."

"And you're trying to change the subject."

"Don't you understand?" Darcy bunched her hands into fists but felt her body heat as Jamie moved against her. "I know what I'm capable of; I know my strength and weaknesses. I've never been good with long term anything; I'll just screw this up."

"No, you won't. I won't let you."

Darcy grabbed Jamie, determined to push her off. "You overestimate yourself."

"No. *You* underestimate yourself."

It's that, Darcy realized as she stopped fighting, *her simple and quiet faith in me leaves me helpless.* She met Jamie's eyes and saw it—the strain and the nervousness in the quiet gray looking back at her. Her answer mattered. She touched Jamie's face. "Dammit. You win."

"I always do."

Darcy frowned. "Don't push it."

Jamie's only reply was a smile against Darcy's neck as her fingers slipped into Darcy again, finding her wet and ready.

Darcy closed her eyes at the wave of pleasure that rose up at Jamie's touch. "But I'm not moving in."

Jamie stroked her. "Okay. But you will."

"I said—"Jamie's mouth closed on Darcy's nipple.

Jamie lifted her head with a smile. "You said?"

"Don't stop," Darcy whispered helplessly. *Don't stop touching me, don't stop loving me.*

"Never."

Chapter
Thirty-five

THE ROADHOUSE WAS tucked back from the highway. Inside, six booths were arranged down one wall. In the middle were about a dozen tables with mismatched chairs haphazardly pushed together and forgotten. The bar was black with age and the floor, beige linoleum faded to gray. The lone waitress was young and bird-thin, her hair a bottle blonde gone bad.

Someone was crooning about lost love from tinny speakers. To Alex it sounded like Willie Nelson, but she was no country music fan and to her, everyone sounded like Willie. Tapping her fingers impatiently on the surface, she sat at the table waiting for Barney, who had become her unofficial investigator after Jamie's abdication. The waitress slowly made her way to the table, and Alex twitched her nose at the cloud of cheap perfume that came with her.

"What'll you have?" Her too red lips stretched in a vague imitation of a smile as her gum snapped.

"What's good here?"

"Nothing." Her gum snapped again.

Alex looked at her and had to smile. "Okay, what's safe?"

"Coffee."

Alex nodded. "I'll have that, then."

The woman returned with a pot and poured her a cup, then threw some creamers on top of the wobbly table and went back to the counter.

Alex toyed with the spoon, irritation growing at the waiting. *He calls me for a meet, at the very least, he could have come on time,* she thought with annoyance. After an hour of fruitless waiting and too many songs about lost love, she gave up. *I'm gonna kill Barney the next time I see him. The jerk probably got drunk somewhere else and forgot about having made plans to meet me.*

She shook her head at his inconsistency. Barney had sounded so urgent when he'd called. He said he had uncovered something about Reynolds' death, related to his extra-curricular

activities. The investigator didn't want to give her details over
the phone, and he didn't want to meet her at any of the joints he
usually frequented. Whatever it was that he had discovered had
scared him. That had gotten Alex's attention; the former cop
didn't scare easily.

Alex threw some money on the table and left. As she stepped
out into the evening and stared into the inky sky, part of her was
disappointed. She had wanted something, anything to kick-start
her stalled investigation into the death of Jamie's father. She was
at a dead end, and that didn't sit well with her at all.

When she heard footsteps moving quickly away from her,
Alex turned, half expecting to see Barney. She saw a car parked
along the alley next to the restaurant. The beat up Chevy looked
familiar, and she cautiously walked to it, her nose wrinkling as
the smell of rotting garbage wrapped around her.

She could see someone sitting behind the wheel and as she
neared, she saw that it was Barney. "Well, it's about damn time
you showed up. I was about to give you up for..." She looked in
the car. Barney was very dead, a bullet hole in his forehead.

Alex sensed movement behind her but didn't have time to
react before an iron forearm clamped around her neck and a
searing pain scalded her lower back, just above her waist. She
tried to jab her elbow backward, but couldn't generate any
significant force. *Why do I feel so weak?*

She felt her knees start to buckle and when the arm around
her neck released her, she fell to the pavement. Pain rocketed
through her skull, then oblivion rolled in like a dense fog. She
saw it coming, welcomed it.

Chapter
Thirty-six

THE RINGING OF the telephone finally penetrated through to Jamie. She groaned as she opened one eye and stared into the darkness, glanced at the clock beside her bed and frowned at the time. *Two o'clock.* For a moment she toyed with the idea of ignoring the insistent clamor, but wondered if it might be Darcy calling her after closing the restaurant. She stretched out a hand and lifted the receiver with a low groan.

"Hello?"

"Jamie?"

The voice was urgent, thick with emotion, and Jamie sprang up, heart thudding. "Megan? What is it?"

"I think something's happened to Alex. They called looking for her mother's phone number. They wouldn't tell me where they've taken her. Jamie, I think..." Megan's voice broke as she started to sob.

"Megan, it's okay. I'll start calling around. Just try and stay calm. I'm sure everything is okay. I'll call you as soon as I have news."

"Oh, my God, I don't know what I'm going to do if—"

"If nothing. You won't have to do anything because she is fine," Jamie interrupted firmly, even as dread spread. "I'll call you, I promise." Shaken, she hung up the phone and swung her legs off the bed. She was barely aware of throwing some clothes together. She dialed a number from memory.

"Gaston? It's Saunders. What's going on?"

"Saunders? What the hell do you want?"

"I got a call that something happened to Alex."

"Ryan's been shot or stabbed. She's at Mass General."

Her heart dropped. "Is she...?"

"I don't know. Who called you?"

"Why in the hell wouldn't you tell her partner?"

"Partner? No one wants to partner with her since you decided to play house. Besides, she was off duty."

"Not that kind of partner, you idiot. Never mind." Jamie clicked off and threw the cordless phone down, then frantically searched for her shoes.

Monster, thinking it was time to get up, bounced around Jamie, tail wagging madly.

"Go lie down." Jamie knew her voice was rougher than usual, and Monster sat down, shaking, looking at her with sad brown eyes. "I'm sorry, buddy. Just go lie down," she choked out, blinking back tears.

Jamie called Megan as she left the house. The phone was answered on the first ring. "Megan, it's Jamie."

"Alex?" The single word was almost a sob.

"They've taken her to Mass General. I'm sorry, but I don't know any more than that. I'm on my way; I'll meet you there."

"Mass General. Thanks, Jamie."

The line went dead just as Jamie reached her car. Fumbling with her keys, she swallowed a scream of frustration, took a deep breath as she started the car, and sped off with a squeal of tires. The minute she was on the road, her mind went completely blank. The adrenaline kicked in and her reactions now were based on her training. Somewhere her fear had frozen over, and been replaced with icy calm.

She punched a number into her cell phone as she turned a corner too fast and fishtailed, missing a parked car by inches. She forced herself to slow down. "Come on. Answer the damn phone," she hissed through clenched teeth. She heard a click. "Darcy, something's happened to Alex. Get everyone. I'm on my way to Mass General. Meet me there." At a time like this, there was no time for pleasantries.

"WHAT THE HELL could be taking so long? She's been in surgery for hours." Jamie pushed up from the yellow plastic chair and started to pace.

The question had been aimed at no one in particular, and no one bothered to answer. It had taken Darcy little time to gather everyone after Jamie's phone call. Now assembled, the group crowded into the small waiting room, fidgeting as time dragged by. Each one struggled with her fear, her feeling of impotence at not being able to do anything but wait.

Megan sat quietly next to her grandmother, Willy, who periodically patted her hand. The diminutive white haired woman struggled against the urge to take out the small flask hidden inside her coat pocket. *Just one little sip would take the edge off.* She moved her hand to her pocket, but glancing at Megan, stopped and instead took her granddaughter's hand.

Megan looked shell shocked, all expression carefully wiped from her face. Of all of the things she had imagined for their future, this was not one of them. Though she knew that Alex faced danger every day, she had never thought about what would happen if Alex were hurt while on duty. Now she fought against the rising panic of facing a life without her partner. The fear clogged her throat and she tried to repress the tears burning behind her eyelids.

Darcy leaned against the wall near the hallway to the surgical suites, reading the same poster over and over again without any of the words registering. She was remembering another phone call in the dead of night, a couple of years earlier. The message then had been equally brief, with the news of another friend who had been gunned down while on duty.

The irony that the call had been about Sam, Alex's late girlfriend, was not lost on Darcy. She glanced at Jamie and gave a silent prayer of thanks that she was no longer on active duty. She couldn't deal with the fear of what Jamie might face every day.

Lauren periodically stood up to go stare down the hallway, looking for any sign of Madison, who was still at work somewhere else in the hospital.

Jamie shoved her hands into her pockets and glared at a watercolor print as she paced.

Aware of the emotion vibrating through Jamie's body, Darcy intercepted her path and massaged Jamie's neck with a gentle hand. "She'll be fine."

At her touch, Jamie leaned back against her for a brief moment, wanting to feel Darcy's arms around her. "What the hell was she doing in that alley? I should have been there."

"Jamie, stop it. Don't do this. You are not responsible."

"What's going on?"

They all turned their attention to the hallway as Madison came dashing in. She had spent the better part of the night at the bedside of a dying patient until the quiet end had come. As an oncologist, unfortunately those times came with ever increasing frequency. She had stayed for a few moments to console the grieving family, then had stepped out...and received the message about Alex. Swaying with fatigue and worry, she tried to read the news from their body language. Lauren jumped up and into her arms as everyone started speaking at once.

The cacophony died down just as quickly as the double doors opened and an older woman entered the room. The sight of her wasn't encouraging. She looked like a battle-scarred soldier who had lost the war. She had pulled on a lab coat, but it didn't hide the bloodstains coloring her scrubs. Strands of hair, damp with sweat, trailed from beneath her cap.

"I'm Dr. Ramsay. Is Alexandra Ryan's family here?"

Megan stepped forward. "How is she?"

Dr. Ramsay tracked her tired eyes to the blond woman. "Are you family?"

"Hi, Louisa. We are all Alex's friends, but Megan is her partner," Madison broke in gently as she wrapped her arm around a trembling Megan who was flanked on the other side by her grandmother.

Dr. Ramsay looked at Madison in surprise. "Maddie. I'm sorry, I didn't see you there." She turned to Megan. "She survived the surgery."

Megan expelled a deep breath and buried her face against her grandmother's shoulder. Lauren wiped tears from her eyes as Jamie and Darcy hugged, both whispering a prayer of thanks.

Dr. Ramsay pushed her hands into the pockets of her coat. "She was stabbed in the back and the wound was deep. The solid part of her right kidney was penetrated. The organ was repaired and should heal without adverse effect."

Megan smiled through her tears. "Can I see her?"

"Come with me." As they all stepped forward, the doctor shook her head with a faint smile. "I didn't mean the entire waiting room. Sorry, only immediate family tonight."

She led Megan and Willy through two sets of automatic sliding doors into the surgical ICU. "She's still under heavy sedation, and I should warn you that she doesn't look very good. She fell on her face."

Megan turned to Dr. Ramsay, eyes wide.

"Apparently, she was attacked from behind," Dr. Ramsay said. "She collapsed and landed hard on the pavement, face first."

Megan went directly to the bed, took one look, and began to cry.

At Megan's tears, her grandmother rushed to her side and took her into her arms.

Alex lay on her right side, propped up by pillows. A breathing tube was taped in place between her lips. The visible side of her face was so badly swollen and bruised that she was hardly recognizable. Her eyes were closed, but she couldn't have opened her left eye if she'd wanted to; it was too swollen.

"Her pulse is steady. We're keeping a close check on her blood pressure. We'll be taking her off the respirator as soon as she regains consciousness. Naturally, she'll be sedated for pain.

She'll remain in ICU for several days, but her prognosis is good. It helps that she was in good physical condition." Dr. Ramsay recited the litany in a voice that sounded mechanical and detached.

They stood looking at Alex in silence for a couple more minutes. Megan felt her heart trip as more tears threatened. "Oh, honey, what happened to you?"

The doctor then motioned them out. "Visitation will be restricted for a few days, until she is stable. Only immediate family for now."

Megan struggled for calm. Now that she had seen Alex, the relief she had expected to feel did not come. Instead, fear settled over her and made her legs wobbly. "Her sister and mother have been notified. They were out of town, but are catching the first available flight."

The doctor nodded once. "I'll leave word with the nurse's station. If you'll excuse me." She left them staring at the closed doors.

Megan leaned her head against her grandmother. "Willy, I could have lost her."

"Yes, but you didn't. It'll take a lot more than this to beat our girl. She's too tough to go quietly."

Megan smiled, but she remained worried.

Chapter
Thirty-seven

JAMIE SAT BESIDE Alex's bed. Megan had gone home to shower and change—Jamie having pushed her out of the door, threatening to physically toss her out if she didn't leave—and would return later. She thought Alex was sleeping.

"My face. Hurts like hell," Alex mumbled.

Jamie couldn't help a wry smile. "I'm not surprised."

"What do I look like? Every time I ask Megan, she starts to cry."

"I won't lie to you. You look like hell."

Alex closed her eyes, then opened them. "Damage?"

"Considerable but reparable."

"Did they get him?"

Jamie shook her head.

"Fuck."

"Apparently you were attacked from behind."

"Right."

"You fell forward and landed hard on your cheek. You're bruised and swollen, but no bones were broken."

"So I'll be as beautiful as ever?"

"Yes, and as conceited, I'm sure." Jamie paused and stared at her friend. "You scared the hell out of me, Alex. Don't do that again."

Alex tried to smile, but the movement caused her discomfort and she closed her eyes. "I promise."

"What the hell were you doing in that alley?"

"I was meeting Barney." Alex opened her eyes. "Barney, he was in the car, and I thought he was..."

Jamie nodded grimly. "He's dead. Shot through the head."

Alex closed her eyes again. "He wanted to tell me about something he found regarding the judge's death."

Jamie's guilt level escalated and she sighed as she studied her bruised friend. She had chosen the easy way out by resigning. *I should never have tried to avoid getting to the truth.*

Maybe if I hadn't, I might have been there, might have prevented Alex from being stabbed.

Almost as if she could hear Jamie's thoughts, Alex opened her good eye and stared at her erstwhile partner. "It wasn't your fault, James."

Though she did not agree, Jamie nodded. She set her face, turning grim with resolve. She felt the fear, white hot, spear through her. It tightened her stomach into knots and constricted her chest, and was followed closely by rage. She was usually slow to anger, but when it came, the rage was often blinding. She had failed. She had not been there to cover her best friend's back.

"I'm coming back, Alex. I'm coming back and I'm going to finish this thing once and for all. No one comes after my best friend."

Her words fell on deaf ears; Alex had fallen asleep.

Hate and rage surged through Jamie as she continued to stare at Alex's bruised face. Her father had been involved in something ugly and sordid and even now, months after his death, his poison was still causing destruction. She had no doubt that Barney's death and the attack on Alex were all related to her father's death, that he was somehow to blame. Even as a victim, he was still the catalyst.

She wanted to escape the smells of sickness and injury, the sounds of voices and phones, the sight of yellow plastic chairs in the waiting area, the stifling box of memories that held so much pain and fear. But she fought off the panic and emptied her mind of all thoughts except one: she would find whoever was responsible and make them pay.

"I'M GOING BACK."

Darcy continued to rinse glasses even as her heart dropped at the words. She didn't have to ask to where. From the determined set of Jamie's face, she knew Jamie meant back to work. "Okay."

"Aren't you going to ask why?" Jamie knew she sounded belligerent. She had expected an argument.

Darcy shrugged. "I don't need to."

Jamie pushed the glass in front of her. "I can't just sit here and pretend that all of this is not happening. I have to do something. I can't turn away and ignore the fact that Alex got hurt while working on a case that I should have been involved in."

"I know you can't. So, you'll go back, and you'll find who is responsible, and then you'll be able to move on."

It was said calmly, logically, and Jamie frowned at that. Needing an outlet for her anger, she had wanted Darcy to argue the point. Now that Darcy was full of understanding, it defused her anger and she wanted, no *needed* to stay mad.

Because Darcy knew Jamie so well, she read all of the emotions that flickered across her face. "Did you really expect me to argue against you going back to work?"

Jamie shrugged.

"Would it make a difference to your decision if I asked you not to go back?"

Jamie hesitated, then shrugged again. "No."

"There you go. So why waste my energy arguing a point I can't win?"

"It never stopped you before."

Darcy sighed, sensing that Jamie was spoiling for a fight and understanding the reasons behind it. But Alex's stabbing had Darcy rattled and scared. And because she was scared for Jamie, Darcy erupted. "Do you really expect me to be happy about you going back? Do you think for one minute, one second, I want what happened to Alex to happen to you? Are you that stupid and clueless?"

"What? I didn't think—"

"No, you didn't, which is typical of you." Darcy had found her own mad and was on a roll. "Do you think it gives me any pleasure to think about you going out there on the streets, in the back alleys? I saw what happened to Alex. I remember what happened to Sam. I sure as hell don't want to lose another friend. Especially one..." *Especially one that I'm in love with.*

Jamie stared at her lover, mesmerized by the sight of Darcy in full fury.

As Jamie gaped at her, Darcy threw up her hands. "Forget it." She turned and headed to the kitchen.

Jamie stood up. "Darcy! Wait." She whispered the last word.

If it had been shouted, it wouldn't have had the desired effect. As it was, the soft plea stopped Darcy, who turned in the kitchen doorway.

Jamie went to Darcy and cupped her face in her hands. She saw frustration in Darcy's eyes, but it was not born of anger. She was used to that combination. What pulled at her and made her touch gentle was that this time the frustration was triggered by fear.

"I'm sorry." She was close enough to Darcy that their breaths mingled as they stared at each other. "I have to do this.

Please don't ask me not to. Don't ask that of me."

Darcy closed her eyes briefly as fear churned deep in her stomach. "I know, Jamie. That's why I didn't want to say anything. I know you have to go back. I'm trying not to think about the fact that two of my closest friends get to carry guns for a living. And one of them, I'm rather fond of."

Jamie closed her mouth on Darcy's and the kiss carried the tenderness that Jamie could not express. She drew back. "Only fond?"

"Yes. I'm rather fond of Alex." Darcy trailed feather light kisses against Jamie's jaw and she felt Jamie's smile. "Promise me you'll be extra careful," Darcy said against her mouth. "Promise me, James."

Jamie pulled back to stare into Darcy's eyes, serious, intent now on soothing. "I promise. Look what I've got to come back to."

Chapter
Thirty-eight

"WHERE IS SHE? Where's my baby?" The voice that pierced the quiet corridor had even Alex wincing.

"Oh no. Quick, move me to another room. Better yet, let's move to Canada. It's not too late," Alex whispered.

Megan smiled. "She would probably hire the Mounties to find you, but it's worth a try. Oops, too late," Megan whispered back as the door swung open and a shorter version of Alex swept in.

"Where is my daughter?" An older woman with salt and pepper hair cut in an elegant bob, a smooth still unlined face, and the same piercing blue eyes as Alex swept into the room. She pushed past a startled Megan to get to the bed, took one look and started to cry.

"Oh my baby. My poor baby. I need a chair. I'm feeling weak." She continued to weep.

"Mom, Mom, I'm okay," Alex protested at the fluttering hands that kept insisting on patting her everywhere.

"Alexandra, I told you this would happen. Being a cop is so foolish. Didn't I warn you about this?"

"So many times," Alex murmured. She closed her eyes and willed her mother away. She loved her dearly, but at a great distance. She opened her eyes and sighed when she saw that not all dreams came true.

Mrs. Ryan produced a tissue that she delicately dabbed against her eyes. She tried to smooth the sheets, all the while shaking her head. "Don't you worry, I'm going to take you home to Virginia and we'll have you fixed up in no time."

"Mom, I'm fine. Plus, when I get to go home, I have Megan to take care of me."

"Yes. Megan. Your les-bi-an partner." Mrs. Ryan had a habit of pronouncing lesbian as if it was a three-syllable word. "How is Megan?"

"She's fine, thanks," Megan replied dryly from the other

side of the bed. "You can just call me partner. Saves time."

Alex started to laugh, then winced as her facial muscles protested the movement.

Mrs. Ryan ignored Megan's comment and turned to her daughter. "Poor baby. What can I get you?"

Megan rolled her eyes, then turned as the door swung open again and Ashley, Alex's older sister, entered.

She reached Megan first and kissed her. Their eyes met and Ashley smiled. "Sorry I'm late, I couldn't keep up. I've never been good at the twenty yard dash."

Ashley approached Alex and looked down at her, eyes filling with tears. "Wow, kid, you look like you lost the fight with a transport truck. What happened?"

"I fell on my face."

Her sister nodded. "Of course you did. Cool. I'm the prettiest now." She kissed Alex.

"Ashley Dawn, what a terrible thing to say. Why, look at her face."

The door opened again and Jamie, Madison, Darcy, and Lauren walked in, interrupting Mrs. Ryan in mid-hysterics.

"The cavalry's here. Thank God," Megan whispered.

"Terrific, now we can have a party," Darcy drawled.

Alex closed her eyes in relief. She felt no shame in needing her friends as a buffer against her mother. For now, she just wanted to sleep.

Mrs. Ryan forgot about her tears as she looked at the spectacular group of women crowding into the small room. "Ah, the les-bi-an friends are here."

"Indeed. We prefer being called a posse, but whatever," Jamie said, grinning. She bent down and kissed the older woman's cheek. "Hi, Mrs. Ryan."

"Jamie, you look...well."

There was almost an accusation in the remark. Jamie was fine but Alex wasn't.

Feeling overly sensitive, Jamie tried to rein in her guilt and anger.

"What the hell is this? Out! Everyone out! This isn't a party. I said immediate family only." Dr. Ramsay stood in the doorway glaring. She caught Madison in a laser sharp gaze. "Maddie, I'm surprised at you."

Madison shrugged sheepishly. "Well, I've always been a follower." The long sweep of dark hair slid against her cheek as she kissed Alex before following the chastised group out.

Megan kissed Alex. "I'll be back later, honey."

Dr. Ramsay strode to the foot of the bed and swept her eyes

over Alex's face, noting the strain that covered the pain. "I would say that visiting hours are over for tonight. My patient needs some rest."

"Are you the doctor?" Mrs. Ryan asked as she stood up.

"Yes. Doctor Ramsay."

"I'm Alex's mother."

"Ma'am."

"Are you a les-bi-an, too?"

"Mom!" Alex groaned.

Dr. Ramsay looked taken aback for a moment, then she caught Ashley's embarrassed look and smiled slightly. "Not the last time I checked. Now please, leave so that Alex can rest. You can come back in the morning."

Dr. Ramsay ushered them out firmly and so smoothly that neither had time to protest the ejection. She then returned to Alex's bedside. "How are you feeling?"

"I will pledge you my undying love and devotion if you will ban my mother from this hospital," Alex whispered, fighting against the fatigue that was making her eyelids heavy.

The doctor's mouth twitched as she deftly probed the bruises. "Tempting offer, but I would imagine your girlfriend would have something to say about that." She lifted the bandages and took a peek.

"You might be right. Then how about using one of those infernal needles to inject her with Valium when she's not looking?" Alex was already falling asleep as the sound of laughter floated around her.

Chapter
Thirty-nine

"JAMIE?" A SURPRISED Shane looked past Jamie's shoulder for the others. There was only Jamie.

"We need to talk."

Shane stepped back and allowed her visitor to enter. She closed the door and leaned against it briefly, steeling herself against whatever was coming, then followed Jamie into the living room. Jamie stood gazing at the framed pictures scattered on the mantel.

"Is this an official visit?"

"In a matter of speaking."

Jamie turned. She took inventory of Shane's appearance—the loosely worn robe, the tousled damp hair—and realized that she had caught her coming out of the shower again. As she glimpsed the bare skin peeking from the opened gap of the bathrobe, she remembered the last time she had surprised Shane.

Shane fluttered her hand to the collar of her robe. She gave a faint smile. "You have me at a disadvantage. If you can wait, I'll get dressed."

Jamie nodded, warding off the memory of Shane's naked body. *Easy now.*

A few minutes later, Shane returned, dressed in faded jeans and a loose sweater. She had quickly brushed her hair and it lay curling against her shoulders. "Can I offer you a cup of coffee or something?"

"No. I'm fine."

Shane stepped closer and Jamie caught her scent. She smelled fresh—of the soap she always used, of something sweet—and her body automatically responded to that stimulus. She frowned at the betrayal.

As if sensing Jamie's reaction, Shane stopped a foot away and looked at Jamie uncertainly. "Should we sit down?"

"Sure." Relieved to have some distance from Shane, Jamie settled on the couch and immediately regretted it as Shane sat down beside her.

"Where is Detective Ryan?" Shane suddenly asked.

"In the hospital." Jamie studied Shane for any sign of guilt.

Shane widened her eyes. "In the hospital? What happened?"

Jamie ignored the question. Instead she turned slightly so she could look more fully at Shane. "Shane, you need to level with me. You need to tell me everything you know about my father."

"Father?" Shane asked, puzzled. After a moment, horror filled her and she jumped up and strode to the other side of the room. "Reynolds...Reynolds was your father?"

Jamie narrowed her eyes. "I use the term loosely."

"Oh, my God...oh, my God...I slept with..." She felt lightheaded at the thought. It was too sordid to even think about.

Jamie felt a bit sorry for Shane. "You slept with both father and daughter, in a matter of speaking," Jamie said, bluntly. She felt it needed to be said out loud for it to lose its impact.

Shane looked physically ill, and Jamie sighed as she went to her, took her by the arm, and led her back to the couch. "Look, sit down. Maybe you should have a drink or something."

"No...no. I'm fine. It's just so unexpected."

"Unexpected is not the word I would use, but okay."

"I...I didn't know *that,* Jamie."

"I know." *Now.*

Their eyes met. "I guess this means that you and I are an impossibility," Shane added quietly.

Jamie swallowed her brief regret and smiled ruefully. "For a variety of reasons."

They sat quietly for a moment, each lost in her own thoughts.

"Was it you that night?" Shane asked.

Jamie glanced at Shane, then away. "No." She sighed. "And I can't elaborate any further than that." She rubbed at a spot on her knee. "Shane, I need to know who else he was blackmailing, where he got the money, everything you know."

Shane leaned her head back against the couch cushion and closed her eyes. "I don't know about the money. I knew he was being paid to swing some votes, but I don't how or how much."

"Which cases were you pressured on? Let's start with that."

Shane was troubled. "Jamie—"

"I'm not trying to get you to implicate yourself. I'm asking because my best friend was almost killed and someone else also died because they kept digging into this case."

Jamie watched Shane toy at her bottom lip with her teeth.

She could so easily picture that mouth on her body. It unsettled her that despite her feelings for Darcy, she could still feel that curl of lust while sitting beside Shane. The thought of Darcy made her stand and pace by the window.

"Some of the decisions I would have agreed with, regardless," Shane finally said.

"Shane," Jamie said in frustration. She released a breath. "Then start with the ones you didn't agree with."

It took a few hours, but by the time they were done, Jamie had a list of about a dozen suspect cases spread over five years. Some were names of corporations she vaguely recognized, others were names she knew nothing about. But as she read through the list, no common denominator jumped out at her. She would need to run them through the system to see if any pattern appeared.

Jamie stood up and her back protested the sudden movement. As she stretched out the kinks, she looked at Shane, who stood staring out of the bay windows. Shane looked shaken and tired.

Almost as if she could feel Jamie's eyes on her, Shane turned around. She gave her a strained smile. "Did you get everything you needed?" She motioned toward the pile of notes and files that she had pulled out of her home office for Jamie to read.

Jamie nodded, putting away her notebook. "Yeah. Thanks for that. I'll work my way through them; maybe something will come out of it." She gazed at Shane again. *She looks worried.* "Don't worry. It won't track back to you."

"Whoever did this may know about me," Shane replied with a faint shrug. "That's all I was thinking."

"I know. I'll keep an eye on things. If you see anything suspicious or if anything seems odd to you, call me." Jamie handed her a business card.

Shane took it and she smiled, almost amused by the preposterous situation in which they found themselves. She followed Jamie to the front door. On an impulse, she gave Jamie a soft, tentative kiss.

Jamie stood rooted to the spot. She hadn't responded, but she hadn't pushed Shane away, either.

Shane ruefully shook her head. "Good night, Jamie."

JAMIE RETURNED TO the office, feeling unsettled. Her foul mood was scarcely improved by finding the assistant district attorney waiting for her.

"Hi, Jamie."

"Stacey." Jamie pushed by her and threw her keys on the

desk. When Stacey followed her into her office, she turned, unable to hide her irritation.

"I wanted to know how Alex is doing."

"Go see her at the hospital." Jamie silently cursed at a momentary flash of hurt on Stacey's face. She flopped down in her chair. Its creak was the only sound as they stared at each other.

"You don't like me much, do you?" Stacey asked.

"Not much."

"Why? What have I ever done to you?"

"Not to me. I just don't agree with the kind of person you are."

"Kind? What am I, a different species?"

"The kind that would screw around with my best friend's girlfriend."

Stacey winced at the blow. "Alex seems to be over it."

Jamie started to sort through the files on her desk, hoping that Stacey would get the hint and leave.

"Love doesn't ask permission before crashing through your life, you know," Stacey said, softly.

Jamie snapped her head up. "What?"

Stacey regarded her calmly. "You heard me. Sorry to have bothered you." She turned to leave.

Jamie thought about Shane and Darcy and sighed. *Who the hell am I to judge anyone for being human?* "Hell, Stacey, wait!" She stood up and shoved a hand through her hair. "I'm being a bitch."

Stacey smiled ever so slightly as she glanced at Jamie. "Agreed."

Jamie whipped her eyes to Stacey. She grinned reluctantly at the neutral look on Stacey's face. "Truce?" She offered her hand.

Stacey went to her and took her hand. "For now. Wouldn't want us to get too comfortable."

Jamie shook her head at the weak attempt at irony.

"So, let's start over. How is Alex?"

"Better. She's still weak and in pain, but she's getting cranky and that's always a good sign."

They exchanged smiles. When the silence lengthened between them, Stacey shifted. "Well, I should go. See you later, Jamie."

As Stacey left the office, Jamie suddenly had a thought. "Do you have any idea what Barney could have found? Did Alex talk to you about it?"

Stacey stopped and turned. "No." Her eyes narrowed. "Are you back on this case?"

Jamie shrugged. "I want to find who did this to Alex."

Stacey nodded. "I do too."

After a brief hesitation, Jamie threw a small notepad, which Stacey caught in mid air. "I went to see Shane earlier today."

Stacey's raised her eyebrows at the familiarity. *Shane?*

Jamie silently cursed herself. "Judge Scott."

"Uh huh."

"I asked her who might have been pressuring or buying the court's favors through Reynolds."

Stacey flipped through the pages and read the scribbled notes, keeping her face impassive.

Jamie studied her. She grudgingly acknowledged that Stacey was a good prosecutor, and more importantly in her mind, Stacey had once been a good detective before she got called to the bar.

Stacey looked up. "There's enough here to indict Judge Scott. Why aren't we?"

"Because I don't think she did it."

Stacey stared at her. "Why do I sense that you're not telling me everything?"

Jamie shrugged.

Stacey flipped through the notes again. She nodded at the notebook before tossing it on the desk. "There is certainly enough in there to continue digging. I'd take a look at the other woman who was used to lure Judge Scott into that hotel room. She couldn't have been an innocent; it seemed too well planned as a set up. Maybe she was used on more than one blackmail job. And look for that photographer. I mean, someone had to take the pictures."

Jamie nodded, half annoyed that she hadn't thought of that angle herself. *I let myself be too distracted by everything else.*

Stacey looked at her and smiled in amusement. "I'd start by getting a sketch from Judge Scott's description of the woman. Who knows, we might get lucky a second time."

Jamie flipped through another folder, buying time as she thought about her next move. For some inexplicable reason, the thought of seeing Shane alone again unnerved her. "Do you want to ride shotgun when I go back to see her?"

Stacey met Jamie's eyes and Jamie looked away. Stacey narrowed her eyes, puzzled by the apparent embarrassment.

As the silence stretched, Jamie wondered if Alex had said anything to Stacey about her involvement with Shane.

"All right. Count me in," Stacey finally replied.

"SAUNDERS!"

The voiced carried enough irritation to have heads turning in curiosity.

Jamie grimaced. Not for the first time, she cursed the city's builders for the paper-thin walls. She took her time walking to the captain's office. *Why rush? Looks like I'm already in trouble.*

"You wanted to see me?"

"Close the door."

She closed the door and remained standing.

"What are you working on right now?"

"Just reviewing the cold cases."

"Mmm. Rumor has it that you're poking around the Reynolds' file."

Jamie didn't answer.

After a moment of flipping through papers on his desk, Captain Hase lifted his head and looked at her. His chin jutted out as he frowned. "Stay away from this case, Saunders. Ryan told me about the relationship."

Jamie blinked. *Alex told him about Shane?* Her heart skittered.

"Why it came from her and not you, we will discuss later, but I can't have one of my detectives investigating the death of a relative. If the defense ever caught wind of that, bias would be the least of their accusations."

Jamie hid her relief. *He was talking about Reynolds.* She almost smiled.

He narrowed his eyes as he studied her. "I want you ten miles away from this case. Understood?" He waited, but when she said nothing, he continued. "What was the DA doing in your office?"

Jamie shrugged. "Checking up on Alex."

"How is she?" Captain Hase asked.

"Better."

He nodded.

Jamie cleared her throat and tried to sound nonchalant. "Who *is* working on the Reynolds' file 'til Alex gets back?"

"McCarthy."

"What? Captain, you can't..." She stopped as she saw his face tighten.

"Saunders, I'm trying to figure out why I'm not suspending you right now. I don't want to hear another word. Get your notes to McCarthy, then go back to the filing I ordered you to do days ago. If I was you, I'd be careful about not giving me another reason to think about suspending your ass."

He turned to read a memo and Jamie knew the meeting was over. She left, closing the door with exaggerated delicacy. Inside she was fuming. McCarthy was a throwback to the fifties where women belonged in the kitchen. She only grudgingly acknowledged that he knew what he was doing. She returned to her office knowing that, regardless of what Captain Hase said, she would still poke around. She had too much invested in seeing the case solved to leave its resolution in the hands of others.

Chapter
Forty

"DON'T STOP. I'M so close."

"I won't."

"Shane, I need you inside me." Jamie groaned as the swelling of her clitoris increased under the knowing hand. She felt the orgasm start and her whole body twitched. Behind her eyelids she felt another presence, the sensation of being watched. She tossed her head from side to side on the pillow and she clenched the sheet as pleasure and pain mixed.

"That's good, sweet pea."

What? Dad...

"No!" Jamie's eyes flew open just as the climax was ripping through her and the horrified scream was dying on her lips. "No."

"Jamie, it's okay."

Jamie looked into concerned blue eyes and she felt the blood drain from her face as her body shuddered on the tail end of her peak. She gulped in air. *A dream. It was just a dream.*

"It was just a dream," Darcy whispered.

Jamie sat up quickly, knowing she was going to be sick. When Darcy tried to rub her back, she shrugged her off and jumped up from the bed. "Don't. Don't touch me."

She fled into the bathroom, leaving behind a stunned Darcy. She leaned weakly against the closed bathroom door then locked it as she felt the nausea increase. She sank down onto the floor and rested her burning face against the cool tile.

Darcy's concerned voice came through the closed door. "Jamie? Are you okay?"

Jamie felt the guilt pierce through her. "I'm fine. I'll be out in a minute."

Her nightmare flashed through her mind. "Oh, my God. Oh, my God," she whispered into the quiet as her body trembled. *What the hell was that?*

She turned on the shower taps and stepped into the spray,

scrubbing vigorously as tears streamed down her face. Every time her mind tried to pull her back to the dream, the nausea returned and she rubbed her body harder.

What the hell is wrong with me? Jamie thought as she swallowed a hysterical sob. She thought of Darcy in the other room and felt her muscles clench. More than anything, she wanted to run back out and into Darcy's arms, and let her warmth and strength soothe her.

Jamie stayed under the spray until most of the hot water had run out. Shivering as the water cooled, knowing she had delayed it as long as she could, she finally turned off the water and stepped out, then toweled herself briskly. She searched for and pulled on a pair of navy sweatpants and a T-shirt, then slowly opened the door and peeked into the dark room.

Darcy was sitting at the foot of the bed, staring down at her hands. She lifted her head at the sound of the door. "Are you okay?"

The voice was uncertain, soft. It didn't sound like Darcy at all. Jamie hesitated in the doorway and with a sigh finally stepped into the room. "Yeah. I had a nightmare and it just freaked me out. I'm better now." She tried to avoid Darcy's searching eyes, afraid of what her own might reveal.

"Jamie—"

"I don't want to talk about it, if that's okay."

"Okay."

There was hurt in that simple word, and it made Jamie feel worse. She sat on the other side of the bed and glanced down at her hands, wanting desperately for Darcy to hold her but unable to find the right way to ask. Her vulnerability overwhelmed her, and yet she flinched when she felt Darcy's hand on her shoulder.

Darcy went rigid at Jamie's reaction and she pulled her hand away as if scalded.

Jamie bit down on her lip as she fought against the tears that threatened again. She felt the mattress shift as Darcy readjusted herself and lay down on her side. She stripped, then slipped in beside her and, from the corner of her eyes, looked at Darcy's back.

Jamie closed her eyes and tried to relax her body. But she was afraid of sleep, afraid of what sleep would bring. Afraid of what the nightmares and dreams would reveal about herself. Again she looked at Darcy and took in the long bare back, the powerful shoulders. She wanted, no needed to feel Darcy next to her. Needs and fear battled. "Darcy?" There was no answer and for a moment, Jamie wondered if Darcy was ignoring her.

"What is it?" the sleepy voice replied.

"Would you? Could you...?" Tears spilled down Jamie's cheek.

Darcy turned to her, and even in the darkness, Jamie felt the intensity of her stare. She felt the mattress dip in as Darcy shifted closer. Then a gentle hand wiped her tears.

"Honey, what is it?"

"I need to...I have to..." She shook her head, unable to put words to her want.

"Come here."

Darcy gathered her close and Jamie wrapped herself tightly around her. She sighed when she felt the strong arms tighten around her. She buried her face into the warm curve of Darcy's neck, inhaling her familiar scent. "I got spooked. I'm sorry."

"It's okay." Darcy rubbed Jamie's back. "It's okay."

Jamie felt the heat from Darcy's body seep into her own, and she pressed closer. Strength met need and need became desperation. She felt the weight of Darcy's breasts against her body, felt the long legs entwine with hers, and almost violently felt her body react to being that close to her lover. Her mind was swamped with sensations. *This is the woman I love; this is safety.*

"Darcy?"

Darcy stilled her hand at the ache in Jamie's voice.

Jamie moved, and with a subtle press of her hips covered Darcy. "I need you, honey. I need you."

"Jamie, wait."

Jamie was like a woman possessed as she tore through Darcy's defenses one by one. Darcy's scent was everywhere, subtle at the curve of her waist, stronger at the gentle underside of her breasts. With open mouthed kisses, Jamie relearned her body. Her mouth, her teeth, her hands covered Darcy's body inch by inch; she wanted her total surrender. She tasted the moistness of Darcy's skin and craved more.

Unable to stop the tidal wave of emotion that rose up between them, Darcy helplessly followed along as her body arched taut and her hands clung.

As Jamie felt Darcy's muscles clench around her fingers and heard the ragged breathing, she knew her lover was close to tumbling. She lowered her hand and stroked herself, matching her movement to that of her tongue as her mouth made love to Darcy. "I want us to come together," she whispered.

Darcy groaned as she felt Jamie touching herself. "Then come up here, honey. Jesus, come here." She urgently moved her hands as the breath caught in her throat, and with an insistent pull she had Jamie turned so that Jamie straddled her mouth.

When Darcy's tongue stroked her, hot and sure, Jamie cried

out and buried her own into Darcy's wet softness. She knew Darcy's need was tangled with love.

Instinctively they matched rhythm, and Jamie was almost deaf and blind to anything but the sensation of wet silk in her mouth and Darcy's tongue inside of her. She felt Darcy grow rigid then push against her mouth with a loud cry, and in almost simultaneous response, her own orgasm came crashing through her. It robbed her of coherence as she bucked against the wave, while her tongue kept time with Darcy's frantic thrusts.

When Jamie tried to pull away from Darcy's mouth, unable to take any more, Darcy grabbed her hips and kept her close as her tongue continued to ravage.

Jamie was almost sobbing into Darcy's wetness. She screamed Darcy's name when the second climax hit. They collapsed back down on the bed, Jamie throwing one arm weakly over her eyes as her body shuddered with aftershocks. She felt Darcy tremble beside her.

"Darcy, you completely wreck me," Jamie managed weakly.

Darcy opened heavy lids to look at her. "I've never... This is the first..." She blushed.

Surprised by Darcy's shyness, Jamie pushed herself up to look at her. "You've never done that before?"

Darcy shook her head as her cheeks heated. "No. I've always sort of taken turns. I've never felt compelled to..."

Jamie flipped back to face Darcy and leaned over to kiss her. "I love you, Darcy." She was surprised at the wetness against her mouth as she felt Darcy's tears against lips that trembled. The love she felt for Darcy swamped her and she gripped her fiercely. *How can I think of anyone but her?*

Afraid, Darcy held her. She had sensed a desperation in Jamie's touch, almost as if she wanted to forget. *Forget what?* She tightened her hold and they fell into a restless sleep.

Chapter
Forty-one

JAMIE ERUPTED WHEN she entered the room. "What the hell do you think you are doing?"

"What does it look like?" a grumpy Alex answered.

She had stayed in ICU for two days. For the past five, she'd been in a private room that afforded her a lovely view of the parking lot. She was now able to lie on her back. It still hurt like hell, especially when she was forced to get up and walk around, which was at least twice a day. Each of those hikes, as she called them, was an ordeal equivalent to climbing Everest. At first she was only able to shuffle slowly around her room, but earlier that day she had managed to make it to the end of the hall and back, which the nursing staff claimed was a major breakthrough. Alex had cursed and asked them where they stored their Nazi uniforms.

She was now just shuffling back to bed after going to the bathroom, and was sweating and feeling as helpless as a baby.

"I had to pee. I refuse to do it in that god awful plastic bowl."

Jamie hid a smile as she helped her into bed. "Where's Megan?"

"I sent her home." It was more like she had thrown her out, irritated by her concern. And just as soon as Megan had left, Alex wanted her back.

When Jamie made a clucking sound, Alex glared at her. Her cheek was still the color of an eggplant going bad, but the swelling had gone down enough for her to see out of both eyes.

"What?" Alex asked grouchily.

"You must be feeling better, you're back to being grumpy."

"Shut up."

"Are you eating?"

"Some. A little. I'm not hungry. Besides, have you seen the crap they try to pass off as food?"

Jamie sat on the chair beside the bed. "Megan said you

should be going home soon."

"Who knows? The evil Doctor Ramsay won't tell me anything." Alex shrugged, feeling guilty about being so mean to Megan. "Have you talked to Megan?"

Jamie smiled. "Yeah, and she's not mad. But you should call her later."

Alex looked sheepish. "I'm a bitch and she should leave me the first chance she gets."

Jamie grinned. "Yeah, that's what I told her. She keeps insisting that you have redeeming qualities. God knows what they are."

They smiled at each other. Jamie looked away briefly, then cleared her throat.

Alex looked at Jamie speculatively at her sign of nervousness. "What's up? Everything okay with you and Darcy?"

"Everything's fine." Jamie hoped she sounded convincing. "I asked Stacey Nash to help me with the case."

Alex lifted a dark brow in surprise. "Stacey? You mean you guys haven't come to blows yet? If you tell me you've become friends, I'll know that I still have a concussion."

Jamie shrugged. "We've come to an understanding. How much does she know about my father?"

Alex sighed. "Nothing that relates to you. And she doesn't know about you and Shane, either." Jamie's eyes flickered and the reaction didn't escape Alex. "Wait a minute, I didn't think you were working this case. What're you up to?"

"Looking into things for you until you are back." She shrugged then stood up, needing to pace. "We got a description of the woman that picked up Shane, and Stacey will poke around the hotel some more. I'm going to track down Barney's last flop. Do you have any idea where he was staying?"

Alex shifted, grimacing as the pain stabbed at her. "I don't know." She paused before she opened her eyes. "Hey, didn't he used to rent a room out of that stupid strip joint? What was it called? Talisman?"

Jamie stopped her pacing. "Talisman? I'll check it out." She walked back to the bed and briefly pressed her fingers on Alex's shoulder. "You should rest. Can I get you anything when I come back?"

"Yeah, a burger. Oh, and fries too." Alex closed her eyes as the pain medication took effect.

Jamie stared down at her friend and smiled foolishly. *It's good to have her back.* She left quietly.

Chapter
Forty-two

A COUPLE OF days later, Jamie sat at the bar at Murphy's, brooding over her coffee. She had just finished searching through Barney's room, and her search had paid no dividends whatsoever. All that she had found were porn videos, moldy take-out boxes, and a pile of fragrant clothing. There was nothing that even hinted at what he had found out about Judge Reynolds, not one scrap of paper or scribbled note indicating what had led to his death. She glared into her coffee cup, knowing full well that she had way too much caffeine already coursing through her blood.

Darcy smiled at the pouting picture Jamie made and was about to say something when the café door opened.

Jamie's heart stuttered as Shane stood framed in the open doorway. Their eyes met and Jamie made as if to stand, but she remained sitting.

Her reaction was not lost on Darcy, who stared curiously at them as Shane approached tentatively and sat down beside Jamie.

"Shane, what are you doing here? This is not a good idea."

Darcy froze midway between the kitchen entry way and the restaurant, then continued into the kitchen.

Shane gently touched Jamie's arm. "I know, but something told me that this is where I could find you. I was going to try at the station, but it appears that you're not formally working on the case, are you?"

"Really?" Jamie shrugged.

"I was visited by a nice detective with a very thick neck."

McCarthy. "I'm working it, just not quite officially," Jamie admitted.

When Shane continued to regard her, Jamie felt the intensity of her stare and felt herself blush. She was uncomfortably aware that Darcy was somewhere in the restaurant, yet she couldn't find it in herself to break the visual contact. Shane was the first to look away, and Jamie frowned down at her cup.

Shane finally spoke. "I had lunch with Mrs. Carter. A nice lady. Lonely."

Jamie raised a brow.

"Judge Reynolds' secretary for ten years until her retirement two years ago. She was only too happy to talk about the good old days." Shane handed her a slip of paper. "This is the photographer that 'his honor' always used for his official portrait." She shrugged, as Jamie's look sharpened. "Could be nothing, but I thought you might want to check it out."

Beaten by an amateur. Jamie didn't know whether to be depressed by that fact or angry. She pocketed the paper.

Darcy returned from the kitchen just in time to see the exchange, and felt the uneasiness stab at her. It wasn't like her to feel unsure. Ordinarily she would have sauntered over and made a show of not caring, but now she stood frozen on the spot, wanting to escape, as instincts screamed warnings of all kinds. She stared as if fascinated by the intimate tableau before her.

Unaware of Darcy's presence, Jamie met Shane's eyes and felt the impact of them again. "Thanks. I'll take a look at it." Her voice was deeper than she wanted it to be.

Shane touched Jamie's arm and smiled slowly as she saw the flush creep up and over Jamie's cheeks.

Darcy had seen enough and turned to leave, her heart hammering in her chest. *See, I told you good things don't last,* she thought furiously.

"Shane," Jamie whispered. "I'm sorry. I'm involved with someone else." Shane's eyes flickered, whether it was from surprise or hurt was unclear.

"Oh?"

"You and I..."

"...are an impossibility," Shane finished.

"Yeah. Bad timing. Somewhere between meeting you and now, I fell in love with someone else."

Shane smiled with regret as she stood up. "I should leave before I make a fool of myself."

"Never that, Shane."

Their eyes met and Shane gave Jamie a quick kiss on the cheek. "She's a lucky woman." She left quickly.

No. I'm the lucky one, Jamie thought.

She looked around for Darcy, but Darcy wasn't anywhere to be seen. She pulled out the slip of paper and looked at it. She tugged her cell phone from her back pocket and dialed a number.

"Stacey? I might have a lead on the photographer."

About an hour later, Darcy returned to the café from the walk around the block she'd taken to clear her head. She saw that Jamie was gone and, finding no message, she felt the tears burn behind her eyelids.

"Fuck. I refuse to cry over a damn woman," she swore, unaware that the tears were already rolling down her cheeks.

JAMIE AND STACEY stood at the door of the small, nondescript grey building. From the looks of the overflowing mailbox, Brian Mayer, photographer, had not been home for several days.

"Now what?" Stacey asked after ringing the buzzer for the second time and getting no response.

"We should go in and take a look around," Jamie replied. As Stacey looked on in surprise, she started to fiddle with the locks.

"Are you breaking in?"

"No. *We* are not breaking anything." Jamie pulled a credit card out of her coat pocket.

Stacey sighed as she quickly looked around. The residential neighborhood was quiet, with most people probably at work. Still... After watching Jamie struggle with the lock and her credit card for a few moments, she pushed her out of the way. "If this gets out, I'm not taking the fall alone," she muttered as she pulled a small black case from her inside pocket and extracted a thin pick. She had the lock snapping open within a few seconds.

Jamie stared at her open mouth. "Wow, Stacey."

"Not one word," Stacey growled.

They entered quickly and shut the door behind them. Stacey flicked on her pen light, and the weak yellow beam flickered in front of them. They were immediately struck with the musty smell of closed in rooms. Jamie sneezed at the dust.

"I'll take upstairs, you take the main floor," Stacey instructed after a cursory look around.

Jamie raised an eyebrow. "I bet you like to be on top," she muttered.

Stacey turned and gave her a heart-stopping smile. "You'll never know."

Jamie shook her head and watched Stacey go up the stairs, then turned her attention to the main floor. It was sparsely furnished and divided on either side by a small hallway. On one side was the living room and what looked like an office; on the right side and to the back was the kitchen, with its efficient appliances. She was surprised by the neatness, and by the fact that not one photograph existed anywhere.

Isn't that strange? If this guy was a photographer, he didn't bring his work home. As Jamie searched further, she was disappointed not to find a dark room. *What kind of photographer doesn't have a darkroom at home?*

She decided to concentrate on the small room that Mr. Mayer had converted into an office. Except for the fine coat of dust on its veneer surface, the functional desk was bare. No computer, no notepads. The garbage can was empty — no envelopes or crunched up notes. It was too clean. She sighed in frustration.

The desk had three drawers. *Three more strikes and I'm out.* The first one was filled with pens, all ball point and black, and a white notepad. Not one doodle or scribble. Blank. *Strike one.* The second drawer was empty. *Strike two.* Sighing, Jamie turned her attention to the third.

It was stuck, and she struggled with it until she was able to slide it open. There was a rustling sound as she poked about with her fingers, but she found it empty. She pulled it out completely to peer inside and fished into the opening, but her fingers touched only dust, or so she wanted to believe. She slid her hand along the sides and again she heard the rustling sound. Finally, after pressing along the sides, she felt the bottom of the drawer give. *What do you know, there's a false bottom.*

She extracted the contents and was only mildly surprised to find a manila envelope that had been secreted in the crevice. She pulled on a pair of thin gloves before peeling open the tab and pulling out the pictures. She was barely aware of the scream that erupted from her throat. Staring back at her was a picture of her father with Sarah Timley, the eight-year-old girl who had gone missing and then turned up in pieces in a duffel bag in the Charles River four months before.

Chapter
Forty-three

IT HAD BEEN two days since Jamie had found the pictures and given them to Stacey. Two days of avoiding all contacts, of hiding out at Madison and Lauren's while her nights were haunted by nightmares. She hadn't spoken to Darcy; she hadn't even talked to Madison about why she had showed up at their front door.

Madison had respected her silence and was waiting it out.

Jamie was unstable, jumpy and distracted. All three moods collided when the door to the bathroom opened while she was sulking in the shower and she saw Madison enter.

"God dammit to hell and back," Jamie yelled. "I'm naked in here."

"I certainly hope so. I'd be even more worried about you if you'd started taking showers with your clothes on. Bathroom's about the only place I figure we can talk without you trying to escape. Especially with you being naked."

Jamie tugged the shower curtain back an inch. Through the steam, she watched Madison drop the lid on the toilet and sit.

"If I'm in the bathroom, it's because I want privacy."

"Exactly so." Madison crossed her legs. "You need to snap out of it."

"Snap out of what?" Jamie yanked the curtain back into place and dunked her head under the spray. "Seems to me, there ought to be a little more respect around here. People bobbing into the bathroom while other people are wet and naked."

"From where I'm sitting, I don't see that as a disadvantage." Madison grinned. "I want to know what is going on with you. The bags under your eyes are big enough to hold a week's worth of groceries; you've lost weight; and somehow all of this is affecting Darcy. Her temper—never sterling to begin with—is getting ugly. And I'm thinking you're the cause. So spill it."

Jamie snarled. "Go away, Doc. It's none of your damn business."

Dismissal was the wrong approach to use with Madison. She rarely let her temper get the better of her, but now it did. She yanked the shower curtain open and stepped in, fully dressed.

"What the hell are you—"

"Shut up, Jamie." Madison pushed her against the wall and held firm.

Jamie, too aware of her nakedness, fought back weakly, embarrassment heating her body.

"What's going on?"

"I told you," Jamie said, her eyes snapping open at Madison's surprising strength.

"You told me squat. My friends, namely you and Darcy, are hurting, so I consider that my business. Dammit, Jamie, you made her cry!" Madison shouted, shaking her a little.

Jamie stopped fighting. "Who? Darcy?"

Madison's hold loosened as the water plastered her dark hair against her scalp and she felt her clothes cling wetly to her body. "You made her cry. Darcy never cries. Not even the time when I beaned her with a baseball."

"Oh, God." Jamie's breath hitched and she started to cry.

"What? No...hey wait."

Madison was panicked. She hated tears. Jamie slid down into the tub and Madison knelt in front of her. "Jesus, Jamie, I'm sorry. I didn't mean..."

"I love her, Maddie. I love her, and yet I think I'm losing my mind."

Madison reached over Jamie and turned off the water. She put her hand on Jamie's bare shoulder. "Whoever said love was supposed to be sane?"

Jamie shook her head. "I'm in love with her, but I keep having dreams that involve someone else. But it's all mixed up with a case. I'm damaged goods."

"Hmm. Maybe you should start at the beginning."

Jamie sighed. "I need to get dressed first. I feel weird discussing anything further with you while I'm buck naked."

"I'm a doctor. I see naked people all the time." Madison smiled and stood up. "And from where I stand, it's not a bad view." She held out her hand and helped Jamie up. Staring down at herself ruefully, she realized that her cashmere sweater was probably ruined. "I need to change, and then hide this sweater. It was a gift from Lauren."

Jamie looked at her and had to smile. "I'd forgotten how fierce you can be when you get pissed."

Madison made a face as she stepped out and grabbed a towel. She handed one to Jamie. "Just don't say anything to

Lauren."

"What? About how we took a shower together and you saw me naked?" Jamie let her smile hold the promise. "It'll be our little secret. Next time though, you strip. It's only fair."

"Deal." Madison toweled her hair, then stood shivering in the clothing that felt like ice against her skin.

As Jamie wrapped a towel around her body and stepped out of the shower, Madison did the same, then went to the bedroom.

Jamie heard her rummaging around.

Madison returned and tossed Jamie a pair of sweats and a sweater. "Okay, let's talk."

JAMIE USED HER key to enter Murphy's. The lights were still on, but the place was quiet. It was just after eleven and Darcy had apparently closed the place early, which was unusual. As she stepped into the café, she found Darcy sitting at a table, an all but empty bottle of wine in front of her. And a glass, half full.

Jamie took a closer look at Darcy's face. "You're plowed."

"Does that mean I'm drunk? If so, I'm forced to agree. I'm very, very, very drunk." Darcy lifted her glass and managed to sip without pouring it down the front of her shirt. "I don't know how it happened. Prob'ly 'cause I kep' drinking."

Christ, she was cute, sprawled in her chair, her blue eyes bright and glowing. *Her smile is, well,* Jamie thought, *stupid.*

"Yep. That'll do it." Jamie gently braced a finger under Darcy's chin to keep it from wobbling. "Did you eat anything?"

"Nope. Can't cook. Sent the chef home." She found that so funny, she sputtered with laughter. "Why are you here? Hi."

"Yeah. Hi." It was impossible to be anything but in love with her. Darcy looked so sweet and so incredibly drunk, and Jamie felt her heart squeeze for the pain she might have caused her by not calling her for two days.

"Let's get you upstairs."

"Aren't you going to kiss me?" Darcy slid gracefully from chair to floor.

With an oath, Jamie hauled her back up.

Darcy might have been drunk, but she had damn good aim. She fastened her mouth on Jamie's and she delivered a long, eye-popping kiss.

"Missed you. I thought you had gone. Left me. It made me sad. See how pissed I am?" Riding on that and on the wine swimming in her head, Darcy flung out her arms to fasten them around Jamie. "Come down, okay? And kiss me again. It just makes my head go all funny and my heart pound. Want to feel my heart pound?" She snatched Jamie's hand and slapped it over her breast. "Feel that?"

"Yeah." Jamie could feel it all right. The heat of it made her fingers tingle. "Cut it out now." Her system was jangled. "You're drunk, honey, and we need to talk first."

"I feel wonderful. Don't you want to feel me?"

Jamie's curse wasn't quite as good-natured. She hauled Darcy up, unable to avoid the cheerful kisses being plastered over her face and neck.

"Stop it, Stretch." Her voice cracked with desperation as her body went on high alert. She was trying hard to remember that she needed to talk to Darcy. Sober. "Behave yourself."

"Don't want to. Tired of behaving. I came face to face with my past this week. I thought I was losing you. Am I?"

"No, of course not. You've got me good, and I'm not that easy to shake off. I'm sorry. I want to tell you about my week."

"No." Darcy shook her head. She fumbled at the buttons of Jamie's shirt. "Just touch me."

Jamie cursed, unable to hold on to Darcy's head as she carried her from the room and up the stairs. Darcy giggled and Jamie nearly yelped when Darcy bit her ear, then stroked it with her tongue, wet and hot.

"I love you, Jamie. I love your mouth. And I love the way your chameleon eyes shift color. The way you feel against me. Can we have wine in bed?"

"No, and you'd better..."

Jamie made the mistake of looking at Darcy and their mouths fused together. The heat ran through, tormenting. With a long desperate moan, Jamie teetered on the stairs as she lost herself in the wonderfully willing lips. "Darcy." Her name was a plea. "You're driving me crazy and I'm trying to remember you're drunk. Please, honey, cooperate."

"You came back."

Jamie stared at her. "Oh, Darcy, I love you so much; you have no idea. You have my heart. But we have to talk."

"No talking. Just kiss me. I want you inside of me. Feel how wet you're making me." Darcy groaned.

For one moment she almost sounded sober.

"Oh, my God." As a prayer it was perfectly sincere. Jamie repeated it over and over again as she dumped her charge on the bed.

Before Jamie could escape, Darcy pulled, tugged, and had Jamie flopping onto the bed, on top of her. "Feels good." She sighed, then arched. "Oh my..."

Jamie moaned. What was left of her mind scrambled and she knew she was moments from coming. "Dammit, I'm not doing this. We have to talk, and you are in no condition to—"

"Okay," Darcy murmured. "Okay." Then she yawned hugely...and passed out.

Jamie lay there for several minutes fighting for breath, fighting for strength. Still vibrating, she levered herself away from the passive body. She looked down at her lover and had to smile. *She's gonna be one sorry woman in the morning.*

THE SUN WAS up by the time Jamie returned to the apartment. She was very surprised to see Darcy already up and making coffee, having expected her to sleep 'til noon, then wake up, pull the covers over her pounding head and pray for a quick, merciful death. It threw her to find Darcy pale, heavy-eyed, still in her robe, but up. Her hair was wet, which meant she'd probably tried to drown herself in the shower.

"Hi there."

Darcy smiled sheepishly. "Hi."

"How are you feeling?"

"Fine. Tired." Cautiously, she cleared her throat. "I guess I got carried away, huh?"

"You were drunk as a skunk."

"I wanted to thank you for carrying me to bed."

Jamie felt completely thrown off stride. She had expected to be the one in control, coming to comfort and then gently explain. The calm woman in front of her was nothing like what she had pictured. She frowned. "No headache?"

"No. I don't really get hangovers." Darcy pushed a hand through her tousled hair, tightened the sash around her bathrobe, then poured cream into her cup.

Jamie shook her head. *No hangovers?* "Do you remember what was said last night?"

Darcy shifted under the intent gray eyes. "Yeah. Most of it."

Jamie studied her. "Darcy, we need to talk."

Darcy nodded, swallowing slowly. *We need to talk.* That was never followed by good news. She knew, having said it to others too many times.

They walked to the living room and sat down. Jamie wanted to pace, but forced herself to sit facing Darcy. She stared at Darcy, trying to find the words, and found herself suddenly nervous under the watchful blue gaze.

"Two days ago, a woman came here to see me. Her name is Shane."

Darcy stiffened and was glad that Jamie didn't see her reaction.

Jamie stared at her hands and couldn't think of how to explain what she had gone through. Her mind scrambled, trying desperately to retrieve the words she had rehearsed on her way over, the words that had fled the moment she had looked at Darcy. Now she felt tongue-tied.

"Shane is the woman I had a one night stand with, the one who was also photographed with my father." She paused. "Well, I was with her more than that one time but...that second time also felt like a one night stand kind of thing."

That didn't come out right, Jamie thought.

Darcy narrowed her eyes. *More than once?* She fought down that first hint of temper.

"She came to see me the other day because she had uncovered the name of a photographer that my father had used. I had been to see her the week before to ask her about it. Then she kissed me and..."

She kissed her? Darcy's anger burned.

"...then I had this dream, and it was all wrapped up in the case and it scared me."

Jamie shifted under Darcy's penetrating gaze. *This is definitely not going as planned.* She cleared her throat and pressed on. "Two days ago we located the photographer, and I found pictures of my father with this little girl who went missing. It messed me up. And I couldn't figure out what to do, but now..."

Jamie stopped as Darcy launched herself from her seat and started to pace.

"Messed up?" Darcy said. "Are you better now? Feeling okay?"

"Yes."

"All your faculties intact?"

Jamie frowned. "Yes."

"She going to kiss you again?"

"No. I told her that –"

"No more one night stands?" Darcy interrupted.

Jamie narrowed her eyes. "No." *This is really, really not going the way I planned.* "Listen, Darcy, I wanted to say I'm sor —"

"Shut up, Jamie," Darcy said as her fury erupted. "You know — I've been sitting for two lousy days feeling sorry for myself. How stupid is that? Now you're calmly sitting here telling me that only days ago you kissed a woman you had a one night stand with. Days ago! And if that's not bad enough, when she showed up again, you disappeared for two days. Without a word to me."

Jamie struggled to get control of the conversation, as well as her own temper. "I said she kissed me, I didn't say I kissed her."

"Whatever. Details." Darcy waved away Jamie's protest. "I'm only going to say this once." She glared at Jamie. "I love you, goddammit. And it's all your fault. There will not be another woman for you or for me. 'Cause the next woman that kisses you who's not related to you better be me, or I'll have to hurt her and you both."

Jamie stood up. "Really?" *Why, she's just perfect,* she thought with delight.

"Yes, really. I know you've had a shitty time of it. I can't even imagine how this case has messed with your mind, or where you can put all that stuff at the end of your day. But the next time you decide to disappear, I'm going to hunt you down."

"Is that right?" Jamie stared. Darcy in full fury was the most breathtaking thing she had ever seen and she felt the arousal spread through her body. "So now you're telling me what to do?"

"Somebody should. Especially when you are acting stupid. I've said my piece. Now what are you going to do about it?"

Jamie smiled slowly. "Well, to put it in terms you will understand, I'm going to fuck your brains out, Stretch."

"HOW ARE THINGS?" Jamie asked.

Alex smiled as she shifted slightly. She was finally home, and that alone had improved her mood. She had lost weight and was still unable to completely lift her left arm without pain, and her bruises were now a nice shade of yellow, but she was home with Megan. That was all that mattered.

"Better. Megan has eased up on her hovering; I've toned down my grumpiness. All in all, not bad." She looked thoughtful for a moment. "Something's not right with Megan, though. She's jumpy. And every time I mention going back to work, she gets this look on her face."

"Give her time, Alex. This was scary for her, too. She almost lost you."

Alex wanted to change the subject. "So, what's been happening?"

"I came face to face with the possibility that I might be the daughter of a monster. That scared me."

"Jamie, you're not him."

Jamie shrugged. "Yeah, but there's a part of him that lives in me."

Alex took her hand. "You and I both know that no one is

pure evil. Tell me what's happened."

"Shane came to me with the name of a photographer that the judge used, a Brian Mayer. Stacey and I tracked down his place, but didn't find him. It looked like he hadn't been around for days."

Alex looked at her. "How did you get in if he wasn't around?"

Jamie grinned. "Don't ask. Let's just say Stacey and I were creative and used all of the investigative tools at our disposal."

Alex frowned, but it was more out of being left out of the fun than actual concern about a law they may have bent.

"We found pictures, though. One in particular—a picture of my father smiling away with his arm around a cute girl." She took a deep breath, the horror of it still fresh. "Sarah Timley."

Alex widened her eyes, then closed them. "No shit?"

"Shook me up some. I mean—what the hell does that mean? McCarthy took over and found out that at some point, the judge was dating this nice paralegal secretary."

"Sarah Timley's mother," they said together.

"Yeah."

"Do we think she killed him?"

"No. It appears she's got a tight alibi." Jamie sighed, her frustration evident. "I'm surrounded by coincidences. And you know how much I can't stand coincidences." They smiled at each other in recognition of their shared familiarity.

"I have a man who abused young girls, dates a woman who has one, then the girl ends up dead, right around the time he winds up with a bullet in his head."

"Those are pretty big coincidences," Alex agreed.

Jamie pushed a hand through her hair. "Yeah. So now I'm thinking about what I need to do next."

"Which will be what?" Alex asked.

Jamie shrugged. "I don't know. I'm not even supposed to be working on this case."

Alex ignored her statement, knowing that a small thing like jurisdiction wouldn't stop Jamie.

"I would think that we have to find the missing photographer."

Jamie and Alex turned at the voice coming from the doorway. Stacey stood there, smiling calmly.

Alex grinned at her. She felt better knowing that Jamie would have help until she was back on her feet.

"We?" Jamie asked, eyebrow lifting.

"Yeah. We. You can't pick a lock worth a damn, so somebody should help you out until Alex is ready to come back."

"Fine." Jamie acted as if she was capitulating, though deep down inside she was relieved to get the help. "You are definitely a top," she muttered.

Stacey's smile would have melted steel.

"Let's just say I like to keep my options open."

Jamie shook her head and turned and caught Alex's chuckle. "Oh sure, both of you laugh it up. But when my boss finds out I'm meddling in a case that isn't mine and the DA is helping me in an investigation, we'll see who has the last laugh."

They continued to grin and Jamie threw up her hands in exasperation. "Fine. I'm going home to wait for Darcy to make up her mind to move in with her stuff."

It took a moment for the words to register, but when they did Alex's mouth dropped open. "What? Darcy is moving in with you?"

Jamie turned at the door and favored Alex with a superior smile. "Oh, did I forget to mention that?"

Chapter
Forty-four

JAMIE AND STACEY settled in at a little all-night diner. Coffee thick enough to walk on came first, served by a sleepy-eyed waitress wearing a cotton candy pink uniform and a plastic nametag that declared her to be Midge.

Jamie perused the hand-written menu under its plastic coating, then propped an elbow on the scarred surface of the coffee-stained, cheap veneer that covered their table.

An ancient country-and-western tune was twanging away on the juke, and the air was redolent with the thick odor of frying grease. Breakfast was served twenty-four hours a day.

Stacey added cream to her coffee and stirred. "Is he dead, do you think?" she asked, continuing their discussion of Mayer.

Jamie chewed the inside of her cheek. "Dead or hiding out. You know what bothers me the most about the whole thing? Where's his studio? He's a photographer, but he's got no studio."

"From what I hear, he worked in hotel rooms."

Jamie toyed with her spoon. "Yeah. But still... And where is his darkroom? He had to develop his pictures somewhere. I mean, that kind of subject matter doesn't allow for walking into a Wal-Mart for their same day processing. Maybe we missed something back at his place."

"Maybe. To be frank, your screaming pretty much stopped my search in its tracks."

Jamie felt the heat touch her cheeks. "I'm sorry about that."

Stacey studied her. "About that, want to talk about it?"

"Nothing personal, Stacey, but no." Jamie looked away.

"Okay." Stacey pulled her notepad from her back pocket. "So, I think we should go back to his place, search it further."

"Okay." Jamie paused, marshaled her thoughts, and made a decision. "Stacey?"

Stacey turned her attention back to Jamie.

"There are things in my past when it comes to my father that are extremely painful for me. The pictures brought it all back."

Stacey frowned. "Sure. No problem."

"No, it's just..." Jamie hesitated, but if she and Stacey were going to get anywhere with the investigation, they had to trust each other. She took a deep breath. "The judge was my father."

Stacey looked at Jamie for a moment with widening eyes, then surprised her by gently touching her hand. "I'm sorry."

"And, I slept with Shane, our suspect, the night of his murder."

Stacey narrowed her eyes a fraction. "Anything else?"

"Well, you already know about my seeing Darcy. Oh yeah. I've been ordered to stay away from this case by my superior." She had to smile at the look on Stacey's face.

"You *are* still a cop right?" Stacey finally said.

"Of course."

"Good. For a minute there I thought things were going to get complicated."

MAYER'S MAILBOX WAS still stuffed with flyers and bills, the air still felt closed in, and yet when Stacey and Jamie broke into the photographer's apartment again, they both knew that someone had been there recently. They looked at each other, then crouched low as they entered the living room. Only silence met their stealthy approach.

After a cursory look around, Jamie relaxed. "Whoever was here is long gone." She led the way back to the small room where she had found the pictures.

"What are we looking for?" Stacey asked. The bottom drawer was still lying on the floor where it had been left due to their previous abrupt departure.

"Anything."

"Well, that narrows it down." Stacey smiled slightly as they started their search.

Jamie went back to the desk and stared at it, then wrenched out another drawer. She searched it, turned it over, checked the underside, the back, then tossed it aside and yanked out another. On the third try, she found another with a false bottom. She had missed it on that first search.

Her quick grunt of approval caused Stacey to turn, and she watched as Jamie took out a penknife and pried at the wood. Giving up her own search, she joined Jamie. By tacit agreement, she gripped the loosened edge and tugged while Jamie worked the knife around. Wood splintered from wood, and they switched jobs. Jamie got a splinter, swore, and continued to peel back the wood. All at once, the false piece popped free.

Jamie took the knife again and cut through the tape affixing a key with a small tag to the back of the drawer. "Safety deposit box, local bank," she muttered.

SITTING ON THE floor of Mayer's apartment, Jamie and Stacey were trying to work out the details of how to get into the safety deposit box at the bank. Stacey put the ball squarely into Jamie's court. "You know that even if you have the key, banks usually require identification, a signature match, or a warrant."

Jamie frowned, irritated that Stacey was right. "I know that. But I can't very well go to a justice of the peace and ask for a warrant. I'm not even supposed to be working on this case." *Well, I could, but not without involving the captain, and then I'd probably be suspended.* "You're a DA. Couldn't you...?"

Stacey raised an eyebrow.

With a sigh, Jamie considered the other two options. Neither of them looked like a Brian Mayer; that left the signature thing. "Any other talent I should know about besides picking locks? How are you at forgery?"

"You don't think that the teller would notice it if one of us signed our name as Brian Mayer? Unless you want to do a quick surgical makeover, that avenue is closed to us," Stacey remarked dryly. When she saw Jamie contemplating the idea, she waved her hand. "Don't even think about it. I like myself just fine, and Darcy would kill you."

Jamie discarded that option but she refused to give up finding out what was inside that safety deposit box. *We are so close to cracking the case; I can feel it.*

With no other viable option, they decided to try flashing their badges and bluffing their way into the vault. Jamie glanced absently at two men who were stepping out of a blue van and opened her mouth to say something to Stacey when the hair on the back of her neck rose. One of the men, the passenger, nodded in their direction, and Jamie knew it meant trouble. "We've been made. Run!"

They dashed to the car, and Jamie was already pulling out as Stacey was diving in. She caught the glint of moonlight off the van as the two men jumped back in and squealed after them.

"Grab on to something," Jamie said.

She spun the car into a fast U-turn, riding two wheels over the opposite curb. Her bumper kissed lightly off the fender of a sedan, and then she screamed down the quiet, suburban street at sixty miles per hour. She took the first turn with the van three lengths behind.

"You remember how to use a gun?"

Stacey threw her a disdainful glance. "Please."

Jamie nodded at the glove box. "Let's hope you don't have to. Put on your seat belt."

Stacey glanced at the side mirror. "They're closing in. Just drive."

Jamie wound through the streets like a snake, tapping the brake, flooring the gas, whipping the wheel so that the tires whined. The challenge of it, the speed, the insanity, had her grinning. "I like to do this to ABBA." And she switched on the CD player and cranked the volume up to blaring.

"You're crazy," Stacey yelled, but found herself grinning as *Dancing Queen* blasted out of the speakers. "Beats being in court any time."

They heard the ping of metal against metal as a bullet hit their rear fender.

"Now they're getting nasty," Jamie muttered.

"I think they are trying to shoot the tires." Stacey grabbed the gun from the glove box, then hung out the window to waist level and fired at their pursuers.

"Are you nuts?" Jamie's heart jumped into her throat and she nearly crashed into a lamppost. "Get your head back in here before you get it blown off."

Grim-eyed, too wired to be afraid, Stacey fired again. "Two can play." With the third shot, she hit a headlight. The fourth got a tire, and the sound of squealing and crunching metal filled the night.

"I hit them. Bastards! I think they are coming to a stop," she shouted, still hanging out of the window.

Jamie watched in the rear view mirror as the van smashed into a parked car and came to a stop, then she threw an amazed look at Stacey. "I can see. I don't need a damn play-by-play. Get back in here. Strap in this time." She hit the on-ramp and sped into the night.

"We lost them." Stacey grinned, eyes a little wild.

Jamie glanced at her, shaking her head.

Stacey leaned over and kissed Jamie on the mouth. "You're good, Saunders."

"Damn right. So are you." They grinned at each other, then Jamie slowed the car to a more respectable speed and started to retrace her path. "Do you have a car? 'Cause we have to ditch this one; they know it. Whoever the hell *they* are."

Stacey grimaced. "No. Mine's in the shop."

Jamie tapped her fingers against the steering wheel as she

considered their next move. She pulled her cell phone from her front pocket and dialed quickly.

"Hey, Darcy. Listen, my car just died. Battery, I think. Can I borrow your...oh... Yeah, okay. No, I have a couple of things left to do still. I was going to drop in on Alex later, too. Sure. See you later." She threw the phone onto the seat and glanced at Stacey, who gave her a questioning look.

"She said, 'You touch my car and you die.'"

Stacey burst out laughing.

Jamie frowned. "I guess we can always borrow Alex's car."

"I guess. Seems safer that way," Stacey said, deadpanned.

Jamie rolled her eyes as she maneuvered the car through traffic at a more law-abiding pace.

JAMIE HAD NO way of knowing who had been chasing them or why, or how much they knew. The fact that there were two bullet holes in her trunk had her temper on the verge of erupting. As a precaution, she and Stacey decided to leave the car a few blocks from Alex's place and walk the rest of the way.

Unexpectedly, Madison and Lauren were at Alex's, enjoying a glass of wine. "Hey!"

Taken aback by their presence, Jamie hesitated in the doorway. She mentally revised her plan to discuss the case with Alex. "You remember Stacey?"

They accepted the glasses of wine that Megan offered. By then, the adrenaline that had kicked in during the chase was dissipating and the reaction of being shot at was settling in. Feeling her legs weaken, Jamie sat down. She glanced quickly at Stacey, who seemed to be bearing up.

At the exchange of looks, Alex, who was watching them, knew that something had happened. "So, how's it going?" she asked casually.

"Just fine," Jamie said. "Listen, I need to borrow your car."

"Why? What's wrong with your car?"

"I...there was a bit of an incident."

"Incident?"

Jamie jumped at the sound of Darcy's voice behind her. "People have got to stop sneaking in and out of rooms," she muttered.

"I was in the washroom. What incident? You told me your battery died."

Jamie shifted. "I didn't want to worry you, that's all." She felt the heat spread up her neck.

"Smooth," Stacey said under her breath.

Jamie ignored her.

"What's wrong with your car, Saunders?"

When Darcy used her last name in just that tone, it was never good. Jamie hunched her shoulders as she watched Darcy cross the room to the fridge and pull out a beer. As she twisted off the cap and took a long gulp, her blue eyes remained steadily on Jamie.

"I'm fine," Jamie reassured her.

"For now."

Darcy's tone implied that this condition would not last long.

"What happened?" Alex asked.

"We went back to the photographer's place to give it another look, and found a key to a safety deposit box. On our way out, we were sort of chased by a couple of guys in a van."

They all erupted. "What?"

"It's fine. We lost them."

"Where's your car now?" Alex asked.

"We ditched it a few blocks away. There're a couple of bullet holes in it." Jamie avoided Darcy's stare, but felt the heat of it, nonetheless.

"Seems to me we need to figure out who shot at you," Alex said, breaking the tense silence.

"What do you mean *we*? It's Stacey and me. You stay put and get better."

"What transportation are you going to use?" Alex asked smugly.

"I'm going to borrow your car, that's what," Jamie replied, temper roiling.

"Not without me in it."

"If you go, I go," Megan cut in, eyes turning frosty. "I'm not letting you out of my sight."

"Count me in," Darcy chimed in.

"Why you, for God's sake?" Jamie asked, exasperated.

"Some thug takes a shot at my girlfriend, it riles me some."

"We will have to retrace your steps," Madison supplied helpfully.

"Figure out who hired this photographer," Megan contributed.

"For the last time, there is no *we*!" Jamie yelled. She had the sudden sensation of having been dropped into a bad French farce or a screwball comedy. She half expected everyone to pile into a tiny Mini to speed off after the bad guys. "Look, you guys, I appreciate you all wanting to help, but this is a police investigation not a party. Leave it to the experts. I mean…"

She turned to Stacey, who sat there amused. "Say

something."

Stacey shrugged. "Hey, it stopped being a typical case the night you slept with our primary suspect."

AT THE BANK where the safety deposit box was located, Stacey approached the counter and waited until the teller was free to help her.

Jamie stood back near the chairs and tried to ignore the attentive stare of the guard. As she watched Stacey chat with the teller, she wondered how she might get a justice of the peace to sign a warrant without being the officer on the case. *Maybe I can get Alex to do it. Or maybe I'll need to get McCarthy involved after all.* She was about to call Alex when Stacey returned with a smirk.

"We're in."

"How did you manage that?" Jamie asked.

"Just showed her my ID." Stacey smiled. "That, and I'm taking her out to dinner one night next week."

"What?" Jamie looked at her in amazement. "I think you're beginning to scare me."

Stacey grinned. "Come on, before she changes her mind."

They entered the tiny vault and were left alone with the box for which they had the key. Before opening it, Jamie shot a questioning look at Stacey, who shrugged as if to say "what the hell."

Jamie lifted the lid and found a bulky manila envelope and an undeveloped roll of exposed film. She shoved the film into her front pocket, held on to the envelope, and put the box back. In case someone might be about to take exception to their presence, she didn't take the time to look inside the envelope. Once they were somewhere safe, they could look at the contents at their leisure.

After a quick exit from the bank, Stacey and Jamie once again found themselves in the diner, being served by a sleepy eyed Midge. She showed no interest whatsoever in getting them more than the coffee they ordered as she went back to the tabloid newspaper she had been reading.

Jamie toyed with the envelope in her hands rather than opening it. Not able to bring herself to look inside, she frowned, lost in thought. Darcy had been pissed, that had been obvious just from the look she had thrown when Jamie had insisted on leaving alone. She couldn't think of a way she could have avoided that. Alex was upset, too. But she couldn't please everybody. She thought it ironic that Stacey was the only one not upset with her at the moment. It was probably just a matter of time.

Stacey patiently watched and waited, but finally she sighed, and took the packet from Jamie's grasp. "Maybe I should take a look."

Jamie made a face, but made no move to stop her.

Stacey pulled the lone picture out of the packet and stared at it for a moment, her expression inscrutable. She handed Jamie the picture.

Heart hammering, Jamie glanced down at it. The picture was of a woman about their age, dark haired and pretty. She was staring into the camera with a sad expression.

"Do you recognize her?" Stacey asked.

Jamie shook her head. "Maybe she's our missing accomplice."

"Maybe. It might be time to pay another visit to your lady judge."

Jamie frowned. "She's not mine."

Stacey shrugged and turned her attention back to the picture. Something tugged at her as she stared at the photograph, but whatever it was, it was illusive, a whisper, thin as a wisp of smoke. Just as quickly, the thought, or whatever it was, evaporated.

Chapter
Forty-five

"THAT'S HER. THAT'S the woman I met that night the photos were taken." Shane stared at the picture.

"Are you sure?" Stacey asked.

"I'm positive." Shane looked at Jamie and their eyes met; Jamie looked away first.

Jamie was uncomfortable sitting next to a woman with whom she had been intimate. A woman for whom she knew, much to her annoyance, a degree of attraction remained. She could feel it pulling at her. It shimmered between them as they sat close. She shifted in her seat and caught Stacey's speculative look.

Stacey turned her attention back to Shane. "Thank you for your time." She stood up and waited for Jamie, who followed her more slowly.

At the door Jamie turned, feeling like she needed to say something. "Shane..."

Shane smiled at her, a smile tinged with regret. "Jamie, just go. It's okay."

Head bowed, Jamie followed Stacey out of the house. At the car, Stacey turned to her. "Want my advice?"

"No."

Stacey smiled. "I'll give it to you anyway. Stay away from her. Sometimes even when we have the best of intentions, the moment gets away from us."

Jamie frowned, annoyed that Stacey could read her so well without really knowing her. "I'm beginning to remember that I don't like you."

Stacey was amused rather than offended by Jamie's response. "Yeah. I get that all the time."

Jamie smiled and Stacey narrowed her eyes. She continued to study Jamie for a long moment. "Well, I'll be damned," she whispered.

"What?" Jamie shifted impatiently as Stacey continued to

stare at her. "Do I have dirt on my face or what?"

"Where's that picture?"

Puzzled, Jamie handed it over.

Stacey studied the photo and then looked at Jamie. She handed the photo back to her. "See anything familiar?" she asked.

Jamie looked at it again and frowned in concentration. "No."

"You. The girl looks like you."

"I SEE IT."

Darcy looked at the picture, then back at her lover. The resemblance was there in the slashing cheekbones, but mostly it was the eyes — the shape of them, the smoky gray color. She left them to go and grab a pot of coffee.

They had gone from Shane's directly to Murphy's. The reason Jamie had given Stacey for the side trip was that they should get a second opinion regarding the photograph. The truth was simply that she wanted to be near Darcy, but would never admit to her need. Her feelings were too complex to analyze. She was unsettled by her persistent reaction to Shane, uneasy about their latest discovery, but more importantly she was desperate for Darcy's touch.

They were sitting at a corner table when Darcy returned. Without thinking about it, she brushed her hand against Jamie's shoulder gently, possessively.

Jamie looked up at her. Their eyes met, and the look in Darcy's eyes eased Jamie's tension. *We're okay. She doesn't look mad anymore.*

Stacey was frowning over the picture. *What the hell do we have now?*

Every time they inched forward in their search, something blew up at them that sent them in a different direction. Now they had found someone she would have laid odds was Jamie's sister. It was also likely that this woman had participated in Judge Reynolds' sick games. Worried, she shifted her eyes to Jamie.

Jamie rubbed at the headache brewing behind her eyes. "I'm so confused that for the life of me I can't figure out what the next step should be."

I have another sister. Instinct told her so. This stranger with the familiar eyes and a familiar wounded expression was related to her; she recognized the look as the same one she had had for years. Nausea burned the back of her throat. She was afraid — no, that wasn't true — she was terrified of what would come next.

Darcy sat down beside them and, sensing Jamie's internal turmoil, took her hand.

Stacey watched them, feeling a pang of envy. Loneliness settled uneasily over her shoulders. She sighed that feeling away. "We need to find her."

Jamie nodded unhappily.

JAMIE TOOK THE roll of film they had recovered and got it developed. There were several candid shots of the mystery woman. A week later they were still looking for answers.

As Alex, Jamie and Stacey pored over them, looking for clues, Stacey fingered one of the photos. "He loves her."

"Who?"

"Whoever took this photo. I'm thinking Mayer. He loves her and she knows it. She's looking directly at him and smiling just for him. Look at the soft focus, the way he framed her. It's different than the other pictures."

Alex nodded. "You might be right." She absently flipped through the rest, then sharpened her gaze on one. "Hey, guys, look at this one. Notice the address?" The woman stood in front of a tidy brownstone. To her left was an oval plaque with a number on it.

"I can't make it out," Jamie said. "Anyone have a magnifying glass?"

"I'll be right back." Stacey trotted out of the house and returned a few minutes later with a magnifying glass. She handed it to Jamie.

Jamie peered at the photo through the glass. "Twenty-one Bank Street." Jamie met Alex's eyes and swallowed hard. "Let's go pay a visit."

Chapter
Forty-six

STACEY DROVE, WITH Alex sitting beside her. Jamie was in the back seat, staring sightlessly out of the window. Her heart was hammering as she wondered if she was strong enough to face the unknown woman, the half sister who might also be their father's killer. More worrisome was the fact that if the woman had done it, she could not hate her for it; she had wished him dead too often herself.

Alex shifted to look at Jamie. She was concerned for her friend, wanting to spare her more pain. "Are you sure about this, Jamie?"

Jamie nodded. "I need to be there; I need to know."

Alex glanced at Stacey, who looked equally worried, and took a deep breath. "Okay." She set her face in that calm detached look that hid all her thoughts, and she saw Jamie shift into the same mode as they arrived at their destination.

They all got out of the car and filed into the building. At the fourth door, they got lucky when they found the tenant home. The woman barely glanced at the photograph before pointing them to the door marked 5B and closing the door in their faces.

"Friendly neighborhood," Stacey whispered.

Alex stood in front of 5B and rapped on the door, while Stacey and Jamie stepped back into the shadows on either side of her. There was a long pause, and they were about to turn away when the door finally opened.

"Hello, I'm Detective Alex Ryan. I was wondering if I could have a few minutes of your time."

The woman from the photograph looked startled, but after a brief hesitation and a quick glance at the badge, stepped back to let Alex enter. Her look of surprise turned to shock when her eyes fell on Jamie. Her gasp was loud in the sudden quiet and her face paled.

"Who are you? What do you want?" she asked.

She looked afraid, panicked.

Jamie's heart twisted. She recognized that trapped look. "I'm Jamie Saunders. We might have someone in common."

They went to the living room where the woman sank onto the couch, her eyes never leaving Jamie. Jamie sat across from her and met the gray eyes. "What is your name?" she asked gently.

"Kelly. Kelly Tanner."

"Kelly, this is difficult, I know. I'm just as shocked as you are. But I think I might be your sister." Jamie was surprised that her voice shook a little. "Was your father Tomas Reynolds?"

"Yes," Kelly whispered.

Her eyes were wide, like those of a deer caught in headlights.

Jamie briefly closed her eyes. "He was my father, too."

"Are you aware that he died a few months ago?" Alex broke in.

Kelly nodded and her face paled even further.

"When was the last time you saw him?" Alex asked.

"A little over two years ago." Kelly looked at Jamie. "He...he was not a very nice man. After years of therapy, I finally was able to exorcise him from my life." She took a breath as she recovered her equilibrium. "Were you close?" she asked Jamie.

"No. He was a bastard. I last saw him thirty years ago." Jamie frowned. She had not expected to feel a tug of emotion for this woman, but she felt it—that tender call to her heart. She tightened her jaw and she forced the feeling away. "How old are you?"

"Twenty-nine."

Younger. I have a younger sister. Jamie felt the headache return and she gave Alex a helpless look.

Alex shifted nearer. "We need to ask you where you were the night of June 26th."

"June 26th?" Kelly frowned. "I don't remember."

"You don't remember?" Stacey asked.

Kelly turned to Stacey with a look of surprise, as if noticing her for the first time.

"No. I don't. But then again I don't remember what I did last night, either." She gave Stacey a half smile, then stood up and walked to a small table where a black briefcase sat. She took out a date book and flipped through the pages. "June 26th, I was in class—Ethics and the Law." At Stacey's questioning look, she shrugged. "I'm studying law."

"Can someone vouch for you being in class?" Alex asked.

"What?" She frowned at Alex. "I suppose my whole class, my professor. We had to write an exam that night, so yeah."

Something suddenly clicked. "Are you asking me if I have an alibi?"

Alex shrugged. "We're still looking for your father's killer. We're questioning everyone. Your whereabouts are of interest to us for a variety of reasons."

She crossed her arms and glared at Alex. "Which are?"

Alex noted that this was no longer the scared woman of a few minutes before. This was a furious, soon-to-be lawyer who looked remarkably like her sister in that anger. Under different circumstances, the resemblance to Jamie would have been amusing. "Do you know a Brian Mayer?"

Kelly was thrown but quickly recovered. "I might."

"Well, we're looking for him too. Do you have any idea where he is?"

The hesitation was brief but was not lost on the three women.

"No."

"Are you sure?" Alex persisted. "Because he hasn't been seen at his house since the murder and so we're wondering if he is okay."

"Like I said, I haven't seen him in ages."

"Well, if he does get in touch with you, we'd appreciate a phone call." Alex handed Kelly a card. "We will also need a list of names — your professor, your classmates." She stood up. "I would strongly recommend that you not leave town, Miss Tanner."

Kelly's eyes flickered but she nodded, then her attention turned once again to Jamie.

"Are you an only child?" she asked

Jamie froze in the doorway. She turned and gave Kelly a sad smile. "No. I have a twin sister. Identical. We'll be in touch."

EACH LOST IN thought, the trio stepped out into the dusk. The stillness of the night was shattered by a gunshot.

Jamie froze, not believing that anything like that could happen twice in such a short time span, outside of the movies. Stacey grabbed her and yanked her down on the sidewalk behind the parked car, and Alex crouched beside them as another bullet whined overhead and buried itself in the trunk.

Alex winced as her sudden movement jarred her still-injured side. She pulled out her gun. "You guys sure are popular."

"Tell me about it," Stacey growled. "It's starting to piss me off."

Alex peered over the hood in the direction the shot had

come from. There was only silence. Whoever it was had either fled after the warning shots, or was out there waiting. She hated waiting. "Anyone feel like running?"

Jamie nodded, automatically understanding what Alex wanted to do. "Let's go."

"Where are we going?" Stacey asked.

"You should stay put. We're going to try and smoke him out. Keep your head down and we'll come back for you."

Stacey shook her head. "No way. I'm not missing out on the fun."

After a brief hesitation, Alex nodded once. "I'll go left, you guys go right. We'll see who he really wants." She shifted, grimacing at the pain. "Now!" she shouted, and they took off running, guns drawn.

Jamie heard footsteps heading away from her and shouted to Alex, "He's running!"

They chased after the shooter. One block, two blocks, then he cut through a backyard and they split up—Jamie followed him, while the others ran around to try and head him off from the other side. He climbed the fence and fired wildly behind him before falling to the other side. The bullet lodged in a tree inches from Jamie.

"You little fuck!" she snarled, following him up and over the fence, gun poised ready to fire as she jumped to the other side. She saw that he hadn't waited, but was running back to the street, directly toward Alex.

"Drop it!" Alex yelled. "Drop the fucking gun!" There was a shot, and then the sound of a scuffle.

By the time a panting Jamie reached them, the gunman was lying face down, his hands cuffed behind his back.

"You shot me," he spat at Alex.

"Barely. Brian Mayer, I presume?"

"Go fuck yourself."

"Tsk...tsk. Now is that the correct attitude to take with someone who just saved your life?" Alex turned to Jamie with a smile. "I'm getting too old for this shit."

"Right back at you." Jamie wiped the sweat from her forehead. "I haven't run this much since that Lewiston robbery. Remember that?"

"Oh yeah. Man, that was a fun one." Alex grimaced. "I'm going to be stiff tomorrow. Megan's going to kill me. We can't tell her that I was in the middle of a foot pursuit, or else I'm going to be single very quickly."

"Deal. And let's not tell Darcy that I was shot at again. I keep telling her that there's only a one in a million chance of it happening."

"Deal."

They both could feel the piece of their friendship that clicked back into place.

"I'm bleeding over here," Mayer whined.

"Only a little." Alex looked down at him. "Now, I'm going to forget that you tried to kill me twice and that I'll have a scar for the rest of my life because of you, you little fuck. So, listen very carefully. You have the right to remain silent and refuse to answer questions. Anything you do say may be used against you in a court of law. You have the right to consult an attorney before speaking to the police and to have an attorney present during questioning now or in the future. If you cannot afford an attorney, one will be appointed for you before any questioning, if you wish. If you decide to answer questions now without an attorney present you will still have the right to stop answering at any time until you talk to an attorney. Now, what the hell were you doing trying to shoot at cops?"

Stacey was staring at them as if they were insane. "Shouldn't we call an ambulance or something?"

"I'm fine," Alex replied. She glanced at their assailant. "Oh, you mean Mayer, here?" She crouched down beside him. "We'll call the ambulance when he tells us why he's been shooting at cops."

"I just wanted to scare you a little. I didn't mean to hurt anyone. I didn't know you was cops."

"Mmm. Well, I appreciate that thoughtfulness. Why try to scare us?"

"I was just trying to protect Kelly."

Alex glanced at Jamie. "Why?"

"I need an ambulance; I'm bleeding to death here."

"In a minute. Why does Kelly need protecting?"

"She...she needs me to look after her. He's been hurting her, you know?"

He shifted, but Alex kept him down with her hand. "Did you shoot her father?"

He glared at her then looked away. "I'm not talking until I get a lawyer."

Alex stood up. "Suit yourself. Let's go pay Kelly a little visit."

Jamie nodded. "Sure. I'm sure she won't mind spending a night being interviewed at the station."

"Leave her alone!" Brian Mayer struggled, trying to get up, and cursed when he was unable to manage it. "I should have aimed for your head, you bitch. You'd better leave her alone."

His voice broke.

Jamie looked down at Mayer and recalled the look in Kelly's eyes at they stared back at her—so much pain, so much anger. She knew the feeling well, that feeling of helplessness because she always seemed to be only one step ahead of the demons.

Jamie knelt next to him. "Brian, I'm her sister, so I don't want her hurt anymore either. Given the chance, I would have killed the bastard myself. Did you shoot him?"

He looked at her and his photographer's eye noted the resemblance; tears started to roll down his cheek. "I didn't mean to kill him. Kelly, she had read about the little girl that turned up dead, and she knew that the judge knew her because she had seen some of my pictures of the two of them together. Well, she started crying and having nightmares and saying he needed to be stopped. I just wanted to scare him, but when I showed up, he was lying there on the floor not moving. I thought he was already dead. I shot him just to make sure. I did it for Kelly, so she could sleep again."

"Why did you shoot at me when I was coming out of your place?"

He winced as the pain shot up his leg. "I panicked. I didn't know you were cops honest. I was just trying to warn you off. I thought you might go after Kelly."

"You suck at this," Alex said. "Usually, you'd try not to call attention to yourself instead of shooting at everybody you meet."

Jamie sighed and rubbed her eyes with a tired hand. She felt Stacey's hand on her shoulder. It was a gesture of comfort, but also of caution. She stood. "Will you tell Shane she's off the hook for the murder then?" she asked Stacey, who nodded. "Call an ambulance. I'm going home." She started walking and didn't look back.

Alex and Stacey didn't try to stop her; they just watched her go.

Chapter
Forty-seven

A WEEK LATER, they were all gathered at Murphy's— Lauren, Madison, Megan, Alex and Stacey, all determined to be part of whatever else needed to be done. They wouldn't let Jamie hide away from them.

Darcy and Jamie stood behind the bar making drinks. Once everyone was served, Jamie grabbed a beer and leaned back against Darcy, who had taken a seat on one of the stools. It felt good to be held.

"You okay...with everything?" Alex asked Jamie.

"I'm living with everything. I still haven't told my mom or my sister about Kelly, but I will. Finding out so late after the fact that you have a half sister takes some adjustment. Once the case against Mayer is over and done with, I might talk to Kelly again."

They all sat quietly sipping their drinks.

"Do you think the judge killed Sarah Timley?"

"I just don't know." She would live with that, too, the never knowing. Justice didn't always come as one expected. Darcy caressed her neck and Jamie let her head fall forward, closed her eyes, and thought back to earlier in the morning.

Darcy stood in the bedroom doorway watching Jamie get dressed, and she smiled. "You know, Saunders, I used to think I wanted you to distraction because you were so contrary. Then when I had you, I decided I still wanted you because I didn't know how long I'd keep you."

"Is that a fact?" Jamie frowned at her.

"That look right there — the one you're wearing on your face right now — when I think it through, that's the one that did it to me."

"Did what?"

"Had me falling in love with you. Then it kept creeping up on me — why no one had ever pulled at me the way you do, ever made me miss them five minutes after I walked out of the door the way you do.

When I heard that someone was shooting at you, it made me crazy. I figure the only way to handle things and keep you safe is to move in with you."

"That's your idea of a proposal?" *Jamie said, but her heart was tripping.*

"You've never had better. No point in saying no; I've got my mind set on it."

"I'm thinking of saying no." *Jamie smiled.*

"I love you. I don't want to live my life without you. You've been *causing me frustration for the last fifteen years. You're bad-tempered and exasperating, but it seems that turns me on." Darcy went to her and with a quick jerk, ripped Jamie's shirt in two.* "You see, that's the *damnedest thing, this loving you. Makes me do crazy things."*

Jamie stepped into Darcy's arms. Her heart was so full, she was surprised it wasn't spilling over. "Hold on, Stretch. Just keep holding on."

Jamie raised her head and looked at her friends gathered around her. She loved them all. She couldn't help herself—even when they drove her crazy. They had cried and fought and barged into each other's lives in the only way they knew how—insisting on being heard; determined not to be ignored; and always, always loving each other despite it all. And somehow when the chips were down, when life got too messy, they rallied around and pushed and pulled and dragged each other back into living it.

Jamie turned to Stacey. "Hey, Stacey, when was the last time you had a date?"

The End

Also available from
Jessica Casavant
and
Yellow Rose Books

Twist of Fate

Journalist Lauren Taylor is sleepwalking through her life and knows it. When her husband, US senator Matt Taylor, announces that he is running for the US Presidency, Lauren knows that she will need to make a decision about her life. Shortly after Matt's bombshell, Lauren attends a funeral where she meets Madison Williams, a doctor who has learned to disengage from life. Intrigued and feeling an immediate connection, the two women start to spend time together, until one weekend when their growing attraction is acted upon. Their affair continues until a devastating discovery and its aftermath, forces Lauren to make a choice. She bows to the inevitability of her life and stays with her husband.

Two years later, Lauren sees her past resurface when Keith McGraw, an ambitious journalist confronts her with proof of her affair with Madison. The threat of exposure starts a chain of events that forces Lauren to re-examine her life's choices and the future path she will take. Does she deny everything, and become what she does not want to be – First Lady? Or does she confront what she has been running away from for years?

Sometimes it takes a twist of fate to shake you out of a self-induced coma or so Lauren Taylor comes to believe.

ISBN 1-932300-07-4

Walking Wounded

When a sudden tragedy turns her life upside down, Alex Ryan resigns as a homicide detective with the Boston PD and goes into hiding to lick her wounds in private. Her self-imposed exile doesn't last long. Life keeps interfering. Her plan goes awry as soon as she moves into her new home. First there is Megan, the gorgeous new neighbor Alex starts to find too distracting, then her best friend Jamie who needs help in solving a murder. That this murder involves Kate, a mysterious blond with a dislike for disco, and a newly discovered interest in women, only adds to the confusion. Add in the cavalry of friends who won't stay on the sidelines for long and Alex finds that even when she tries hard to disengage from life, life has a way of barging in and demanding attention.

ISBN 1-932300-20-1

Jessica Casavant is an award-winning recording engineer who the night a fist fight broke out between two actors, decided she had had enough. There is only so much of someone else's vision a woman should take. She now works in the television industry while spinning stories on the side. Her other published works include *Twist of Fate* and *Walking Wounded*. She can be reached at cdjc @sympatico.ca or www.jessicacasavant.com.